Born of Swords

A Gorias La Gaul Novel

Also by Steven L. Shrewsbury

Novels
Philistine
Hell Billy
Overkill
Thrall
Stronger Than Death
Tormentor
Hawg
Godforsaken
With Brian Keene
King of the Bastards
With Nate Southard
Bad Magick
With Peter Welmerink
Bedlam Unleashed

Collections
Blood & Steel: Volume I
Thoroughbred
Bulletproof Soul
Depths of Savagery
Nocturnal Vacations

Novellas
Widowmaker's Apprentice

Weird Western Tales
The Black Bible of Juarez

Born of Swords
A Gorias La Gaul Novel

Steven L. Shrewsbury

Cover art: Enggar Adirasa

Editor: Joshua H. Leet

Published by Seventh Star Press, LLC.

ISBN Number: 978-1-941706-85-5

Seventh Star Press
www.seventhstarpress.com
info@seventhstarpress.com

Printed in the United States of America

First Edition

Acknowledgements

Thanks to Stephen Zimmer, Jessica Lay, Brady Allen, Mark Shrewsbury Sr, Chris & Angie Fulbright, Jim Mcleod, Debbie Weaver, Ron Kelly, Shane Montgomery, Peter Welmerink, B.J. McPherson & Erica Benjamin, Rhonda & Craig Rettig, Matt Perry, Diane Eaton, Sharon Durham, Alicia Justice, Eric S. Brown, Cheryl Lynne Staley, Donnise Park, Paul-Noigeoverlord, Julie Lauth, Michael West, Cherry Wanders, Lisa Mannetti, Alex Adams, Bonnie Stewart, Walt Hicks, Angela Bodine, Elizabeth Donald, Andrew Leonard, Val, Gina Ranalli, Ty Schwamburger, Elizadeth Hetherington, DezM, Jennifer Willis, Maurice Broaddus, Mari Adkins, Mark Sr, Mark Jr & Amy Shrewsbury, Dean Harrison, Thom Erb, Trisha, Brandie, and Renee.

Thanks always to my family, Stacey, John and Aaron.

Shrews
Rural Central Illinois

Dedication

In memory of my Schnauzer, Benny, 1991-2004
He was a very good dog

And

Jessica Lay and Kriss Morton
Who thought of interviewing Gorias La Gaul
And then the idea got out of control

Cheers, girls
I owe you coffee
And bacon

Lots of bacon

BOOK ONE

Blades and Spells

"I loathe humanity,
For I deem myself paramount among them,
And I recognize how terrible I am."
UNKNOWN
Inscription found in ruins at Larak

CHAPTER ONE
Meeting La Gaul

The doors of the tavern burst out from their hinges, but the flying debris didn't knock down the redheaded woman on the porch; the flying body of a white-haired man did. Arms spread wide, this burly projectile impacted on the girl, but grabbed her in a fierce embrace and kept on going, his momentum carrying them out into the dirt street of Segesta. Once they stopped rolling, the young lady looked up into the face of the older man. He wasn't a frail codger ready for the sentence of a rocking chair and hearth, but sported a thick body covered in scaled armor and cloak. His face, pieced together with rugged scars and a bushy beard, wore some pain, but also a great deal of excitement.

His arms released her, and then he stayed atop her in push-up position. She glanced down at his long frame and her thin fingers reached out, touching his chest. A bluish armor plating covered the man's chest. The texture of the scales felt alien, not unlike polished bronze but with a quality not dissimilar from the shell of a lobster. He squinted his eyes shut and the girl didn't understand why the thug didn't roll off until another body came flying from the tavern doors. This one impacted the back of the older man and flopped beside them. Her head turned, flat to the ground and she screamed. The newcomer on the dirt street, though a younger man with a long mustache and tan skin, this man was only a torso, savagely vivisected just below the belly button.

"Gorias La Gaul!" came the scream from within the tavern.

She stopped crying out as the big man twisted off her and took a knee in the street. "That voice," she rasped, breathing hard, green eyes ablaze at the opening.

"Yeah, I know," the big man replied as he swept hair out of his face and disengaged twin short swords from his backpack. "It ain't human."

"I'm Jessica," the girl mumbled, eyes wide. "Gorias La Gaul?"

Gorias winked at her but stayed focused on the door, where a hunched over woman wearing a brown hooded robe first appeared, then was swept aside, also deposited in the street by the next person out of the tavern.

From the doorway emerged a colossal figure. The shape ducked its head to manage the trick of exiting. It stood a full foot taller than the brutish Gorias in the dirt lane. The elongated head of the figure on the porch came near to disappearing up into the rafters, but the girl saw what that visage looked like: two red eyes high up where the forehead should be, two tiny holes for a nose right below them and a head dominated by an enormous maw, swinging open to show a rack of teeth not unlike the contents of a fully assembled butcher's block. Long arms, almost touching the ground, terminated in fingernails that resembled the teeth; the same feature graced its toenails presently tapping the porch flooring. The skin ran an aqua-greenish color, and glistened, but she didn't wager the thing wet, only oily like a reptile. Behind its buttocks swung a swishing tail, until suddenly it went erect, rattling.

"What is it?" Jessica gasped.

"He's a Newolik, but that isn't important."

Hands behind her back, pushing herself into a sitting position, Jessica asked, "And they serve those in the bar?"

Gorias stood, half grinning, swords at the ready, and stepped in front of her. Jessica thought she heard him laugh at her words. "Old boy looked a lot different when he came in there."

The rattling tail of the Newolik stopped, bulged and burst open to reveal a bloody crescent rising out of the creature's flesh. The tail swung around and the new stinger pointed at Gorias.

"Aw crap, didn't see that coming." Gorias dug in his boots, swords swiping off each other. "Deliverance shall come."

Absently, Jessica wondered if the thing smiled as it started to move forward.

Gorias didn't wait; he took the fight to the Newolik, a move which seemed to make it stop in its advance. Jessica scooted, away from the torso and more toward the woman cast aside, who looked to be suffering from an injury to her right hand by the way she cradled her arm. Jessica gathered up her long kilt as her boots kicked her along in the dirt, hoping the monster panicked at Gorias' audacity. When Gorias advanced to the porch steps, the Newolik's tail stabbed at him, but drew back fast. Gorias swiped with his right sword and the creature pulled back its stinger, knowing the warrior sought to remove it.

Jaws wide, the creature splayed wide its rows of long teeth again, and a long tongue shot from the mouth like a frog's.

Jessica could smell the Newolik. It reeked of spoiled eggs.

Gorias stopped his advance, held up his left forearm, giving it a target. The creature took it, wrapping his tongue about the armored armlet, but the screech became louder when Gorias pulled back on his forearm, and then swiped across the tongue with his other forearm. The tongue cut free, sending the creature into a shaking fit of pain and anger.

Jessica saw a sharp object not unlike a dew nail sticking from the forearm armor that Gorias used.

With no time to think, the Newolik wrapped its tail about one of the porch roof posts as Gorias slashed and stabbed forward with his swords. The long claws of the beast fended him off, striking at the flats of his blades until the porch post broke under the tail's pressure. The post flew toward Gorias and he parried the timber with his right sword, lodging the blade in the wood. The creature squealed and swiped at his midsection with a hand full of claws suddenly extending as long as its teeth.

Gorias didn't react in pain from the claws. The swipe had no effect save to shred a section of the navy blue overcloak flowing about him. He stabbed forth with his left blade and the creature slashed across its body with its left claw, jabbing at the flat of the blade and, indeed, shoving the sword down. However, Gorias took a step in and ran the left blade up the side of the creature's right calf, scaling off some knobby protuberances on its skin, but stopping at the kneecap. As the small wounds oozed fluid, Gorias dropped to his haunches on the steps. Using the right sword still stuck in the post to circumvent the Newolik's claws, he twisted his left blade, carving a half circle in the creature's knee cap before it could push him off and back into the dirt.

The screams rang inconceivably loud, both from the beast and a portly woman with black hair who bustled up the street into the scene. "What are you doing to my saloon?" she bellowed, not frightened in the slightest that the thing on her porch gripping its bloody knee wasn't human.

Jessica swallowed hard, wishing she could disappear. She heard the hooded woman begin to chant as a set of wicked eyes faced Gorias.

The warrior got up fast, snatched his one blade from the wood and joined it to its mate at the handles, forming a long, single weapon that sported sharp points on each end. When the creature started down the steps, still holding its knee, Gorias spun the weapon like a vortex. The creature grabbed up the fallen post and threw it at him, trying to disturb the spin of the weapon. Gorias turned about, taking the brunt of the projectile on his back. The wooden beam bounced off his armored spine and, turning around, he kept moving, his spinning swords still aiming at the Newolik.

The beast tried to angle itself and go low with its free claw, but the revolving weapon was impossible to miss. The blade cleaved into the edge of its left shoulder, shearing off a few large hunks of flesh before the Newolik dived to the ground, out of Gorias' way.

La Gaul stood over the Newolik, still spinning the weapon. The warrior shook his head as if to clear his mind, then glared at the wounded woman from the bar who muttered still near Jessica. Ignoring the other arrival in the street, he stopped spinning his swords. The creature roared, turning its face and claws up. Gorias separated the weapon again as the claws came up toward his groin. Gorias' knees snapped closed, pressing together the long fingernails of the creature tightly with the plates of his thighs, and he drove the blades down like daggers. The monster twisted in an effort to avoid fate. Gorias' left sword went through its right bicep, only slitting in a quarter inch of flesh. The other blade found its mark better, driving full through the creature's collarbone and out its back, embedding in the dirt street.

"Do you know what I had to do to get this saloon?" The husky woman screamed at Gorias as he ripped his left blade out to the side, tearing loose the muscle of the bicep. He jabbed in again lower, piercing the thing's side and aiming for a kidney.

As Gorias drew the sword in the collarbone out, the Newolik's long maw snapped at his hand. He offered it his forearm and the creature complied, all teeth snapping onto armor plate. Jessica saw that the look in its eyes of dull recognition didn't mirror Gorias' own look of excitement. The girl saw it. All of the villagers drawing close to gape saw it too as Gorias stepped back, breaking off a mouthful of teeth on his armlet and, at the same time, tearing out the kidney of the creature with his left sword.

La Gaul faced the muttering woman near Jessica, still cradling her arm under her robes. "Shut you cake hole, damn you," he shouted at her. "If your spells could stop me I wouldn't have bested you already."

Still, Jessica thought whatever the woman conjured irritated Gorias, but couldn't harm him.

"You owe me, you bastard!" the tavern owner in the street yelled, not even looking at what he'd done to the monster or spellcaster.

As a strong odor of urine filled the air, Jessica wretched. The crowd in the street, formed from various shops emptying at the ruckus, stayed cautious, gawking at Gorias as he stared down at the beast.

The Newolik trembled and started to moan, then drew in on itself, becoming somewhat smaller to the naked eye. Gorias left his right sword in his foe as it lost the monstrous form and slowly transformed back into a human being, still sporting the terrible wounds Gorias imparted.

"See?" Gorias said to Jessica. "He's a guy again. Oh, the curse of Damballah isn't as sexy as Lycanthropy, but just as impressive."

The spell-casting woman rose up, her left hand out from her robe, but right arm still curled in. With her left she made signs with her fingers and spouted words Jessica didn't understand.

Anger boiling in his face, Gorias strode over and squared his shoulders to her. "Damn it, I gave ya a chance when you tried to screw me over for the tablets." Gorias spread his arms out, shaking and slashed then together at the spellcaster's neck. The blades scraped across each other as she lost her head, the orb turning and flopping on the dirt, quickly joined by its body. The act sent a ripple of cries through the crowd, but they soon went silent as Gorias knelt by the fallen form, cleaned his swords on her skirt and returned them to the scabbards. He turned, faced the crowd, and the mass of humanity moved away from him as one being.

"You sonofabitch! What about my saloon?" the big woman screeched, until Gorias turned, disengaged a sword and held it to her throat.

"This fella is gonna die a man. He was cursed to be what he is and had killed quite a few folks over yonder in the far country. At sunset, he's gonna be dead and a man again. You, on the other hand...." He used the bleating woman's apron to further clean off his sword. "You are still gonna be an obnoxious bitch. Now get, before my good nature leaves me."

Wide eyed and mouth frozen open, the woman looked at her apron spattered with blood. She screamed horrifically as if her voice could hurt Gorias, then ran past him to the saloon doors and started swearing once inside.

"Well, that wasn't how I wanted my noon drink to go." Gorias shrugged as he placed his swords back up into the scabbard on the side of his backpack. He stood a yard from the redheaded girl and placed his hands on his waist. "Who are you again?"

"Jessica. I'm a scribe undergraduate from Nineveh School."

He glanced back at the tavern and smirked, probably at the continued screams of the saloon woman. "Nineveh proper-like or a place named after the city?"

"From the city." She swallowed loudly. "Why did you wipe that on her?"

"To piss her off." He held out his right elbow to her. "C'mon. Walk with me. Ya got no business being around here alone. This city is fucked up."

With some reluctance she slipped her tiny hand under his arm and gripped Gorias' elbow. She walked next to him cautiously, careful the big man didn't step on her with his boots.

"Why the hell are you here in Segesta anyways? Nineveh is far but not a world away, still quite a bit for young gal alone." He looked down at her. "Are ya alone?"

"To find you." Jessica nodded. "I had a few escorts, but lost them on the way. One of a fever, another by bandits, but I still carry some enchantments of protection."

"And you made it here to find me? Why? A job of some sort?" Gorias waved at a few children who pointed at him from the hitching posts of the shops along the street.

"No, really. I came to interview you for the university."

Gorias stopped. She took a few more steps but didn't let go of him, nearly wrapping herself about to crash into him. "Excuse me? You came that far to interview me?" He threw back his head and laughed, once, then lost all humor when he faced her. "That dog won't hunt, little sister. Gimme a better story than that. Who the hell would send a girl out into this rotten world for that? I'm not easy to find. Ya here to lull me to sleep with your feminine charms and then cut my throat in my sleep?"

"No," Jessica disagreed with pursed lips. "I've read a great deal about you, Gorias La Gaul. Do you think every woman you meet wants to sleep with you?"

"I dunno. Then again, I haven't met every woman on Earth." He jerked his left thumb over his shoulder at the bar. "That big ol' gal from the saloon? I'd say my chances are dim."

Jessica relaxed and smiled. "No. I'm not here for that. I can show you the seal of my professor. He said he knew you centuries ago when you studied there." She reached in her robes, came out with a thin, stone circle and handed it to Gorias.

"Huh," Gorias squinted at the flat object. "Doc Allard still alive, is he?"

"Yes, very much so."

"He must be pushin' 800."

"835 actually. He said you were very young when you studied and worked as a guard for the royal family of Nineveh."

Fingers pinching the seal, Gorias nodded. "About 675

years ago, maybe. He's got a long memory. What does he want with me?" He glanced behind them and saw a few men on horseback approach the bar. "Let's keep walkin', all right?"

They returned to walking arm & arm and she explained, "He doesn't need you for a service but wants to know for the sake of posterity if the tales about you are true."

"There's really no way of proving anything, dear, so why bother?" Gorias' voice ran lazy but composed. "My word over the ballads of drunk singers of songs? Does it really matter?"

"Dr. Allard thinks a true transcript from you would be a valuable testament or an exciting chronicle for future generations."

"I think you came a long way for a waste of time, sister, but I am headin' out east-ways to Eryx and then further on for a yearly duty."

Jessica nodded vigorously. "Yes, that's how we knew to find you."

He stopped and this time let her wheel around to crash into him. She bounced off and backed away. "Did ya now?"

"Allard said there is no way of knowing why you are in this territory each year at this time but legends abound that every year you are seen in this area."

Eyebrow raised, he offered, "Coincidence."

"Over 600 times?"

He rubbed both eyes with his right thumb and index finger. "Never wagered on being so predictable. Yer fancy Doc know why I'm here?"

"No, just that you pass through the region."

"Whatever." He turned but didn't offer his elbow again. "Yer a long way from home, little sister, and I won't leave you to the wolves of the street. I ain't a complete asshole."

"I can ride along and we can talk," Jessica offered, keeping up with him.

"That's about all I need, talk." His calm voice had left him.

They trudged past many grubby people as the street narrowed and they made a longer way around a trench reeking of fecal matter.

Jessica said, "I'm no trouble and I can feed myself."

"I can hope so at your age. What are ya, twenty, twenty-five?"

"Twenty-one."

"Damn," Gorias mumbled and his head titled far to one side, cracked loud and righted itself.

"This is a scholarly study." Again she reached in her inner robes but this time produced a tiny, green felt bag. "I can pay you for your time as well."

Gorias stopped again, looked down at her, and then moved her by the shoulders as a skinny man staggered past reeking of ale and passing wind loud. "That sounds better at least." He took the small bag Jessica held up and opened it. "Damn my hide, those are raw diamonds. Worth a fortune." He squinted at her and leaned down. "Jessica, is it?"

"Yes?"

"Ya bought yerself some boring stories and a rough ride. I gotta be gettin' outta here and on to the next town."

She reached down her top and searched, fumbling about the wrap to her breasts. Gorias raised an eyebrow but stayed quiet. "What? No comments?"

"None I care to share. Ya need a hand?"

Her hand came into the afternoon light holding four tiny gems. Dull, purple, and flat, they didn't sparkle in the sun.

Gorias reached out and took one. "Eyes of the Dragon, huh?"

She smiled. "Allard said you'd know what they were."

"This will make my stories more plausible."

Jessica beamed. "I have used others to see visions of the past, episodes in the life of the one pressing it to their head. It's an amazing experience."

Gorias gave her the jewels back and coughed. "Careful what ya wish for, little girl."

Hand back in her top to stow the jewels, Jessica wondered, "I figured you were here to collect a bounty back there on that creature or whatever."

"No, I was paid in advance to kill him."

"Who by?" she asked as they stepped onto the porch of a three-story building billed on its marquee as a boarding house.

"That changeling fella's own brother," Gorias clarified as they went inside. He nodded to the innkeeper and said, "I'll be gettin' out tonight. Keep the payment for tomorrow."

Behind the counter, by a rack of huge keys, stood a man so hairy, Jessica could barely find his eyes and mouth in the fur. "Yessir. It's been a pleasure."

"Yeah, thanks," Gorias answered listlessly, but a menace lurked in his tone as he ordered, "Have Traveler brought up and saddled suitable. Anyone fucks with him and ya all die, savvy?"

The bearish man nodded and yellow teeth appeared in the mass of hair. "We wouldn't dream of harming him. It's been an honor, and truly, we wish we had a souvenir to remember you by."

Gorias set his boots loud on the hardwood floor and stared at the innkeeper for a few moments before saying,

"Once I get my gear and head out, what I leave in my room will be memory enough. To yer health, fella."

After he started up the steps, Jessica followed, but she soon stopped as Gorias turned.

"What?"

"Ya really should stay down here. I just gotta grab a few saddle bags."

"Why?"

Gorias frowned. "Our relationship might be at an end fast-like. My life isn't a fantasy adventure, sweetheart; it's horror, pure and simple."

"I understand, Lord La Gaul."

"I ain't a Lord any more. But if ya want, I guess ya can see the room."

Once at the top of the stairs Gorias took a deep breath and walked to the third door on the right. He fished in a pouch on his belt, produced a huge metal key and undid the hanging lock on the door. Opening the door, he walked to the left side of the small room. While he leaned down to grab a pack, Jessica stepped to the doorway but didn't venture inside. The rancid odor struck fast and the scribe's right hand covered her mouth.

In a chair carved out from an old tree stump sat a man, dead, headless, his left arm missing at the shoulder joint. If alive, he still wasn't going anywhere for he'd been bound to the chair with ropes and a burlap belt that may have even been his own. Though fresh dead by the wetness of his wounds, the body stank and flies had started to build colonies in the wound where the neck stopped.

"It's the brother of that thing out there," Gorias said blithely as he turned around, arming up his saddlebags and kicking into view something that had been obscured to her until then: the man's head.

Though her eyes widened at first, a look of curiosity came over her, then shock when she glared at Gorias.

"Yeah, I killed him in mid-transformation. See? His teeth were growing already. Never knew how they do that, morph folks, ya know? They must feed off something in their bodies to create more mass but that's a greater mystery than my mind can solve easy."

"This is the brother of the other one?"

"Yeah, they were twins."

"What's their story?"

"Dunno. Who cares really? Twins cursed to be monsters, not much of a story in the grand scheme of celestial pissing matches."

"How can you say that? It sounds amazing! Who contracted you to kill them?"

Gorias kicked the head again and it flopped over, facing away. "He did. Something noble still lived inside him. As cursed as he and his sibling were by some asshead Mage of Damballah from way down south, he wanted no more part of it."

"So he paid you to kill his brother, and him, too?"

"Yeah. That wasn't my only reason for being here." He opened his cloak, revealing a belt about his waist that housed a few orderly leather pockets. A wadded up cloth was crudely jammed behind the belt. Pulling the bundle out, he unwrapped it and Jessica stepped back.

"The right hand of that spellcaster?"

"Yeah, it's a long story as well, but I need this for a future endeavor. C'mon. Let's go."

Once in the hallway, Gorias eyed her. She blinked up at him and half smiled.

"Ya took that better than I thought."

"I'm screaming on the inside, Lord La Gaul."

"Call me Gorias," he told her as they started down the stairs.

"I have to ride with you now," she half laughed.

Gorias smiled at her humor. "Really? What for?"

"My guards are dead, my enchantments spent and after today, I don't know if I can ever feel truly safe again."

"I might could take you along to Nineveh, but I have other stuff to do, all right?"

"So you don't care if I ask you things on the trip?"

They stepped outside and walked back to the stables area. "Knock yourself out."

Her eyes widened at the great white stallion being saddled. "This is Traveler?"

Gorias waved to the grubby-faced youth securing the tack on the horse and slung the saddlebags over to him. "That's what I call all my horses. I get them from a good stock. I've lost a few but always return to that bloodline. They are great horses."

Jessica gushed and clapped her hands once. "Excellent. That's one story. I thought I'd heard a crazy tale that your mount was immortal."

He turned and smirked at her. "Yeah? Go figure. I assume you have a horse someplace?"

"Yes, sir, uh, Gorias."

"Let's get it and get going. Though it's noon, I wanna head outta of here, darkness coming later or no."

"You plan to sleep outside?"

Gorias shrugged. "Been doing it for centuries, sister. Surely you had to on your trip here."

"Several times yes, but...."

"Skittish after that monster, huh?"

"Are such things common here in this region?"

"In Sicani? Probably not. The world is a bad place, so every so often ya run into real badness if that makes sense. That was uncommon but not unknown. The gal who owned the bar?"

"Yes?"

"That's more common place. She's an Elymian, not native to this land but have usurped this corner of it. The Sicanis further over in Eryx, they are easier to deal with. That's more of a religious place than a politician hellhole like here in Segesta."

"I see. You'd rather deal with religious people than politicians?"

"Both can be equally as crooked, but I at least know those guys better."

"Fine."

"Can't stomach those Elymians though. Obnoxious bitch? Ya don't need a curse from a wizard for that to appear in ya. It just shows up in some folks."

CHAPTER TWO
Day of Iniquity

Once Gorias saw that Jessica sat astride her mount, a beautiful roan several hands shorter than Traveler, he reined his horse about and started trotting for the edge of town. Segesta, a quiet village composed of many brick buildings in its truly clean and metropolitan center, degenerated quickly in the outer reaches as the streets turned rougher and the homes became made of logs.

"One would think the external limits of a village might be where the new houses start," Gorias related, a final glance over his shoulder. "It seems they build new places on the foundations of old places, when it suits them."

Jessica gripped her reins and looked back as well for a moment. "Why is that, do you think?"

"Perhaps familiarity. Maybe folks don't wanna leave a spot. Maybe just bein' lazy. Maybe the ancients knew what they were doing. Who knows?"

"Do you ever dream of the place of your birth?"

Eyes ahead, Gorias' voice held no emotion when he replied, "No. My boyhood home, maybe a little, but not where I was born."

"Do you miss family and friends?"

"My family back there where I grew up are all dead and what friends I have are scattered."

"Both of your parents are dead?"

Gorias shot her a sour look. "This is gonna be a great time hangin' out with you. Traveling alone provides a kinda silence rough diamonds can't buy."

"I'd love to hear about your parents." Jessica produced a tiny scroll, spread it across a stone tablet balanced on her saddle horn and then pulled out a quill from her robe.

"Ya write with that?"

"Certainly. It scribes on the parchment and I rub it in later with filler."

"Amazin', I say," Gorias deadpanned.

"Was your father a great warrior?"

"Yeah, but he was a chief of our folks in that region of Thule." He gazed off into the rolling countryside and distant trees as he recalled. "We seldom fought unless for a good reason, but every so often, such an event popped up. That guy, he'd travel half a world away to get what he wanted. Took most of the village with him on such treks. He got pissed, he stomped on the reason." Gorias eyed her and asked, "You all right? Ya look like ya got lost all of a sudden."

Jessica turned her face from him and her gaze wandered in the sparse open grasslands before them. "You're giving me hints, not tangible tales."

"The tangible tales of Gorias La Gaul," he chuckled. "I wouldn't pay to hear that even if half drunk. All right, once we get bedded down, ya can use one of them Eyes of the Dragon and I'll show you a story about my father and mother."

Jessica looked to him again. "Is it a romance?"

"There's some love to it," Gorias affirmed, eyebrows raised in recollection. "Haven't thought about them in a while."

Jessica smiled wide then tried to repress it, taking on a

studious look. "You will place the eye to your head and pass on that vision to me?"

"Sure. Glad to see you can't contain your excitement. Lemme warn ya, sister, be ready. My visions and the stuff folks told me about that forms most of the story ain't pretty."

"The eyes pick up real events seen by those there or their blood kin in spirit."

"That's the theory about those Eyes of the Dragon anyway."

"You sound doubtful."

Gorias sighed as they passed on over a great crest and headed down into a valley. "In every Eye of the Dragon is a negligible flicker of dragon-fire, a part of the soul of all dragons. They desire a window into the life of a person. They got to see plenty of me, so I really don't fret over myself."

"But you do me?"

"Someone has gotta."

Her dainty hand on her chest for a moment, she winked. "I'm touched."

"I'd feel pretty bad if ya got screwy in the head over the things I could show ya and your spirit is tainted by the dragon-fire."

"Nonsense." Her forehead furrowed and she took on a somber expression. "The goddess Ishtar will preserve me."

Gorias' smirk faded. "Good luck."

*****

"This area is pretty harmless," Gorias assured her as Jessica spread out her bedroll near a small campfire in the darkness.

"In reading up on this area, it seemed reasonably devoid of beastie stories."

Gorias stopped for a moment as he removed Traveler's saddle. "Beasties?" he said quietly and then stowed the saddle. "Yeah, the further inland we get, the worse that is, but we're safe for now."

Jessica's face lightened up, made almost angelic in the glow of the fireplace as she pulled the Eyes of the Dragon from between her breasts. "What have I to fear? I'm riding with Gorias La Gaul!"

He turned and wondered aloud, "Ya been nippin' at the wine flask already?"

She wore a hurt expression, bottom lip pouting. "I had some brandywine, but not enough to obscure any coming vision."

He pondered her words, and how she only feared a night monster or a snake maybe, but not the amorous advances of one of the world's greatest lovers. Such was life....

"Well, get comfy and we'll try this out," Gorias told her as he saw she had already settled in a cross-legged, sitting position with a blanket about her legs. She was all ready to get his vision. He thought it was lucky for the gal he was a slight gentlemen, as while one is in a vision with the Eyes, folks could be easily taken advantage of, as they were entranced for a long time.

He took the tiny bag of Dragon jewels, shook one out and frowned at it in the palm of his hand. He soon sat before her, but not in the same position.

"What?" she wondered aloud as he groaned, pulling his cloak off and dropping to his buttocks, facing the fire.

"I ain't as nimble as I once was. You live 700 years and try that sitting style ya got working."

Jessica's eyes widened as he picked a jewel, her anticipation high.

Gorias placed it to his forehead, closed his eyes and then yanked it away. "Here. Go crazy."

She clicked her tongue in her mouth and grinned. "That easy?"

"Ya need to lay off the brandywine, missy."

Jessica rocked her hips, swept back her hair and placed the jewel to her head.

And the rest was history.

*****

"You throw down an olden woman in front of the Son of God himself, and expect information?" the deep voice pondered before stopping to chuckle. "You truly are from the lands of the north near Thule, Chief Ambiorix. Only one from there would have the stones to do such a thing."

Steely fingers held the writhing body of the woman on the slab. These weathered digits attached firm to the muscled arms of an enormous man. Beneath his heavy mustache, his lips curled back and he grunted, "It's you who sets the price of accurate tidings, Neurath. Besides, what makes you so special? There are many sons of the gods running across this planet."

The flickering firelight in the cavern only showed the massive outline of the giant Son of God as he leaned forward. From these shadows came the sound of nostrils flaring and the wet scrape of steel on stone. Though Ambiorix stood very tall, the figure that stood up dwarfed him. The air soon gasped as a heavy blade passed through it. Ambiorix never flinched as the Nephilum Neurath brought down the axe head the size of a man's chest onto the stone slab. The naked woman wheezed and then let out an earsplitting cry before her sobs exploded into insane squeals. Neurath clumsily dropped the axe beside the block. He reached down, picked up the skinny leg freed from the body, and put the bloody edge to his huge mouth.

"Good enough?" Ambiorix asked, still holding the woman down solid.

Neurath sighed. "It will do for starters." The giant then seized the tiny figure on the stone, careful not to drop the leg, and Ambiorix released her. The behemoth turned and hanged her on metal hooks screwed into the stone wall. As the hooks pierced through her back and protruded under her collarbones, Neurath yawned, "So, Ingaevone tribesman, what is it you require of me?"

"What no one else can give," Ambiorix replied, a hand on the grip of a short sword sheathed at his waist. "I need to know where the cult of Ensibzianna hides. It's said the malevolent son, Alagar, leads these folk at the moment."

Neurath sat back on a cushioned outcropping in the cave, still chewing his food, and soon said through crimson teeth, "You come to a Nephilum for such a boon? You have stones in those russet trousers, I will grant you that, Ingaevone." Swallowing, he gestured with the leg and muttered, "Alagar, curse me running, that damnable imbecile."

"I know the charge of one who thinks he's descended of the gods," Ambiorix stated and motioned to the cave entrance. Two husky men, nearly copies of Ambiorix in large build and hirsute body, carried in a struggling figure, but this time, it was an old man. They stripped him of his scarlet cotehardie, then his gypon, and again, Ambiorix held his offering down on the granite wedge.

Neurath arched an already serrated monobrow. "You came prepared. So the primitives from beyond the Zenghaus

Mountains are learning, eh?"

"I'd never travel this close to Shynar unless it was vital to me or my kindred," Ambiorix said as maintained his pinning clutch on the oldster.

With a single nod, Neurath scooped up his axe and reared back. The old woman hanging behind them gagged and passed out at last. The axe fell and this time the giant extracted a left forearm from the stone block. Sampling this meat and wearing a more appreciative look, Neurath declared, "Very good, Ingaevone. This mage is from afar." Neurath then arose and hung this man on a set of hooks near to the old woman. The tongue of the aged man screamed curses unto the Ingaevone, their mothers and the offspring of fallen angels.

Ambiorix waited patiently, never speaking.

Neurath noted Ambiorix's patience. The again reclining giant gnawed on raw tissue. "I admire you, primitive human. You hold your tongue." He wiped a ruddy-skinned forearm over his bloody maw and asked, "You knew the price was blood and provender?"

"As is the cost with anything," Ambiorix replied with a calm voice. "All matters come down to blood."

Gulping with a stiff grunt, Neurath sucked on the forearm and wore a reflective expression. "Ensibzianna, aye? A cult indeed worships my half brother Alagar from the heavens. His ego is overloading his ass, truth be told." He fanned himself with the bone and licked marrow from his upper lip. "I know where he awaits oblations from his foolish admirers."

Since the pause was so long, Ambiorix sighed and turned to his men. They exited the cave and returned with another screaming contribution. Again, this woman was older, but not as ancient as the first one Ambiorix lay down before Neurath.

Neurath's hawkish nose twitched. "You keep the fatter ones for later? You are wise," he snorted, watching the men place her under Ambiorix's hold.

This woman did not cry, but cursed Ambiorix and Neurath. "I invoke the names of Asmodeous and Azathoth to burn out your eyes!" she yelled with enormous malediction. "May Tiphereth mate with your mother! May Belial pass water in the face of your sister and all of her children fall from her belly before it is time!"

Neurath belched a bored groan as he picked up the axe. "Mouthy one, no?"

Ambiorix held her with great difficulty as she made signals with her fingers, blaspheming heavily. Frowning, Ambiorix said, "I'll throw in a few more if you cut off her head."

With a slight snigger, Neurath chopped and she yelped. He took her left foot off and promptly placed the woman on the wall. Though wailing in agony, she still uttered profanity and curses at them. The old man next to her had gone unconscious from loss of blood now painting the wall. The giant eyed her and then Ambiorix. "Maybe you are correct." He then picked up the foot and started to pick as his teeth with the appendage's little toe. "This cult is located in the ruins of Larak at the edge of the desert of Dundayin. This is most certainly true."

Ambiorix nodded and started to turn away.

"Tell me," Neurath mused, teeth grinding on the cold toes amid the ear-piercing curses of the woman. "Amuse me, Ingaevone. Why does the cult of Ensibzianna enrage you enough to bring sacrifice unto a Son of God that is not of your faith? Why travel all this way from home in Thule?"

"My god is Wodan," Ambiorix responded with assurance. "He gives strength the moment one is planted in your mother's belly and watches us to see if we'll stray from the good course. If I were not smart enough to find my lost blood amongst the cult, Wodan would not show his favor to me."

Neurath nodded, as if lost in thought. He then supposed, "And yet you had no trepidation of bringing these ones in for me? You fear not their powers? They are all necromancers and witches, as it were, every last one."

Ambiorix shrugged. "Why should I be afraid? I don't believe in their gods."

The cackling laughter of Neurath echoed out of the cavern as Ambiorix exited.

Just outside the cave, the acolytes of Neurath frowned at the savages. The three women were tall, quite fleshy and dressed in green samite robes. The youngest one stepped forward, her black tresses shaking, and said to Ambiorix, "You fancy yourselves real men? You do not know what it is to be a true man."

Ambiorix didn't reply, but one of his men, a fireplug-shaped warrior called Garretson, cursed her and told her, "You fuckin' have courage because you can fuckin' take in a giant? Wodan craps fuckin' knives on you."

They climbed on their horses, but the woman persisted, wishing blight on Ambiorix. Looking down, the chief retorted, "What kind of woman lays down with what is not human?"

She snapped back, "What kind of man brings in old ladies to sacrifice for his desires?"

"One in love?" Ambiorix shrugged. "They were just witches. They said they could tell me whereby true love was located." He then smiled wolfishly. "They lied. Take care that I find my love at Larak, or we shall be back."

The other plump acolyte put her arm around the cursing

girl and said to Ambiorix, "She's young."

Garretson pulled on his face wrap to ward off the trail dust and muttered, "She may not get much fuckin' older."

The young woman said, "To give up lives for meat, just for your true love, that is barbaric!"

Ambiorix and his kindred laughed. "We are barbarians," Ambiorix informed her as they left.

*****

This vision shifted to a broad, open place. A grizzled man, ancient of years, opened the door to his home. The small abode, made of mud bricks, was the only structure aside from a grain storage bin at the oasis. Several palm trees and a long pool of bubbling water made the oasis unique on the edge of the vast desert of Dundayin. Wobbling, using a withered branch for support, the hermit faced the mounted barbarian horde alone.

"Good day, men," the old one said, shielding his eyes to the sun. The watcher then saw several women dismount from amongst the great force. Not much smaller than the men, these sturdy built females carried sheathed swords, too. He lost count of how many walked in the pack.

The host of hairy men and women climbed off their horses and led them to the water. There were so many of the barbarians that they refreshed their horses and themselves in shifts.

From out of these strangers emerged two blue-eyed men. Removing the dark cloth from their faces, they nodded at the watcher and shook off the dust.

"I am Ambiorix and this is Garretson. We shall use your water."

Looking back the way they came, the watcher said, "Far from home, I see."

Ambiorix went to the bubbling spring and buried his face in the water. Emerging with a wild gleam in his eye, hair whipped over his head, he looked at the pool and then directed his eyes south of the oasis. "Larak is not far from here. I can see the ruins in the distance."

The watcher coughed in agreement and then sat in a wooden chair made of sanded-down palm tree trunks. "Not much there, young man."

Never taking his eyes from the distant site, Ambiorix murmured, "All that matters is there, oldster." He then gestured to his men. They unloaded a few long rolls of cloth and laid them at the door of the watcher. "There's dried meat and nuts in there. We remember who honors us."

"I thank you for that and my life."

Ambiorix's eyes still ignored him, but his mouth replied, "No use killing an aged watchman, is there?"

"I suppose not."

"Previous owners of the food have no more use for it. Call it a gift from Wodan."

The watcher faced back to the North. "Wodan? My, you are far from home. By your fair hair and blue eyes, I'd guess you were of the tribes far beyond the Caucasus Mountains nearest here."

"You would guess correctly."

The old man fell silent. He took a few breaths and then looked toward Larak.

Ambiorix waved for the women to refill the skins of water and at last faced the watcher. "And you wonder why we are here, from a world away, so far south?"

Shrugging, the watchman said, "I'd deduce it has to do with the faction of Ensibzianna in Larak. They absorb many followers and hold up in the ruins. There certainly isn't anything to rob or rape in the remains of Larak."

Ambiorix's huge hands curled into fists. "That's not why I…we are here." He bent over and leered at the watcher. "Why are you out here at the edge of the desert?"

"My father before me lived here and tended this oasis. It's my life. This is where I live and belong. I do as I was taught. Surely, even you folk of the north know to honor your father and his wishes."

"We know of blood, old man," Ambiorix nodded and walked to his horse. "My niece here is twice the fighter most men are and worth dying for."

The watcher eyed the stout, blonde girl barely covered in buckskin clothes and cloaks to keep off the sand. "Take care. There's a gang of fighters in Larak."

Ambiorix smiled. "That's all right. I brought my own."

With a snicker, the watcher wished, "Be of fine fortune then, even if you meet your death. If you seek after your kin, I hope you find them."

"I will," Ambiorix promised. "If they send my ass back to Thule, they won't send it back alive. The fools in Larak plan a sacrifice tomorrow, a grand hecatomb of children and infants. I know through their by-laws and their slavery to the shifts in the lights of the sky. If anything, these religious dolts are dogmatic and prisoners to their rules. We'll take them all to Hell before any of my kin falls."

"God be with you," the watcher wished him.

"God loves men like me," Ambiorix said, half jovial. "Whoever you think the supreme God is."

"Why is that?"

Ambiorix shrugged. "He just does."

As the barbarian leader walked away, the other blonde man Garretson looked at the watcher and proclaimed, "God has balls. So does Ambiorix. God respects that."

*****

Stopping a fair distance from the ruins of Larak, Ambiorix surveyed the scene. He saw heavyset men and boys, sorry excuses for guards or pickets, scurrying to tell that a massive force stood at the doorway to the despoiled city. That didn't concern Ambiorix at all. "They need to keep what I want alive," he muttered to no one. "Don't they, now, princess?"

The city of Larak was once a great spectacle, Ambiorix heard tell, but destruction fell on it long before he drew a breath. Previously, his warrior grandfather, Gorian, told him a raging sea once covered the desert of Dundayin. Off to their left, an endless wasteland hemmed in a more fertile ground around Larak. Fertile as to say weeds and some plants grew there.

One of the warriors called out, "Looks as if that land over yonder is the piss bucket of the gods!"

After the laughter subsided, Ambiorix nodded toward the ruins ahead. "My grandfather told me around the fire that Larak was destroyed and he didn't lie. But what sort of creatures could have done that?"

While rows of obelisks remained, several blocks of these phallic stones lay knocked every way as if a child destroyed a playground sand sculpture. Numerous high stonewalls slumped, some broken and jagged, whereas others still formed corners. The ceilings of many of these buildings, Ambiorix guessed them temples, had caved in, spilling light and sand through the breeches. Grim, chaotic visions swam in the primitive skulls of the foreigners to the desert. Ambiorix's heart started to beat faster, but he never would have admitted to such a fact. It was as if the structures toppled in a pattern, he thought.

"What vanity," Ambiorix declared, pondering the configurations not overthrown by human hands. "To build up marble houses for their gods to live in. Huh, looks like one of them grew angry enough to knock down the habitations."

"Shall we send the new squatters to their fuckin' gods?" Garretson asked, causing a cheer to arise from the multitude.

With serenity in his manner, Ambiorix griped the handle of a sword on his back. "Yes."

Whichever riders rode two at a time let their spare dismount. As these lines of footmen assembled behind the procession of horsemen, those inhabiting the ruins of Larak scuttled like disturbed rats. Unorganized and half dressed, these residents created unity only in their communal fear…at the battle cries of the northern ruffians, heralding their berserk charge.

Shouting with insane vehemence, the invading folk moved en mass toward the broken granite carcass of Larak. Ambiorix felt his blood leap in his veins as the thunder in his ears became drowned out by the cacophony of hooves.

A few dozen valiant souls actually stepped forward to fight. This force of cultists swiftly retreated when they realized the size of the tide of livid humanity bearing down on them.

Swinging long swords, bludgeons, and stabbing spears, the multitude rode into the crumbling streets, slaying whomever they encountered. Ambiorix led them in first, removing the skullcap of a baldheaded man. This man swung a curved footman's axe at him and missed badly. After one swipe from Ambiorix, a slop of brains painted the nearest fallen obelisk. The ancient mosaic of creatures half man and half squid was further obscured by the gray gruel.

No organized resistance flowed from the cult of Ensibzianna. Since the attack lacked great order, it made the melee additionally turbulent. Most of the savage host leapt from their mounts, dragging downward running members of the religious assemblage. Punching, stabbing and slashing, Ambiorix's people made rapid work of anyone unlucky enough to be caught.

Ambiorix and Garretson met, gathering their troops behind their backs. In front of them stood one of the more complete edifices, hardly cracked by whatever destroyed the city. From this cracked structure poured an armed fighting force, lean men all in thin chain mail and brandishing shields, axes and short scimitars. Prepared for their deaths, Ambiorix's tribe screamed for *Wodan* and charged.

Blood spattered the ancient pillars anew and the dust became muddy in the spilled ichor. Ambiorix looked down at a fallen Ensibzianna cultist. The mouth stretched open too far, crimson sparkling as it ran out fast like vomit. Helmets flew and heads rolled free from them as the barbarians forced their way forward. Links of chainmail bent or shattered under the strength of their strong blows.

A press of fresh bodies forced Ambiorix's back to a huge block of stone. While three held him in place, one shorthaired man grinned and stepped away from the throng. He held up a flail and spun the metal spiked head around in victory. He gloated too long before delivering the deathblow, for this gave

Garretson time to make a diagonal slash and remove the head of the cultist, nearly taking off his shoulder as well. Ambiorix pushed off one of the cultists and this man landed on the end of Garretson's sword. Only impaled through the kidney, the man howled and slipped off the blade. Garretson cursed. Soon, his left hand swung around, wielding a war hammer. Though the cultist's head did not explode, it did give a loud, wet pop sound as the body under it plummeted.

Swiftly dispensing with the two left to him via his dagger and sword, Ambiorix nodded to Garretson and they moved closer to the center of Larak.

Through the massive slaughter, the tribesmen ran amok and prevailed. Shoulder to shoulder, though, they advanced to the main shelter of the cult of Ensibzianna.

Suddenly, a huge shape stumbled out of the break in the wall. The invaders froze for a moment, but their tension soon passed. Alagar himself had entered the fray. However, this giant, twice as tall as even the hulking Ambiorix, was no fiend incarnate. His muscle tone had gone and his elongated limbs slacked at the biceps. His stomach hung low over the green silken kilt that covered his nakedness.

"Fuck but he's seen better days," Garretson remarked, holding back a smile.

Alagar staggered, trying to hold up his huge mace to fight.

Ambiorix said, "He was once a lover of great capacity."

Garretson affirmed, "Butcher me to fuckin' Hell if I end up as such."

"Agreed," Ambiorix guaranteed him and waved an arm at the youths in the tribe. These boys, barely in their man-making stage, were along on this trip to help complete that particular male journey. They launched spears at the immense

Alagar. Many of the lances broke, stubbled off on Alagar's thick skin, but a few of them held in his belly. This distraction was all the tribe needed to thrust ahead. Despite the fact that Alagar swung down, crushing the spine of one attacker, the folk swarmed his legs, chopping with great battle axes, taking his toes and ankles out with ease.

Alagar fell to his knees and swiped his mighty arms, shoving several off himself. Ambiorix and Garretson attacked as one, both swinging their swords down at the top of his shoulders. Ambiorix's overhand swing removed the left arm of Alagar. Garretson's blade swung into the joint of the right shoulder. The giant lowered his brow and thumped Garretson to the dirt. His head swayed to Ambiorix, and with a clumsy impact, caused the leader to drop his sword. Frantic, needing a weapon, Ambiorix performed as all barbarians do and fought with what was at hand. He grabbed the wrist of the giant's dismembered arm and shouted a wordless war cry. Swinging the limb up, he slammed the bloody stump of the arm into Alagar's jaw. As if he were stabbed, the Nephilum grabbed his mouth, his injured right arm flailing, and blood spurted out. It was an orange fluid. Ambiorix assumed the giant bit his tongue off from the blow. In moments, Alagar felt the points of a dozen spears in his chest and belly. He slumped back abruptly and breathed his last.

"At least he fuckin' came out and fought," Garretson commented, sucking air, winded by the struggle.

"He had courage, perhaps as much as any cornered beast, aye?" said Ambiorix as he turned and saw further members of the cult stream out of the pillar-lined streets. Screwing up their audacity, they meant to retaliate.

Rushing forward, the counteroffensive had some teeth

to it, at least until they beheld their dead Lord Alagar. At the spectacle of his bloated corpse full of spears, they shrieked and fled.

"The day is fuckin' ours!" Garretson rejoiced and many jumped in the air.

Ambiorix looked into the main shelter. "Almost."

Drawing near to Ambiorix, Garretson said in a low voice, "Do you think Neurath warned Alagar that we were coming?"

Peering into the lopsided stone structure, Ambiorix shook his head from side to side. "No. They were ill-prepared for a strong assault. Besides, how could Neurath have done that?"

Garretson thought for a second and answered, "Perhaps a power of the fuckin' mind? They have unearthly parents."

Ambiorix gave him a distasteful glance and motioned for him to follow along on inside. "I doubt that. Besides, the Nephilum all hate each other."

"Why is that?"

"Imagine a family where all of the children think they are God."

Grunting a little, Garretson surveyed the interior of the barren building. "I see. Still, we killed his brother."

"Neurath will not care," Ambiorix promised as he walked, unarmed, towards the front of the building. "One less sibling to worry about. Neurath would applaud me if I brought Alagar's head to him."

"Will you?"

Ambiorix glanced at him and smirked. "No."

At the echo of their voices, a few people scrambled from behind a crumpled tapestry. These few older men didn't make it out alive, running into a line of thickset savages. Ambiorix and Garretson never concerned themselves with them. The fallen tapestry revealed a vulgar, decaying stone altar. Once, this small platform was an oversized pair of breasts divided by a phallic symbol. An unstable world or whatever trashed Larak had ruptured the floor in places, thus making the altar uneven and pinched together, crushing the penis between the breasts. This amused the chief, but when Ambiorix walked behind the slab, his smile faded.

"Come on out, dog," Ambiorix snarled.

The figures popped up so quickly, Garretson stepped back and held up his sword. One person was a man of great age. His eyes flared with vitality as he easily subdued the woman under his grip. One arm around her neck, his other hand held a curved blade.

The flaring eyes of the man danced as he promised, "Come closer and she dies, dirty pig!"

The woman was much taller than the elderly man. Her ginger-colored hair hung disheveled about a grimy face. She wore a single-piece cloak, but this simple cover couldn't hide her advanced state of pregnancy. The look in her eyes was one of terror at the sight of the warriors.

Ambiorix scowled at them and his gaze focused on her. Eyes dancing over her appearance, he reached out an arm to Garretson and took the short sword.

The older man shouted with vigor, "Stop, or I will sever the cow's throat! I will do it as sure as you live. I don't care if she's from the royal house of Transalpina. I am a priest of Alagar and ready to die, so back away or I shall cut her from ear to ear."

The blade of the short sword bounced off Ambiorix's thigh. He said coldly, "Do as you must."

Confusion reigned in the eyes of the priest as his gaze

went from Ambiorix to Garretson. From out of the tresses, the woman's face also registered bewilderment. Tears started to flow from her bulging eyes.

"I said," the old cleric repeated, "I will kill her!"

"Kill her then," Ambiorix told him and stepped forward. The priest and woman bumped into the stone slab as Ambiorix's left hand reached out. However, he neither grabbed at the old man nor the woman's arm to pull her free. Instead, he placed his hand lower, on the flat in her middle, below her breasts, above her stomach. With an almost elegant thrust, Ambiorix sliced a crescent wound around the belly of the struggling woman. The priest released her, his voice caught in his throat, and she sprawled on the altar, screaming in horror as Ambiorix carved the baby out of her midsection.

Through a mess of screams, spewing cherry-colored fluid and pulpy gray tissue, Ambiorix performed his duty. Stepping back in a moment with the infant, Ambiorix felt the child contort as more pliable gore fell away. With his pinkie finger, he cleared the tiny mouth and then held the baby up. By means of a scream, the child's voice joined the throng of barbarians now gathered in the inner temple room. With great happiness, they shouted a welcome to their blood, led in cheers by the clapping niece of the chief, herself sporting a bloody nose and gore staining her blouse. Another cut was made to the cord still stringing the babe to his mother and Ambiorix turned, showing them all. Quickly, word spread that it was a boy. He handed the child to his niece.

"You...bastard..." the celebrant of Alagar stammered as he glared at the dying woman, who tried to fix her guts back into her belly a few times before the agony overtook her.

Ambiorix watched as his niece removed the upper flap of

her chain mail, and then her bloody blouse. With no hesitation, she placed the child to her left breast and it fed. Smiling, she then bowed her head to her uncle and said, "Though this isn't my daughter who died weeks ago, I shall raise him as my son."

"Good," Garretson said as the crowd applauded. "Then he'll not have a mother who tried to sacrifice him to a filthy fuckin' god for gold."

Laughter rippled through the chamber as the priest gaped at the suffering woman. He was about to cut her throat in mercy when Ambiorix slashed at the priest's wrist. The cleric dropped the knife as blood gouted from his forearm.

"No compassion for her," Ambiorix said ruefully. "Let her die as all traitors and the unfaithful must."

The mass of hirsute humanity started to recede from the temple and the priest shouted, "That is it? You are just going to leave?"

"I have what I came for," Ambiorix replied, waving at his son, feeding and mewling at his niece's breast. "My one true love."

"You destroyed all of my magnificent plans, all of my dreams of power at the great day of sacrifice," the priest screamed, fists hitting the altar and the dying woman's head alternately. "I could have beaconed the demons to bestow me proper power and you slew all of them, all of the other carriers of the seed, for what? For that barbarian bastard?"

Ambiorix stopped, turned and said, "All that matters is blood. Isn't that what all of you rubbish priests say? Isn't that what all of your demon lords require for happiness? Hell, isn't that what the one, true God supposedly desires for the forgiveness of sins—blood? Yet, you find it so hard to understand that we would do all of this for blood. You have not the right to survive."

Drawing the old priest's focus, Ambiorix walked back across the room. With a fast motion, his niece drew back and threw a dagger. End over end, the blade flew true and struck the priest's throat. The old man instinctively removed the blade, tearing loose his Adam's apple. The priest fell, choking and writhing in the dust by the ruined altar of big tits.

They turned their backs on the dead priest and the bloody woman. The tribe left the ruins of Larak.

Before they set out for their mountainous home, they stopped at the oasis to water their horses. Again, the old watcher came out of his home to see Ambiorix. This time, the watcher's eyes widened at the sight of the new baby.

"So," the watcher said, pondering the significance of what he saw. "You have found your love that was lost in the ruins at Larak?"

"Yes," Ambiorix proclaimed with pride in his voice. "This is my son; the only thing truly conjured in the day of iniquity wrought at Larak." Buoyant laughter traveled through the crowd. "Let that be a lesson to all, old man. If you try to use blood for blood, the wrong thing may come unto you."

The watcher nodded and stared at the child. "How is this one to be named?"

Ambiorix reached out and his huge hand touched the chest of the boy. Tiny fingers gripped the still bloodied hand of the warrior, and turned into fists. The boy's bluish-green eyes blinked and peered up at his father.

"He shall be called Gorias, after my grandfather. The name means *King of the Bastards*. Born into a world of blood and violence, let him get his mouth full of it. He better get used to it."

Born of Swords

The barbarian horde then extolled Wodan and entreated him to bless Gorias, son of Ambiorix, with life and strength.

Gorias cried out as well to the clear, afternoon sky. The infant studied the blood on his hands and, years later, Ambiorix's niece swore unto Wodan that little Gorias *laughed*.

CHAPTER THREE
Catching the Treetop Rapist

Back on horseback and heading down the trail the next morning, Gorias didn't bother looking at Jessica when he asked, "You doin' all right?"

Eyes ahead, she answered, "Fine."

"Ya haven't said dick since before the vision last night."

She frowned but kept her eyes forward. "Dick. Are you happy?"

Gorias tilted his head a little. "I know it's probably not easy to watch all that."

"I've seen many bad things, great wars and mass suicides via the Eyes of the Dragon...." Her voice that started off strong trailed off.

"But?"

Eyes down at her reins, then off to the left where a thicket of knotty fallen timber loomed, Jessica opened her mouth but the words failed her.

"Take your time."

Her head snapped to face him. "Don't treat me like a child."

"You are a child," Gorias mumbled, watching the road. "I respect your vast learning from stone tablets and scrolls.

Hell, I'm sure you're smarter than me by far on any exam to be given. But there's something to be said for all the years I've lived and endured. If my manner is rough, tough, you invited this deal on yerself, sister."

"He chopped you from her body," Jessica said silently, looking away from him.

"Yeah. That's what he thought was the right thing to do."

"He came all that way and did that to get you back?"

"That's love, huh?" Gorias had humor in his voice when he spoke.

Her dander fell. "You two must have been so close."

"Not specially," reflected Gorias. "He never said those words to me, *I love you*, in my entire life. That wasn't our way. But his actions spoke louder than sticky words."

"Yes, I can accept that."

"Did you think me born in a palace with lots of attendants and priests waiting? C'mon, sister, ya know that ain't gonna be the case. Surely there are tales of my birth or origins?"

Jessica frowned, eyes spotting the ringlets of smoke in the air beyond the trees in front of them. "I hadn't took you for barbaric beginnings. The tales of you in Nineveh and close by struck the reader as a young man of breeding and some culture, with a distant drop of blood from the royal house of Transalpina."

Gorias threw back his head and laughed loud, causing birds to fly from nearby pine trees. "Some culture? Well, hell, I'll drink to that!" He pulled out his flask and took a swig.

Jessica gave him scant notice but kept her eyes focused ahead. "A tad early for that?"

Gorias stowed his flask. "For wine? Hell no. It's great for yer innards, or so they tell me." He paused, wiped his mouth with the back of his hand and added, "In Nineveh, if I recall."

"Your words carry a bit of disdain for the cultured and refined world."

"Not at all," Gorias scoffed and made a big show of that reaction. "I love the clean places out there. The world is a shit pile. Sweetheart, I adore sparkling cities and smart folks. They are outnumbered by a swarm of assheads all about them. Please don't think my tribe in Thule a bunch of inbred freaks or tree-worshiping fools. They were good folks, one with the world, god-fearing, but maybe not the gods ya might know, and really an honorable bunch. They give their women a damn sight more respect than those cultured dickheads you work for. I'm shocked they let you out, unless they wanted you out of the way."

Jessica's eyes widened and she glared at him. "How dare you imply such a thing!"

"Oh, I know that sounds a bit much," said Gorias, chin pointed to the sky for a moment as his eyes roved the heavens, then his look focused again on the rough road and grasslands ahead. "There are easier ways of gettin' rid of a problem."

"Are you implying I'm a problem?"

"Ya kinda seem to possess the ability to grow into one. Nonetheless, I think even an educated fella would pay to have ya smothered in your sleep rather than send ya off on a quest like this."

Jessica frowned and turned to gaze across the tall grasses and wild wheat stalks.

Gorias let it lay for a few minutes and then added, "Not everyone likes a person, ya know? Ya can't please everyone, I know."

"Where are we going next?"

"I'm headed to Eryx to see some monks across the next couple valleys. It's part of my yearly, predictable thing, I hear tell."

"Any observances of you weren't so specific."

"I gotta pay some respects. I'll fill ya in as we go." Shifting in the saddle, Gorias replied, "Huh. These are wild lands, but not barbarian territories, of course. The bandits here are little fuckers and easier to kill."

"How many have your slain?"

"Bandits or people in all?"

"You have them categorized?" Jessica's look lightened.

"Generally, but not numerically. Some people ya hope God forgives ya for killing, but others, hell, they have it coming. I can't believe there are too many survivors to tell of my yearly trip."

"It irritates you people might be watching?"

"It irritates me I gotta share the world with so many idiots."

After an hour's ride the road flattened out and more wooded areas cropped up, but the trees were of a shorter variety, not towering oaks or maples. Gorias allowed Jessica off her mount to go into the woods and perform a necessity. He slung himself down off Traveler and did likewise, but didn't go into the woods. Subsequent to a few stretches, Gorias climbed back in the saddle.

She returned, adjusting her tunic, and jumped back onto her horse. Eyes to Gorias, who stared at her intently, Jessica snapped, "What?"

Facing the road again, Gorias pulled his overcloak about himself and gripped the reins. "Nuthin', sister."

"How was it a member of a royal family created you along

with a Thule chieftain?"

"Oh, she was kidnapped in our territory by unsavory folks and my dad accidentally saved her, one thing led to another."

"A woman of breeding fell for a hairy thug?"

Gorias winked. "Happens more than you might think."

She laughed as she put her boot in the stirrup. "Don't delude yourself."

"Just sayin', sister. Guess he didn't foresee her batshit crazy side. Ah well. A pretty face and a great ass can fool the best of us."

As the road crested, Gorias pulled Traveler to a halt. Jessica went ahead a few paces, unready for his move. She grimaced at him and then at the road ahead, which carried on into a dreary grouping of willow trees, sadly all hunched over and overgrown, all sweeping the ground by the road. The trees wouldn't impede their progress, and didn't hide the smoke from chimneys beyond.

"What is it? You smell a rat?"

His right hand in his saddlebag, Gorias said, "A nest of them." He drew out a tubular object sheathed in brown leather. His hand off the reins, he pulled the tube and twisted, making it extend. Gorias then held it to his eye and Jessica gave him mocking applause.

"A scope? Aren't you progressive."

Eye squinting at the viewing hole, Gorias mumbled, "Not so much, but the guy I killed and took this from was."

Her mirth vanished, and she peered at the distance for signs of life. "What is it?"

"Ever get a bad feeling? Intuition? I hear women have it."

"Are you scared of feeling like a woman?"

Still looking down the scope, Gorias confessed, "If I had

the girly parts, I'd never leave the bed mat all day. No, I got a bad, prickly feeling all over, a dreaded thing in my head just now."

"Are you familiar with this village?"

Scanning, he said, "I've passed through it several times and watered my horse. They have a river running alongside that snakes through this country." He lowered the scope and sighed. "That is why most villages are near it, ya know?"

"That makes sense."

After an eye roll, Gorias raised the scope again. "These people are only memorable in how they try and purify the water more from the river, boiling it so much. I think their chief or leader was a neatness guy, a progressive as you called him."

"Nothing wrong in that."

"I didn't imply there was, just that he didn't care for shitty water."

"Must you be so vulgar?"

Gorias stopped moving the scope and studied a spot in the distance. "It just kinda happens, vulgarity." He put the scope away. "A lifetime of livin' will make it common to yer regular vocabulary."

"You must try and restrict that talk," Jessica chided him.

He kicked Traveler a bit and said, "Ya ain't my wife."

Jessica kept with him as they gradually headed into the edges of the village. "You've had a wife?"

"A few."

"What happened?"

Gorias let out a loud sigh. "Disease, war, beheadings, hell, lots of things. I'd rather tell you about that ogre I killed when I was a lad. That is a good tale. Polish up yer jewels for that one."

Frustrated but letting it pass, Jessica eyed the weeping trees at the edge of the village and wondered, "Tell me how you came about that armor of yours."

Chin raised a little, Gorias conceded, "That's a good story, too."

"In the Chronicle of Morton, it is written that you slew a brood mother of blue dragons with your great swords, took the pieces to Jericho and they were crafted into this suit you wear."

His look intense, Gorias ducked his head a little as if wary of a hawk as they left the open places. Beyond the willows, numerous trees dotted the village but no more willows. Many had been burnt but stood, their charred branches bare, others chopped down and left to rot.

"That's all bullsh--uh, not true, m'lady," Gorias even mocked a high tone. He then spoke with his usual steady voice when he told her, "I didn't even have my swords yet, not for centuries. Damn, someone about here has a hard-on for trees."

Her nose wrinkled. "Yes, so it seems. The place reeks of sulfur."

Gorias stopped Traveler and Jessica followed suit. "Tell me, little girl, what does that tell you from your learned studies?"

"Plague of some sort? Are they burning to disinfect the air or area? Killing trees to stave off an infection or source of the sickness?"

"Could be. We best be gettin' the hell outta here, though. I told you this felt wrong."

As they started forward again, Jessica asked, "You've went on your life's journeys based on feelings, or intuitions?"

"If I go against them, huh, sister, it can be murder."

The closer they came to the series of cottages, more signs of life appeared in the persons of women clad in woolen skirts and deerskin overcloaks. Some two-dozen people left the homes and a building that just barely passed for a shop due to the mossy overgrowth. All but three villagers were women or teen girls. The others were old men, favoring canes.

A tall, slender lady of some bearing in how she carried herself stepped from the group. She bore a long face, but high eyebrows and blue eyes that glowed like ice. Though getting on in age, Gorias thought, she probably was a looker hundreds of years before.

"Ma'am," Gorias said, sounding tired. "We're just passin' through."

The woman blinked, looked at Jessica and then back to Gorias. "You are a fighting man?"

Gorias glanced the crowd over and then the rest of the village. "Where are your fighting men?"

"Too afraid to come out."

"I'm not that mean, ma'am."

"You misunderstand, they fear the treetop rapist."

Gorias then let his eyes rest on her. "I beg yer pardon?"

She nodded fast. "I'm Kilpatrick, wife of the late chieftain, Dimatta. The treetop rapist has had us in a state of terror for weeks and many are ready to abandon this town."

Jessica scanned the trees and half-smiled as Gorias did the same. "Ya have a rapist in the trees problem?"

"One that only prefers men."

Gorias chuckled but he laughed alone. "Yer serious?"

"Deadly. It isn't exactly human but we aren't sure what it is."

"I see you've tried to get its habitat to a minimum."

"Fruitless." Kilpatrick set depressing eyes on the burnt-out and gutted trees. "One never knows where it will strike."

"Never bothers the girls?"

"Not as such."

Gorias turned to Jessica. "So much for using you as bait." Again, he looked the area over and then the meager populace once again. "So, no one is man enough to come out or kill this thing?"

"It isn't an it so much as a he, but I wouldn't call it entirely human."

Right arm extended, Gorias pointed to the row of buildings made of wood planks, not logs like the houses of the town. "What is that?"

"The gaming hall is a part of it down the way. Many a trophy and stag head adorns the interior, but all the men are unwilling to hunt this thing, now."

He started to move Traveler to the edge of the community, toward a tree that wept so much a body hung from it. Jessica and the women followed.

Gorias swung his leg off Traveler and set his boots on the tall grasses by the edge of the forest. He pulled back his cloak over one shoulder and placed one hand on his left hip as he observed the body hanging from the tree. The crowd gasped at the armor on his body and Jessica looked away to hide her smile, seeing the manner in which Gorias let himself be displayed to the crowd.

"So who is this?"

Kilpatrick's look followed Gorias to the body in the tree. "He's Toushard, from the greater plains beyond Sobruk to the south."

Gorias walked about the form hanging from the tree. "Big fucker, ain't he?"

Hands folded in front of her belly, Kilpatrick frowned. "He was."

"The treetop rapist hung him? The fella doin' yer attacks must have more dexterity than I assumed."

"The rapist didn't do this." Kilpatrick wobbled a little on her cane and Gorias offered his right arm. She gladly took it, gleaning smiles from the populace and an eye roll from Jessica. "Thank you."

"No worries," Gorias smiled and then looked back to the body. "How'd he get strung up out here then?"

The lady sighed. "Toushard did it to himself."

"Toushard?" Gorias stared serenely at the body as if searching it for an answer. "What a punk."

Kilpatrick scowled at him. "That's a callous statement from a fellow mercenary."

"I'm a very callous guy," came Gorias voice, smooth as butter.

"Had you heard of him?"

"No."

"Word on the wind he was one of the best around, the next big thing in the business of killing and mercenary fighting."

"Never heard his name, but that's all right. I'm sure the aborigines over by where Lemuria is supposed to be have never heard of me."

"Where?"

"Lemuria, a place like Atlantis only it isn't real, just a campfire story made up by Atlantean rejects. I'm joking. Anyways. A merc, huh? Well, there's no union to join, but he did the craft a bad service by killing himself. Ya gonna let me guess why for?"

Jessica tugged on Gorias' other elbow. "Aren't we bound for Ey-rex."

"Eryx.

"Whatever. Why…?"

Gorias' eyes narrowed at her. "Ya wonder how the stories of my life happen? This is how."

"You stop in towns and take care of problems?"

"Seldom, really, but I stumble across things."

"Are they going to pay you?"

He pulled free of both women and went to the hanging body again. He reached up and fumbled in the pockets of the dead man. "Did ya pay him?"

Kilpatrick said, "Yes, but…."

"He didn't spend it already," Gorias snapped, menace hot in his voice that made a few young boys flee the mob. "Ya peckerheads stripped the body already."

Her face going pallid, Kilpatrick replied, "So?"

"Gimme what Toushard was paid."

The older woman turned and nodded to a few of the older girls, then turned back to La Gaul. "And you will kill the treetop rapist?"

His voice much calmer, Gorias muttered, "Maybe."

The girls returned and held out two small coin bags to Gorias. He opened each, peeked within and grunted. "All right." He threw one of the bags at Jessica, who caught it, but held it like a dead rat.

"My cut?"

"I don't care. I hate to carry so much." He glowered at Kilpatrick. "Less for them to frisk me for once I'm buggered to death, huh?"

Jessica put the bag in her belt pouch. "I don't think this is about money, is it?"

Gorias cleared his throat and turned back to the hanging body. "How the fuck does a guy keep his head shaved these days?"

"What?"

He pointed at the body, bald above the rings of ropes that broke the neck. "Shiny-headed bastard, but he has a rough beard. Wonder why ya'd keep it so neat. Ticks? Dunno."

Jessica shook her head and even sent Kilpatrick a confused look at this observation.

Gorias continued, addressing Jessica. "So this community has been hiding inside for weeks? Doesn't this thing ever try to get inside the cottages?"

Kilpatrick spoke up loud. "Yes, we are in hiding. No it doesn't."

Gorias replied, "I doubt there are any men here."

"But yes, there…oh, I see." Hands to her hips, Kilpatrick's look hardened. "You belittle the courage of our men?"

Gorias stopped in his walk about the body and he sighed this time. "Yeah, ma'am, I sure do."

"Our chief was a great hunter." She pointed to the long ranch-style hall to their left that denoted the center of the town. "That hall is full of his kills, of his conquests in the field."

"But he couldn't manage to hunt and kill this thing in life?"

"They have tried, and failed badly."

Gorias squinted at the great hall, moldering around the downspouts at the rain barrels. "Those long bones over the main door?"

"Yes?"

"How old are they?"

Jessica stepped around Gorias to take a closer look at the remains that draped the entrance as Kilpatrick answered, "A few months. Why do you ask?"

Hands rubbing his spine for a few seconds, Gorias soon asked, "Did your chief say what they came from?"

"A great winged beast, a hooved thing unnamed that they cornered in the night with its mate in the high country."

Gorias' eyes turned to Jessica and drilled holes in her face. Her humor faded. He looked back at Kilpatrick. "While I'd love to see what passes for a man in this town, I think I'll ferret out yer problem and move on through." He pulled his cloak apart, hands to his waist, revealing his armored body again. A great chorus of "Oooo's" echoed in the crowd, causing Jessica to put her hand to her mouth and restrain a laugh.

"What can I do to help, Lord La Gaul?" Jessica said in a cloying, overly sweet voice.

Gorias turned to her and grabbed his crotch. "Help me reverse my codpiece, would you?"

The women receded as Gorias took off his cloak and let Jessica refit his dragon armored codpiece in reverse, the main dip covering his buttocks. She reached about Gorias' big frame and pulled at the cinch straps.

"No jokes?"

"On the contrary," she said in earnest. "This is brilliant, even if you should let these fools rot. You're taking no chances?"

"I seldom do, though it might not look like it."

"You plan on being attacked from the rear. What a great idea."

"Again, I take no chances. "

Jessica's eyes stayed on her task, but her voice lowered. "You know better what those wings came from, don't you?"

"Yeah, and it wasn't a winged hoofed beast." His face screwed up in pain. "Hey, careful with the straps. I plan on using my balls again someday."

"Sorry, your majesty."

Gorias looked off to the groves of trees. "Don't call me that. I ain't never playin' that game again."

"You were a king, weren't you, for a brief time?"

"Is that what your tablets say?"

She stepped back, cracked her knuckles and picked up his cloak. "I do remember that."

"Not a king, not exactly. I guarded the heir during his regency, but it all got pretty ugly."

"In Albion?"

"Transalpina. Close."

"You were there in the great war against the Pryten uprising?"

"It started out to be something else, but yes, I led the armies to exterminate the Prytens later on. We got most of them but it was like trying to kill all the inhabitants of an anthill. They breed like rats and, after another generation, I just saw some in Transalpina a month or so back."

His cloak over her arm, she said, "You must tell me that tale and show it to me in the jewels."

Gorias winked. "Get yer crossbow, missy, and get ready to reload it. I'm going for a walk in the woods over yonder."

"You think the women of this Earth so taken with you that now a beast will be unable to resist?" Her voice rang soft, sexy and barely able to suppress humor.

"I think that thing wants any man."

"Guess I'm lucky it doesn't coddle to the women?" "Probably eats them."

Her face flushed. "Probably?"

"That'd be my guess, so watch your skinny ass, all right?"

They stepped closer to where the grove of trees thickened. She whispered although all were out of earshot anyway, "What is it?" "Could be a couple things, but I'm hoping it's a wounded gargoyle, nothing worse. That's what the wings look like. I reckon the chief cut the wings from a gargoyle and it has come back to um, well...."

"Take a pound of flesh back?"

"Via the backway, yeah."

Jessica smirked. "You speak funny for a man about to be sodomized by a monster for people he doesn't know well."

Gorias drew out his blades. "I like my odds. Now load your bow and follow at a good clip."

"Do you think this thing will really drop out of the trees on you? It can't be that easy."

Gorias nodded, nostrils wide. "I can smell it. It's near. Gimme my helmet while you are at it."

"I can't smell anything." Her eyes enlarged as she went to Traveler. "You fool with me. You couldn't be that cool under pressure." She undid his helm from the saddle and threw it underhanded. The helmet landed badly a few yards from him and Gorias frowned at her. "I throw like a girl, sorry."

"Oh, I dunno." He scooped the helm up, slid it on, but didn't take time to tuck his long hair in under it nor did he close the visor. He started into the denser grove at the edge of the village.

Jessica jogged to her horse, placed Gorias' cloak over the

saddle and pulled her crossbow down. She notched an arrow and ran back just in time to see Gorias, swords out at the ready on either side, have a dark, humanoid shape drop from the trees onto his back. She screamed, for the tree didn't look able to hold anything up in the faint spring leaves, although the twisted branches may have hidden something…it had to, that is what she told herself…surely the thing couldn't have appeared in this reality from another place. She ran to shoot at the form on Gorias' back.

Why didn't I freeze? she asked herself. Was she so convinced Gorias would take this thing that she had no such fears for her own safety? No, she was terrified and acted anyhow, for the creature straddled Gorias spine, long stringy arms swiping down on his wrists, knocking both swords to the grass. Long legs wrapped about Gorias' thighs, securing its base as the long arms wrapped about Gorias' helmeted head.

Her feet moved, the boots jerking to regular motions as she tried to take it all in, what *it* even was at all. The previous night, she'd lived a horrific vision from La Gaul's infamy, and now, reality slammed into her eyes. Not being a feeble lady of the manor or palace, Jessica held the grips of the crossbow lightly, and tried to relive days of hunting deer. The scent of the thing on Gorias wouldn't make any stag hunter happy, for it reeked of cabbage and rotten eggs.

With the idea of gargoyles set in her head, though, Jessica thought the thing would be gray like stone effigies back home. This creature's body, while trimmed with reptilian scaled ridges, bore a skin tone aping that of tree bark. Brown, weathered and nearly sporting a grain to it, the creature looked like a portion of the tree when it fell on Gorias and started thrusting against him.

Apparently, Gorias' codpiece idea worked, for the big man stood up and gyrated, then grabbed the creature by its flailing wrists. One of the claws pulled free of his grip and started to bat at his head, an unearthly squeal filling the air. Gorias staggered, blocking Jessica's shot with his own body. He then fell backward, and all of his weight pinned the creature beneath him.

Jessica stopped a few yards away, hoping the beast slain by the heavy impact of Gorias' big frame and harsh armor. La Gaul rolled over and she prayed it meant the beast done with him, but the creature slithered out from under the warrior. She swallowed hard, as it got to its three-pronged feet. Jessica raised the crossbow, but never fired, enthralled by the face of the beast glaring at her.

Whatever it was, a gargoyle or not, it resembled a hideous fish with fangs and a mouth like a diamond, opening farther out than looked comfortable. A few teeth were missing, and a black blood ran from the gaps. Had it tried to bite Gorias' head and found the helm made of dragonskin armor? The lips about that maw ran pulpy like a painted whore, and though the nose receded into the smallish skull, Jessica counted two nostrils on either side of a finn-ish divider up the face. The eyes made her the most afraid for they looked human, white with a brown iris. The arms and legs, though thin, held the dexterity to snap back and not be crushed by Gorias' rude fall.

Gorias planted a knee and started to push himself up.

The crossbow steady, Jessica fired.

The creature swerved itself to the left and the arrow struck Gorias in the shoulder. His right arm snapped up so fast, Jessica thought he caught the missile. As the monster screeched at Jessica, legs farther apart, she noticed two distinct things: First,

Gorias slapped and fumbled with the arrow, crushing the shaft on his shoulder plates. Second, the creature howling at her had two swinging male appendages, no, four, no…eight…as they kept dividing and spinning like a wheel…then back to the original two.

She notched another arrow, mind afire at what any victim of this beast endured under such genitals. Jessica had little time to think about much more than raising the crossbow for the creature leapt at her, arms outstretched. The trigger squeezed and she didn't know if the arrow found a mark, but she saw Gorias spring after the thing. It tackled her and wrapped about her body fast like it had a dozen arms, twisting her to the ground, sharp claws and odd appendages ripping holes in her clothes as they tumbled. Her back on the ground, the creature was face to face with her, but it was only for a split second and then Gorias' heaviness crushed them both down. The air left her lungs and the world tilted. Suddenly, the weight was gone and she felt an inrush of air. On her side, she choked and watched as Gorias slammed the arrow point from her bow into the top of the thing's skull and swatted it in further with his palm.

An uneven squeal echoed about them, and the thing seemed to fracture, its limbs doing the same act like its penis, dividing and wrapping about Gorias like a spider. His left hand on its throat, he swung his right fist down, smashing into its face. It tore at his armor and the sound of the claws on dragon skin echoed like fingernails on slate boards. It battered his head, knocking Gorias' helmet askew about the time Jessica leapt up, and found her legs didn't quite work yet.

She staggered and saw Gorias' helm fall off, but as the spinning limbs went for his head, Gorias' forearm blocked a dozen of the long tendrils and he shouted, "My swords!"

Feeling silly that she forgot the obvious weapons, Jessica ran to the tree and grabbed the nearest of his dropped blades. She almost fell backwards picking it up, as she expected a greater weight, but the blade almost seemed to not be there. The gleam bewitched her, an unearthly blue shine on the sword, and then Jessica wanted the other story, to know if these really came from angel wings.

"Sister, I'll let ya screw that sword later, but c'mere with it!"

Broken from her trance, Jessica ran over and stopped a few feet from them. She didn't wait for orders, but got in close, held the sword back and slashed, chopping off long reedy pieces that soon morphed back into a single reptilian leg. She hacked again, but missed. The creature squirted out of Gorias grip and returned to a more regular form, but discovered fleeing wouldn't work on one leg. It fell, began to morph into a better form to crawl, and grabbed Jessica's ankle. She screamed, slashing the sword, but fell herself and lost the sword. The thing started to mount up on her but her left hand groped round, gripped Gorias' nearby fallen helmet, and swung it. The helm connected, bouncing off the thing's head, causing it to shamble back...where Gorias stood with the sword she dropped.

"Deliverance is not an issue," Gorias mumbled and stabbed true once, striking through the creature. It stopped shifting and went still, the blade piercing its spine. Gorias had hit a crucial nerve and it couldn't move. He twisted the blade, ground out a large hole in its back and inserted the dew nail on his left armlet into the hole to tear more flesh away. Gorias tore the creature in half. It mouthed off aplenty, jaws working, except by no means did it make a sound as it fell dead.

Lungs sucking air, Jessica jumped up and ran to Gorias, clutching his chest, letting his left arm embrace her. She presently leapt back from him, blinking many times.

"It's all right, you were magnificent," he said, eyes alight at her as if speaking to a woman in the sheets.

"I'm sorry, I...."

"Nuthin' to be sorry 'bout, little sister. Ya done great. Ain't every day ya gotta deal with that. See its back? The thing had wings. I bet the great puss hunter of the village ripped its wings out and caused all this."

"Are you going to ask?"

"We got their money. To hell with 'em."

Jessica kept studying the back of the dead thing until Gorias retrieved the crossbow and nudged her hip with the butt of it.

"Thanks," she took it as he retrieved his helm and other sword.

"Nice shootin' for a scholar. I figured they trained ya up some before lettin' ya loose on the world."

"Since I could walk, not just for this trip."

"Good. That might come in handy again."

Once they had returned to the horses, the villagers started to seep out of their dwellings, led by Kilpatrick.

Jessica leapt into her saddle and started away, but held up after noticing Gorias sat atop Traveler, not moving. She returned to him quickly.

"What is it?"

"I wanna see what passes for a man in this town."

A smile on her tired face, she wondered, "What was that story about an ogre?"

"Huh? Ya know that one?"

"No, but you mentioned it a while back."

"It's not much of a tale, just me fightin' an ogre in a bar."

She glanced back at the carcass of the creature and then the villagers dancing. After fishing in her blouse for another Eye of the Dragon, she asked, "Is it good enough to see as I ride?"

He took the jewel. "I suppose. Let's get outta here. My curious nature will get me killed someday."

"Did a seer tell you that?"

"Yer fulla questions, huh? No, I just figure it." He touched the jewel on his forehead for a few moments and then handed it back to her.

Jessica waited until they got out of the village before placing it to her head.

CHAPTER FOUR
Jawbone of an Ass

The jewel in her palm, Jessica closed her fingers over it and then her eyes.

Though he'd been watching her, Gorias focused ahead. "Wishin' upon a star? Yer gonna have to wait a bit. The day is long before us."

"No, just saying a prayer to steady my heart."

His mane of hair shifting from side to side a little, Gorias stated, "Yer about the most centered gal I've seen in quite a time. Ya didn't run away from that monster, ya stood yer ground. I half expected you to flee, but nope, ya shot and took yer medicine. I like that."

Eyes still closed, Jessica answered, "Thank you so much."

Gorias went quiet for a bit and then added, "Thinking pure thoughts to yer goddess?"

Eyes open and glaring at the big man beside her, Jessica replied, "Yes. After that last vision…."

He didn't face her as he said, "Yer lyin' to me."

"What?" she almost yelped.

"Ya aren't prayin' at all."

"I am so!"

"Yer lyin' to me. Don't bullshit a bullshitter."

Her face wore a stern look, ready to protest further, but soon her dander fell. "How could you possibility know that?"

"Ya move yer lips when ya pray, when ya close yer eyes. Ya do it when yer walkin' and prayin' fer real. You were still as death there. Yer mind is on somethin' else, missy."

A high-pitched sigh later, she mockingly applauded him. "Your vision and observation skills are not diminished."

Eyes still forward, Gorias responded, "I try. I've been reading faces for centuries."

"Can you tell me what I was doing?"

"I'll give it a stab. Ya were focusing on yer mind, a focus point, an inner strength, maybe a nice event as a little girl to keep yer brain clear."

Her jaw dropped.

Gorias added, "Ya don't really believe in the goddess, Ishtar."

"But I do!" she protested loud, but then relaxed. "I am a bad card player, hmm?"

"Ya suck ass, deary dear. That's okay. Ya can't be good at everything."

"But it isn't okay," she snapped back, bottom lip pouting. "I've been in service of the goddess for ages...."

"But ya don't believe, not anymore, huh?"

Composed again, Jessica stated, "I've studied for years, understanding that men are fools and there must be a rational reason for this world."

"And gods that want blood are likely crap? Good for you."

"But then I meet you, and see these crazy monsters, beings fathered by angels or demons, creatures unreal, and think there must be something to it."

"Relax, hon. There is something to it. If ya live long

enough, ya might see a little bit more."

"That isn't very reassuring."

"It's all I got. Now do the crystal Eye there. The ogre ya will see is nothin' supernatural, just a big ugly fuck."

"No demons?"

"No demons."

"No gods?"

"Nope, but there's a wizard in there I think. Yeah, that's right. Go on ahead. It won't bite. Ya get to observe something that hurt like hell for me. Go on."

Just before she raised the jewel, Jessica asked, "Are you going to explain where we are going exactly and why?"

The flask in his hand again, Gorias undid the top and drank. "I figure it will all become apparent, if ya live long enough to make it there with me."

Eyes off the jewel, a frown on her round face, Jessica replied, "That's reassuring."

"And yet," said Gorias, pointing the flask at her twice, "ya don't act too scared."

"Does that show I have courage?"

Another drink went down and Gorias put the flask away. "Maybe, or little brains, but I'll favor the former. Ya done right swell with that creature back there."

Her hand held the jewel to her stomach, her eyes focused on his face as he again seemed to be looking at something else down the trail, far away. "You weren't afraid. You went right in there and did that."

"I'm a good actor. Yer always a little afraid, sister."

The jewel gripped tightly, she shook her fist at Gorias. "Are you putting me on?"

His mane swung about and some caught in his beard as

he stared at her. "Ya think I set up a town to be sodomized by a wingless creature for yer benefit to see me fight? C'mon. Yer not that damned important and Hell, I didn't know ya until the other danged day." He grinned wide. "See? I'm tryin' to act gentlemanly again. I didn't say fuck once."

"No, I meant with these jewels."

Hands tight in the reins, he answered, "Ya brought 'em."

"But a sly fox like you? I'd bet you'd learned something or two about manipulating what I see."

"Maybe I'm leavin' clues to our endgame in the things I choose to recall."

Jessica smiled. "Are you?"

Gorias winked. "Naw, but that's a nice idea. Go on ahead. This is sort of a funny story."

She pressed the jewel to her head and closed her eyes again.

*****

The sunshine over the green plains and the forests peeled back and Jessica's mind filled with drab colors, a scene surely in the evening at a locale of dirty sand. She thought it a series of hovels built in peculiar honor to a few rude buildings made of bricks. It resembled Shynar's backwaters, not the areas of reading and thought, but places of drinking and whoredom. She spotted two figures outside of a building and near a series of mounts, both men wrapped up in dirty road garb, and speaking clear.

"It's decided then, Heson," one figured muttered, yanking a deerskin cover closer. "We subdue the warlock, Ashtok Sarkis, once he's drunk, and cut his heart out if he doesn't surrender the information. There may be a market for pieces of his flesh as a poultice."

Heson placed his hand on the crude door of warped boards, shuddering in the wind. "Syroc, as limber as the old cuss is with curses, mayhap we should cut out his tongue first."

Syroc frowned, glancing back at their sturdy cart full of hardly covered cages. A sound like withered boards creaking emerged from it. "If we do that, how can he tell us where the gate is at?"

Heson shrugged. "He can write, can't he?"

"Heh. Agreed."

"What if we have to force him off a woman?" Heson asked, glancing at the cart as a high-pitched mewl escaped from the cover. "He won't be in a disposition for talking."

Syroc then grinned darkly, his jagged smile appearing amidst his tangled black beard. He patted his hip. "A blade will remove anything connected to a man and his slut. Don't fuss, Heson. Ever see a man of magic busy with women?" He gestured at the covered wagon nearby, strapped down with a tarp. It sat amongst many horses tied up to the warped hitching posts. "I'd raid his wagon, yet I fear his magic would get us with some eldritch snare. Better to tarry until he's plowed."

With a nod, Heson pushed the tavern door open. "The secret of the gate we seek is worth the jeopardy. We'll be rich with that information. Witches, wizards and men trying to rid themselves of their enemies or debtors will pay us to know the location of the gate." Then he muttered, "Oh, damn, the ogre is here."

Nostrils flaring at the scent of sweat and fusty ale, Syroc rubbed his hawkish nose. "We aren't the ogre's concern. Find me Ashtok Sarkis." He scanned the dim tavern, well populated but faintly lit by candles, a few torches, and the hearth. "Let that mouthy-assed beast talk."

Once inside, the ogre of the town did just that.

"I am the strongest one in all of Chanoch," the huge individual near the end of the bar blustered. He loomed larger than any in the bar. "None is badder, or a bigger lover than I, Vukkah Tiosaqqel."

The two travelers closed the doors and moved away from the bragging creature. They rested near a group of older men sitting with a single youth. All of them were shrouded in overcloaks due to the chilly wind that evening. As the litany of Vukkah continued, Heson eyed a man in the far corner, away from the rest.

"I laugh at the shaking of spears!" Vukkah ranted. "My manhood is longer than anyone's here. Stand up and I will buy drinks all night if you surpass me. What? No takers? Cowards and women you all are."

"He's an ogre," the young man near Syroc said, his voice buried by the other revelers of the bar. "Figures he would be the biggest one around."

Many aged men nodded at the words of the young man. The two travelers looked the boy over and Syroc asked, "You're a stranger here, yes?"

The foreigner nodded and said nothing more. He sipped a flagon and watched the ogre with irritation.

"He speaks the truth," an elderly man said in a low voice. "But take care, all of you. Vukkah would rather torture a foreigner than slay him, for truth."

"I see," Syroc muttered, sizing up the ogre, and then quickly noting the wizard they hunted in the far north corner of the tavern. Heson nodded at his partner, understanding that the stout, ginger-haired man in a dusty trousers and faded jerkin was their quarry, Ashtok Sarkis.

"Yes," a rather portly man with a balding head agreed, slapping the shoulder of the drinking outsider. "We see all kinds in here, but sometimes one must stomach wickedness to drink in tranquility."

"I came in to have ale," the foreign youth said without lowering his voice, now glaring at the two rough men who'd just entered. He watched them staring at Ashtok Sarkis. "Not to hear the bullshit of that mistake of nature."

The young man had spoken during a short lull in the background noise, and his words echoed through the place. Conversations and games of chance stopped, and even juvenile men discussing whores held their breath. A pair of old men by the entrance walked out backwards, their faces masks of terror. Another aged man with a long white beard let his wine spill from his lips in amazement. Even Ashtok looked up from his parchment and took his hand away from his bottled spirits.

Vukkah swung his immense girth around, facing the segment of the bar where the youth sat. Adjusting the girdle under his great abdomen, Vukkah growled, "Who values their life no more than that?" The flames of the hearth cast extra light on the repugnant features of the ogre, inducing a few to look away in revulsion. Vukkah's flesh, the color of deerskin, shined mauve in areas above his jaws. His jowls hung flabby on the spacious skull, and his general countenance favored more kinship with a bulldog than any human. Vukkah's face hung longer than any dog, though, and his grinding maw crowned a tree trunk midsection bloated by food and drink.

Syroc and Heson moved across the room, flanking Ashtok, pretending to shift away from the scene. Ashtok didn't regard them, but wore a bemused look, staring at the towering ogre leering at the youth.

As the older men scooted from the boy, one of them said, "We tried to warn you, pup. He dislocated the limbs of the last man who crossed him, dragged him around town for hours."

The eyes of the youth glowed inside his hood. "How long did it take for that man to die?"

Vukkah drank more, showing his lack of concern as the balding man nearby said curtly, "We don't know. Vukkah still feeds him and keeps him alive for taunting pleasure."

"Who are you, cur?" the ogre asked, the hoggish ears on the back of his rhombus skull twitching. The mammoth jaw of the creature ground away as his ruby eyes focused on the youth.

"One who wants to drink in peace, ogre," the outsider answered, no fear in his voice.

Syroc and Heson exchanged glances. Each look said, *We could use this for cover.*

Squinting at the stranger, Vukkah replied, "Who are you and where are you from, *auslander*? I generally like to know where men are from before I slaughter them. If I don't ask, I can't incorporate it in my next sermon to the bar."

"The entire hall is exhausted of your mouth," the youth said and straightened out his body. No more than twenty-five winters, this youth indeed stood quite tall, well over six foot, though still a foot shorter than the ogre. "Only a man from the Zenghaus Mountains would have the guts to say it."

"Guts can be ripped out and used to clean between my teeth." Vukkah clucked heavily in his throat, unimpressed. "Usually it is a matter of no brains, youngster. You are but a feral savage who walks upright on a jaunt away from the mountains…to die here? You are dense, boy. Who are you?"

Loosening his heavy veneer, but not removing it, the boy responded, "I am Gorias." Under his cover, Gorias wore a thick belt, showing the metallic tips of various objects. "I tell you so that when you fall into eternity, you will know who killed your ugly ass."

The patrons drew a collective breath, but Vukkah laughed shallowly. He flexed his burly fingers. "Words from a Thule blacksmith? Are they your only weapons? How did you drag yourself this far?"

Gorias said, "I'm a smith. I work in metals. I can find work anywhere."

"No future in dying," Vukkah grinned, his rack of shark-like teeth dripping drool over his hairy bottom lip.

"I'm not troubled by your fantasies," Gorias responded plainly. "I've killed bigger monsters than you."

Vukkah raised a curved eyebrow and started to reach for the sword at his hip. "There's a set of balls on you, that's for sure. Nevertheless, youth has clouded your judgment. That is a fatal error. Why, in the olden days..."

Gorias dropped his cloak and bolted forward. Stunned at the move, the ogre abandoned his reach for his weapon and swung both his arms together to block the youth's approach. Gorias ducked low. The immense, meaty thews of the ogre slapped only into each other. Gorias leapt up, hands slamming into Vukkah' face on either side of the huge maw, and blood gouted from the spots he touched the ogre. When Gorias yanked and then released his hands, the onlookers could see he clasped curved blacksmith tools. He left his utensils in an instant once they inserted deep in either side of the ogre's massive face.

Balanced on Vukkah's voluminous belly, Gorias would

have fallen off Vukkah save for the fact the ogre flailed, embracing him slightly. Constricted for but a moment, Gorias leaned forward with an open mouth and bit into the ogre's nose. Not only did this move support the young man's heavy body, but also it provided him the moment he needed to pull another article from his cincture. Gorias used his weight to his advantage and pulled back against the crazed ogre. Vukkah, screaming in agony, seized Gorias' arms. In all of his pain, Vukkah never considered his next act. Gorias had clamped a small set of iron tongs under the ogre's mouth. With Gorias repelling away from him with all his might, Vukkah pushed him away and inadvertently ripped his own jaw out of his skull.

His flailing paws slapped the boy down as the massive being stomped frantically in every direction. Most people ran, save for the drunken warlock and the two travelers, who retreated back from the wild scene, but watched in sadistic glee.

Gorias rolled on the floor. He drew no steel, but stayed out of the shambling path of the ogre. As Vukkah moved, the first two implements stabbed in his face, two pritchells, fell out of the hinge of his jaw.

Syroc and Heson jumped on Ashtok Sarkis. Syroc hit him with a lead bludgeon concealed in his coat. The wizard briefly looked confused, then his eyes rolled back and he collapsed under the attack. The two travelers would have made a fast exit, save for the bloody exhibition in front of them.

Vukkah howled and cursed, but the words were lost, for he could say little with no lower jaw. His agony made him stumble, incoherent, until at last his head cleared. The ogre drew steel from his hip at last and went after the youth.

"Vukkah means wise or learned," Gorias taunted him, hopping his backside onto the bar, avoiding the heavy blade of the ogre. Vukkah squatted on his haunches like a cat, missing another strike. "Were your parents as stupid as you are homely, hanging such a name on a freak like yourself?"

Swinging his weapon, Vukkah groaned in rage and swiped at Gorias again. The youth leapt over Vukkah, grabbed his shoulders and flipped over his back.

The ogre spun fast, livened by his distress, his fist striking Gorias in the shoulder before the youth could set his feet. Gorias stumbled, boots shifting, but did not fall as Vukkah's huge frame shifted to face him. The ogre charged, arms outstretched, but Gorias slipped out of his way at the last moment. Vukkah collided with a table and two wooden chairs, splintering them. He lost his blade in the debris, sliding on his own blood in the process. He swung his head around to see where Gorias went, a long line of crimson gushing from his face.

Gorias laughed at the ogre, throwing a small table, and then a mug of mead at the bleeding beast. "Brag to me now, you fat fool."

Vukkah flung himself at Gorias, sending them both through tables and chairs. Before the youth could rise up, the ogre boxed his ears. From the ferocity of the slap, the onlookers expected Gorias' head to burst. Gorias proved thickheaded and simply fell to the floor, limp.

Syroc and Heson froze in place, unwilling to cross the path of the brawl with their warlock prize in tow.

Those huddled at the door of the tavern looked at Vukkah rise up over Gorias, legs on either side of him. Many sighed, knowing this would be all for the brash youngster. Still bleeding profusely, Vukkah glared down and interlocked his thick fingers. Raising his fists to the ceiling, Vukkah crashed the bony bludgeon toward the pit of Gorias' back.

Gorias coiled to his right, curling his body around Vukkah's shin as the blow hit the floor. With a thick forearm, Gorias struck up fast into the groin of the ogre. Vukkah flinched, but didn't fall. Vukkah' right hand swatted, clipping Gorias' scalp. The shot knocked the youth, head over heels, and left him sitting upright on his buttocks, blood creeping from his scalp.

Vukkah charged and Gorias ran to the bar. Gorias evaded him, trekking down the bar, laughing as blood trickled into his facial features. He darted about the enclosed space, laughing and taunting. With a liquid bellow, Vukkah caught up to him at last. His huge hands enclosed Gorias' head. Going to his knees on top of Gorias, Vukkah roared and fell forward. Gorias gasped and suddenly, cried for help.

"Get this thing off me," Gorias growled, but there was not great fright in his voice. "Vukkah Tiosaqqel is dead."

Cautiously, a half-dozen men peeled themselves away from the exit. They eyed the immobile ogre.

"Are you going to help me or screw his corpse?" Gorias grunted and lifted the body partially off himself, but he couldn't remove the ogre entirely.

As if that was the sign that Vukkah was truly dead, the patrons of the bar pulled at Vukkah's shoulder. With enough wriggle room, Gorias escaped the death embrace of the ogre. Stumbling backwards, Gorias hit the bar and stood up. He sucked air and let his hand rest on his belt.

Open-mouthed, Syroc stepped forward, no longer holding Ashtok's arm, and said, "Nergal be damned! The young pup never even drew steel."

Heson chuckled. "The barbarian bled him to death. Paint my ass red."

Gorias looked at the returning bartender and asked, "Will that earn me a drink?"

Terrified, the bartender's yellowy eyes bulged. "Are you serious? Once his kindred hear of Vukkah's demise, we shall all die for this! You are a foreign-born man. You can run from this, but have sealed our fate."

Confusion at the words swelled on his face, but Gorias dismissed him with a wave. "Bah, you deserve to die then. To live in fear of what's *not* at your doorstep...." Gorias then reached over and grabbed a skin of wine. The barkeep made no attempt to stop him. The local wasn't about to tangle with a man who slew an ogre.

From the rear of the tavern, a new noise split the air. The bartender screamed, afraid his destiny came nigh. Gorias faced the future, and it arrived in the form of the old wizard Ashtok. Eyes starting to literally look aflame, the warlock raised his arms and began an incantation.

Syroc and Heson, caught unaware by the wizard, were on the floor. Up to their knees quickly, they fumbled in their robes, pulling out ropes for restraints. Ashtok's hands began to glow orange.

Abruptly, Ashtok's spell stopped. His eyes flared as his incantation was trapped forever in his throat. A blade had flashed twice before him at lightning speed, trailing a spray of scarlet. Ashtok gaped at his wrists; both of his glowing hands were gone, severed by what Gorias kept hidden in the back of his robe.

Gorias had reached behind his head and drawn out a

very short two-edged machete. With a shout his overhand swing split the head of the wizard in two pieces, spattering the abductors on either side with the mage's brains. The left side of the face fell away, caught in the downswing of the blade's thrall; the right side remained stiff for a few moments, frozen in a look of shock. Brains ran down the dead man's shoulder. Gorias kicked Ashtok's left knee and the old one collapsed.

Wiping the blade clean on the wizard's trousers, Gorias remained unaware or uncaring that most of the patrons left for good.

Both Syroc and Heson were on their feet and near to stuttering when they spoke to Gorias. Syroc stammered, "What in the…why…?"

Gorias shrugged and placed the machete in the sleeve behind his back. "He was a damned wizard. They should all hang."

Heson stepped forward, his finger extended, then decided against jabbing it under Gorias' nose. He backed away, but rage spurred him to speak. "You insolent pup! That marvelous mage meant much gold to us. You've slain a man that had enormous secrets and prevailing knowledge of the ages!"

Gorias checked his girdle to make certain his smith tools remained, gave the two men a mild shrug and returned to the bar for his skin of wine.

Arms in the air, Syroc exclaimed, "You say nothing to us? That's your answer?"

Gorias paused before drinking, saying, "My throat hungers for this wine almost as much as I lust for a woman. What do I care for a spell-casting man?"

Hands holding his turban, Heson slapped his own head and blurted out, "But he knew the location to the gates of Hell itself!"

Gorias eyed him as he drank. He took a deep swallow, causing them to fidget more. "Who'd wanna know such a thing?" He then tugged his cloak tight about himself and headed for the door, wineskin in hand.

"Damn you!" Syroc persisted, jumping after Gorias, but Heson held him back.

Once outside, Gorias faced the street and said, "You're fools to attack a necromancer and not slay him outright. Best to kill them where you find them. How in the name of Wodan would you secure his knowledge?"

Heson blinked and murmured, "Wodan? You are from far away."

Syroc's breath was ragged in his throat as he shouted, "You savage! If we couldn't wring from the magus what we wanted, we know he would have bartered with us for the information."

Gorias walked toward his horse, a great white stallion, and then eyed the two men again. "Barter with a wizard? That sounds bad."

Syroc spat at Gorias' boots. "You know not the ways of the world or magic. You're not even curious about what he might have told us, are you?"

Gorias untied his horse and shrugged again. "Not really. I have drunk my fill and need to leave this place. Raid the conjure man's wagon if you dare." He looked back at the tavern. The bartender pointed at Gorias and talked in low tones with a knot of people. The traveler from Thule muttered, "Chanoch is no place for me, it seems."

Heson walked over to their carts and motioned Syroc away from Gorias. Still Syroc focused on him, angry over what he lost. As Heson untied his mount, a high-pitched whine rose from their carts. Heson slapped the side of the wagon and swore.

Facing the cart, Gorias tilted his head. The mewling sound continued from the wagon. Heson took out a long walking stick from the seat of the cart and inserted it through the cages in back. A sharp cry stabbed the air and Gorias left his horse. He walked over to the wagons casually, although he frowned.

Shifting from sandal to sandal, Syroc grinned at Gorias. "You see, boy, even wizards have their needs."

Gorias studied the cart and perceived a writhing mass of bodies, all clothed in rags. Their mouths bound up, their hands tied, their eyes streaked with tears. Not a one of them was over ten years of age.

"You would trade these children for your heart's desire," Gorias wondered without hostility, "just to find the location to the gates of Hell?"

Syroc said, "Old Ashtok is not as young as he used to be, barbarian. He cannot snatch up children for his sacrifices or means. Don't look too shocked. Most cultures spill blood for magic."

"I'm not a barbarian." Gorias looked into the eyes of the children and asked, "They are from here?"

"You think us dimwits?" Heson chimed in and laughed. "We took them from the southern city of Dolram."

"Well," Gorias sighed, stepping back from the cart, "good fortune on your quest for the gates of Hell."

*****

In the morning sunshine, Gorias watered his horse outside the main hall in Dolram. He looked into the face of the magistrate of that city, an astonished man whose eyes and mouth hung open, stretching his pencil-thin beard.

"You can keep the cart and horses of those shits, if you so wish. I'd burn the carts to banish the memory, but that's me."

Climbing into the saddle, Gorias heard the magistrate say, "My thanks. You're a rare man to do this. May God and all of his Holy Angels bless you always."

Looking at the faces of women, men, and the children, all weeping in joy as they embraced, crying out to gods and goddesses for thanks, Gorias replied, "What would I do with a dozen crying children? Take better care of them, you all. A ten-year-old child of Thule would have killed the sorry excuses for men who stole this lot."

The magistrate asked with wry humor in his voice, "Need I ask what became of those dealers?"

Gorias looked down from his mount. "I gave them their heart's desire, what they really wanted and searched for. I showed them the location of the gates of Hell."

"Where is that?"

Gorias' hands clenched into fists around the reins, but a smile played on his lips. "Could be anywhere."

CHAPTER FIVE
Night Howlers

Jessica emerged from the vision, her horse still on the mud road, and gasping for air faster than she even thought possible. To her left and right, the rolling fields were gone as well as the forest ahead. The sun, overhead when they left the city of cowards, now hung near to setting beyond a village of many homes just ahead of them. She looked behind herself to see a thick forest and Traveler, sans Gorias.

"I guess we passed through the forest, but where is my guardian angel?" Jessica wondered as she placed the jewel back in her pouch. Her gaze quickly found Gorias, several yards off the trail, hacking at the ground with both swords. The strikes weren't crazed, but measured, precise, like he practiced. She cleared her throat.

Gorias turned fast, like a youth caught with his manhood out. His confident demeanor returned in a moment and he sheathed his swords. "How was that for ya?"

"You were close to my age in that vision in the city of Cain's son."

His face sour, Gorias told her, "Don't say that name."

"A dashing youth, very brave, but I wonder if it happened, was it real? Seems like I have heard that tale before, about a youth slaying an ogre in a bar? If you had a gutless episode would you show me? Would you show me only your great days and not getting your tail handed to you? I don't know if I think that was a real story about you. Fun, though. And typical, I suppose." From his lack of response, she doubted it. Jessica rubbed her back and then slipped from the saddle. "How long was I out?"

"Quite a few hours, the afternoon kinda got away from ya."

She glanced around and frowned.

Gorias patted Traveler's mane. "I know ya gotta go, sweetheart. Just squat and go. We're on the trail."

Arms folded, Jessica replied, "Your clairvoyance on bodily functions is amazing, but I can't see doing that in front of you."

Eyes to the sky, Gorias said, "Ain't like I'm gonna watch, dear. I love women but I ain't weird."

"I am *not* your sweetheart, dear or honey." She went to the other side of her horse and started to fumble with her garments.

Eyes away from her and taking in the surrounding lands clearly eaten down by grazing sheep, Gorias commented, "Ya almost laughed when ya said that."

Trying to keep from giggling, she replied, "Stop making me laugh, I can't pee while I laugh." Gorias remained quiet for a bit and then she stood, shaking her head at him. "What?"

"Hey, I have no jokes. C'mon."

"How much further to Erex?"

"Eryx. It'll be another day at least."

Back in the saddle, Jessica faced the town. "Are we staying in that spot tonight?"

Boot in the stirrup, Gorias paused and joined her look.

"Naw, that's Godly."

"It sounds friendly."

"It isn't."

"Godly. Is that supposed to mean something?"

"To me it does." Once in the saddle, he let out a groan, shifted and stated, "They keep to themselves and no outsider is welcome. I had hoped to navigate through Godly before nightfall and be past yonder forest, as it is full of spirits and whatnot." He gripped the reins, giving her a sideways glance. "But I had not reckoned on you slowing me down."

"The treetop rapist slowed you down."

They started toward Godly and Gorias muttered, "My better nature has slowed me down, takin' you on and bein' curious is all. We'll get through here and take our chances with the spirits in the forest."

"What is so special about the forest beyond? The spirits are bound to it? Why don't they fly over and terrorize the raped men of that town behind us?"

"Some spirits like where they are, or are cursed to the locations." He eyed her again for a moment. "No words for me besting that ogre in the vision?"

"That was impressive," she granted him. "Equally your mercy on the children. You have a bigger heart than you let on."

"My heart is gettin' tired."

Their horses' hooves clattered the nearer they drew to the town. A deposit of crushed gravel and sand provided an even layer for the main avenue of the town. This also coated the side roads that forked off the main grid. Jessica mentioned this to Gorias who was dismissive.

"Ain't they tryin' to be fancy."

Although several people shuffled about the town, they soon disappeared at the presence of the two riders. "They don't spend much on clothes." Her nose wrinkled as the wind changed. "Or sanitation."

Although his head didn't stray from the road through the middle of town, Gorias noted, "They are a grubby bunch. Godly my ass, huh? Did ya notice the troughs?"

Their pace unslackened, Jessica did see the series of short water troughs that accompanied hitching posts by local business shops. Each had a canvas cover over it.

"That's not very friendly."

Gorias let out a fake couple coughs before saying, "They don't even like each other."

"Figure it would be tough to do business that way."

"People are screwy, little girl. I'll water the horses before we go. Hope I don't have to kill anyone."

She frowned as they stopped in front of a shop near to the edge of town. "It's just water, not worth dying over."

Gorias climbed down, eyed the shopkeepers that vanished nearby and yanked tarps down to cover their windows. "Ya never can tell. I fought in a war once started over beer." He reached down and jerked the covering off the water trough, swished his fingers in it and tasted it.

"Over beer?" she threw back her head and laughed. "It had to be more complicated than that."

"I think there was a woman involved, there usually is," Gorias said quietly and then shouted at the woman barring the door to her shop. "We're using your water, ya daft cunt." As the woman babbled something, Gorias muttered, "To yer lovely husband as well, ya stupid fuck."

Her eyebrows raised a little at his words, Jessica remained

quiet.

After the horses drank their full, Gorias mounted up.

Jessica gave Gorias a questioning look as he turned Traveler from the main row of shops. "It's getting late."

Gorias declared, "I'll take my chances in the woods this night."

Next door down, a stout merchant shuffled from drapes that still hemmed in the just-unlocked panels to his shop and he waved at them. "Be not placing your soul against the night, good folk." Behind him emerged a tall woman, her black hair splayed about like a lion's mane, her breasts barely kept in tow by a suffering clasp on a gown made of shiny red material.

Gorias let out a loud sigh and motioned for Jessica to come with him. Instead she let her mount meander over to the merchant and his woman, who petted the horse's muzzle. Gorias snapped, "We don't have time for his crap, sister."

The plump man removed his round felt hat, let a mane of frazzled locks fall out, bowed to the Jessica and announced, "I am Zimms, the last dealer of this hamlet."

She gave him a gracious mock curtsey from the saddle. "Unquestionably the most agreeable." Though Jessica smiled at the woman, she returned only a rueful look, like Jessica owed her money.

Gorias rolled his eyes to the heavens and kept staring there. "Gimme a break, Lord, and strike me fuckin' dead."

Jessica ignored him. "Mr. Zimms, what is it you sell here at the last shop before the wild country?"

He doffed his purple hat to her a second time and then pulled back the tarps on some low shelves built into the front of his shop. Cages and entrapments lined the shelves, all opening back to the inner portion of the shop and allowing easy access to take care of the creatures within via that route.

Her eyes squinted at the cages and she held her hand over her brow to focus more. "What are they?"

"Sacrifices for the spirits and fallen saints of the countryside." Zimms' smile beamed from his beard so one could nearly read by it. Though his woman kept a hand full of painted nails walking up his back, she stared at Gorias quizzically.

Jessica frowned again. "I beg your pardon?"

Gorias moved up near Jessica and explained, "These are tiny creatures that appease the spirits in the night where we'll be traveling. That's the theory and selling point."

Unconcerned, Jessica asked, "Will they need appeasing?"

Gorias looked off at the encroaching trees of the hilly country beyond. "That's a supposition. I'd ride all night but dunno if you can do that. If there are any spirits about, they prey on the sleeping and immobile more than those passing by."

Zimms nodded to Gorias. "You know, if you do just ride, it might help to have one of these pretties along anyway. It is better to be safe than tempting the night howlers, great warrior."

"Get off my leg, fella. Just fork over one, cheap, and we'll be going. Only this girl is your means to a sale."

Zimms grinned, well aware of his craft and that of those before him. "Of course. I sell hope, and many little Mortons for sacrifice." He picked up one of the cages holding a gray creature that sported a turtle-like shell. Six shiny legs slithered about a pair of batish wings trimmed in reddish hair and protruding from its back. When its head did extend from the oblong shell, a hooked beak and three eyes peeked at Jessica. A hand to her mouth, she gasped.

Gorias threw him a few of the coins from Kilpatrick. "That monstrosity better make the ghastly spirits happy." No earnest threat floated in Gorias' tone, more apathy.

"The Morton will," Zimms attested and gave the small cage to the girl. "I promise." The woman behind Zimms clucked her tongue in her mouth, but said nothing.

"It'd better." Gorias snorted with no faith in his words until he promised, "Or I'll come back and kill you."

Zimms bowed to them again, still smiling. "You won't be coming back."

Jessica found herself giving the cage to Gorias before she mounted up, and never asked for the creature back.

They turned about and headed out of the town. Once they reached the edges of the forest beyond, Jessica turned. "Would you really do that?"

"What?"

"Go back and kill him."

"No. I'd come back and kill his family. That'd hurt more."

She stared at him for a bit. "You are serious?"

Gorias shrugged. "Probably not. I'd kill him and sell his kids to the army."

"That's horrible."

"The world needs buglers, teamsters and ditch diggers, young lady. There are worse lives to have. That'd beat selling sacrifices to strangers in the butt crack of the world, I'd say."

Her mouth opened, but she soon closed it, unwilling to ask if he was serious. Instead, she nibbled on some candies stored in her pouch. Gorias refused any sweets. She looked at the woods that soon surrounded them. "Nice territory."

"It ain't bad. Kinda close trees and all, really. Too dense

to ride through if this road hadn't been chopped out by some studious folks years ago." He then stopped and pointed. "See over there? The icon?"

She stopped for a moment, peering into the dense woods. "I almost didn't see that structure in there. It's like a clothing cabinet holding a statue of...."

Gorias drew a large flask from his saddlebags, started to refill his smaller flask and took a swig. "Yeah, sister, what is that exactly?"

Jessica moved in a little closer and grimaced. "Some sort of ugly god?"

"I honestly dunno which forgotten deity that might be, but he's probably around somewhere."

"I beg your pardon?"

He drank again and stowed the larger flask. "That's a clear resin on the case, not a piece of flattened glass. We might be looking right at whatever is left of that dude."

"But it looks well maintained, not vandalized, even if mummified...and like his mother knew a badger intimately."

"I reckon there's a monk who tends all these icons, this forest is full of them--uh, icons, not monks. Worshiping dead people, that's just weird. Hope no one does that for me once I'm scattered on the wind."

"Aren't we full of ourselves?"

Gorias winked and scratched his beard at the chin. "Maybe they will name a day of the week for me at whorehouses from Albion to Jomon. Conversely, I think if ya dishonor the territory where this guy is right here, well, I bet his spirit will tear you to shreds. S'true. That's why Zimms sold you the creature for sacrifice. It appeases the guy's shade."

"Really?"

"That's a theory on angry ghosts and spirits, but many sleep better with the sacrifices laid out. That thing before ya might be a doll covered in amber or it might be the housing for a really pissed off, dead wizard. We need to pass on by and pick a better spot to camp in, sister."

"Agreed. Surely there are more pleasant spirits about."

"Not really, but we can see."

Jessica watched Gorias balance the tiny cage on his lap and then pick it up, extend his arm and offer it to her.

"What am I supposed to do with it?"

Gorias half tossed the tiny cage to her, and she readily caught it, somewhat revolted by the tiny thing inside. "You manage it. It'll be educational."

"How do you figure?"

Gorias settled in the saddle as they rode on into the encroaching forest. "Tell me what that thing is, dear."

Eyes narrow, she studied it for a few seconds. "Zimms said it was a Morton. That doesn't sound correct to me. It looks like what we'd call a Kuhn back home."

"And what's a Kuhn, exactly?"

"What this looks like: a little birdish thing that doesn't know if it's a bird, lizard or turtle, has scales, sports reddish tufts of hair, always looks bitter."

"Different regions, different names. What are they known for around yer homeland?"

"They are rare, but I hear very chattery, and a rare delicacy. This one is very quiet."

Gorias nodded but didn't look over. "Zimms cut its vocal cords."

Her face flushed. "That's ghastly."

"You'd wanna cut 'em too if ya had to listen to them little

fuckers chatter. They are worse then locusts or cicadas."

"Zimms thinks this will be an apt sacrifice? I wonder why?"

"Yeah. They're delicious, I hear tell, but have never ate one. Maybe the spirits like 'em, too."

"Oh? I figured there wasn't much you haven't devoured in your many trials and trails."

Readjusting in the saddle, Gorias reflected, "That's a fact, but be careful what ya eat when given the choice. Those little things, well, I stay away from things that lesser gods or spirits find yummy."

"What makes them so special that the gods would want them or deem them good for a proper sacrifice?"

"I was hopin' maybe you'd heard why. Dunno. I don't know everything, ya know."

Jessica observed the creature for a little while. It sat, content to nip at its wings with its crooked beak. "There's a tale amongst children where the Kuhns are mentioned in an Eden story."

"Oh?" Gorias cracked the knuckles of his right hand. "I've heard a few of them, but not that one."

"There is a great epic where a hero searches for eternal life and approaches thegates of Eden. He finds Cherubim there." She looked over at Gorias. "Angels."

Eyes sullen, Gorias' expression went grim. "I know what the damned Cherubim are."

Undaunted, Jessica questioned him. "You've met some, haven't you?"

His manner not softening, he ordered, "Finish yer story."

Jessica settled herself in and looked at the darkening sky as if that's where the tale was written. "The hero of the epic wants the fruit of the tree of life, but fails and is cast out of Eden. The Kuhn birds are mentioned as being in Eden, still. Perhaps they have special significance to the old spirits, I can't say."

Eyes closed for a bit, head nodding slowly, Gorias recalled, "I think I've heard that story, but the birds were left out. Huh, it'd be weird to see one of them things fly."

"You don't have any bird stories?"

His disposition lighter, Gorias said, "I could tell ya the one about the Harpy Lady I fought way down south centuries ago. Every damn time I go to that continent there's trouble, but I digress. Naw. I have better tales to tell or show ya with those Eyes of the Dragon."

"Will this thing really be a sacrifice in these creepy hills? Why would a wandering spirit accept it over us? Why eat a bird or suck its life out when one can have Gorias freaking La Gaul?"

Those words made him smirk again. "Ya sleep outside a few times in yer trips?"

"Yes, I told you before."

"The guards every put a lasso around your bedding?"

Jessica smiled. "It wards off snakes."

"They aren't supposed to wanna crawl over it."

"Yes?"

"That's bunk, prolly, but it's reassuring in the night."

"Are you saying we'll sleep better thinking this little thing is a proper sacrifice to whatever lurks in the night?"

Eyes on the road again, he said, "Yer sharp for a city girl."

"I'd like to think so."

Gorias smile soon faded as the looming trees closed in even more. "There aren't many pleasant nights out here. Just gotta warn ya."

"It doesn't look friendly, all the icons. Look, there are many more out there. They almost look like coffins or people watching us."

"Lots of bad magick here, spirits wander and sorcerers' spells linger. There's really no way of getting past it all. I'm not much afraid, as I'm old hat at it, but for you, well, I'll try to sleep with one eye open."

"Not much afraid?"

"Not much. Oh, I can feel fear. Only a stupid ass thinks he's afraid of nothing."

"Are you afraid of death?"

"No, not as such. I hope my life matters. I've cast my life a certain way and have to hazard the die and all that hogwash. In the end, I hope God is a sport and doesn't just want skinny birds for lunch."

*****

Hours rolled on and so did the forest, so they had to stop. They bedded down for the night in an open grove around an icon marked for Ryta the Small. The horses unsaddled and tethered over to the left of the grove, Gorias settled in, putting his back to a stout tree opposite the empty expanse in the tiny circle of maples. He faced the back of the wooden icon box of Ryta and let Jessica sleep in the open on her roll, surrounded by the rope. The tiny creature sat in it cage, mouthing silent calls, to the right hand of the icon. All around them the forest crowded in like gapers.

Jessica peered up from her roll. "Are you sure you're all right sitting up like that?"

Gorias nodded, both swords disengaged and lying by

each thigh. "Yeah, it's better for my back, at least tonight. I can sleep just about anywhere."

She talked a bit more, but soon sleep claimed her. Gorias figured her more exhausted than her chatty mouth let on.

He closed his eyes and relaxed, letting the sounds of the forest lull him to sleep. Gorias slept light as always, ready for what he figured the night was going to bring.

He imagined Jessica interviewing him, laughing at the line of questioning. He asked himself if he oft felt unsafe in the night. Sure, always did.

Have you been attacked while camping?

He even had a jaunty answer for what he did that wasn't camping, and thought of telling a huge lie about screwing in the bed mat in a forest and being attacked by army ants… regretting his lover was consumed by the insects while he escaped…but his secret hilarity was punctuated by a real occurrence. His eyes flittered at the movement by the icon case.

Hands dropping to the pommels of his swords, curse words formed in his mind as he saw the hooded shape in the night make for the tiny Morton cage. No fear grabbed him as the hands that seized the cage were really dirty, easily seen in the moonlight that the trees let fall. He wagered the gods or goddesses of the valley were a lot more tidy than that.

Lurching up, Gorias grabbed his sword pommels tight, stumbled trying to rise, and thus gave the night invader ample time to grab the creature's cage and move toward the road. Gorias leapt across Jessica and held up his swords, but the fight left him.

"Damn ya." He let the blade tips lower toward the ground, but still held them tight. "Well, I hope the spirits have a sense of humor."

Jessica slept through it all.

Gorias peered down at her and gently kicked her in the side. She roused, blinked and yawned. Her eyes were suddenly wide as she looked straight up at a standing Gorias straddling her, but facing away.

"What?"

"We were robbed."

"I'm not comfortable with you on top of me."

"I'm not used to hearing that," Gorias answered and stepped off her, still looking into the night past the icon case.

Jessica sat up, her hands planted behind her. "What happened?"

"You were sleeping soundly," Gorias remarked and pointed his right blade at the icon case. "Some dirty robber lifted Zimms' sacrifice."

Her legs curled under her behind, Jessica rubbed her eyes. "Why would they steal it? Maybe it's a scam from Zimms."

Swords scraping together, Gorias snapped, "I can't see him stupid enough to screw me like that." Rage boiled in Gorias as he promised, "I'll skull fuck him and not kill him if that's the truth."

A frown marring her face in the moonlight, Jessica stated, "You certainly know how to make a lady feel special as she awakes."

"I'll try not to make ya feel dead."

She yawned again and covered her mouth. "Thank you for protecting me. That looked very valiant."

"Yeah, whatever."

Gorias crouched beside her, still holding his swords, but letting the blades lay on the ground. She followed his gaze.

"What are you expecting?"

"I don't know. This night is getting deeper."

"Well, I'm up now. Why not give me another vision with the Eyes of the Dragon?"

"Ya wouldn't care for my bedtime tales. Ya didn't before."

"It's so much better than hearing you tell them."

Eyes still facing out of the grove, Gorias spat, "Yer all heart."

"Oh, you're a fanciful storyteller, but seeing the episodes play out, that is so amazing."

Blade flats hopping on the grass, Gorias muttered, "Maybe tomorrow."

Jessica's face screwed into a mask of anger for an instant, clearly frustrated at his words. "You know best?"

"Tonight I do."

She watched him for a few minutes, staring out in silence, then asked, "You're waiting for something, aren't you?"

"You *are* educated real good, huh? Figured that out without too much research." He stuck his chin out and stood up. "See that beam of moonlight filtering in the outer woods?"

Jessica stood but stayed behind Gorias. "There's no wind, so how are the branches moving...." Her voice trailed off. "Gods, what is it? That isn't the moonlight at all!"

He didn't react to her grabbing the dew nail on his armlet for security. "Since it's gettin' a little closer, I'm betting Ryta the Small might be coming for her little sacrifice."

"Damn," she whispered, panic apparent in her voice.

Gorias spoke regularly as the glowing beam of light traveled closer to them. "I think it knows we are here, so whispering won't help."

The glow widened and started to take on a female shape.

Steven L. Shrewsbury

Naked, supple hips, pointed breasts, but entirely hairless, both in her pubic region and on her head. The face wasn't remarkable, lacking any real features to set it off any more than a statue or relief come to life. The skin, glowing like alabaster aflame, maintained a consistent hue all over. Her feet, that sported no toenails, stayed above the ground a few inches. Her arms hung at her sides, and the eyes, also white lights, never blinked.

Jessica's hands moved from Gorias' armlet to his backpack. "What can you do to fight her?"

"Not much."

"Not much?!" Her voice shrilled. "What are you saying?"

"What the fuck did you think we brought the sacrifice for?"

The image's head tilted, looking at them intently.

Gorias said, "I leave the spirit-fighting to the wizards and fools who think they can control them. More often than not, those idiots all fall in such battles."

Deflated, she mouthed, "Terrific."

"The idiot I trust the most, Ivor, the Oracle of Wodan, is quite a ways away, so this is gonna be rough."

"So, it wants its sacrifice?"

"It wants *a* sacrifice."

"She does?"

"Yeah."

Arms off Gorias and folded across her breasts, Jessica asked, "Why?"

"What do ya mean?"

"Why do the spirits, demons or whoever always want a sacrifice?"

"I'm not sure all the particulars."

"Are they hungry?"

The spirit kept staring at them, quizzically.

Gorias shot her a sour look. "What are you gettin' at?"

Confidence and some indignation in her voice, Jessica put out, "Why should she be pissed at us? Because we are sleeping on a plot of ground made in honor of her? What makes her so great?"

"This mountainside is full of spirits."

"And why the heck do they care about us? Why terrorize the living?"

"Because the dead are so bored and they want us all to be dead too?"

"That's weak."

Gorias lowered his swords. "It is."

Hands to her tiny hips, Jessica stepped around Gorias and said loud to the spirit, "Go on, get out of here. Go attack the bandit that stole your sacrifice. We tried to do right by your traditions passing through, but some jerk-off that didn't respect anything interfered. Go on and get. We have to try and find some sleep."

The image righted its head at them, turned and retreated into the night. It floated into the trees and disappeared.

"Sonofabitch." Gorias holstered his swords. "Ya look right pleased with yerself, sister."

Jessica clapped her hands once in front of Gorias' chest. "I am, providing she doesn't come back."

"And they think I have balls...."

*****

Though they slept fitfully, each did get several hours of rest. Closer to dawn, they set off again, but within an hour they stopped near a pair of boots lying in the road. In the breaking sunlight, they could see a grim reality. The boots still had feet in them, and the legs too. Gorias didn't get out of the saddle as he peered into the bushes.

Jessica hung back some, her view obscured by the huge form of Traveler. "What is it? Who is that?"

"I'm betting the bandit from last night." Gorias wheeled Traveler around, faced her and said, "Ya can look if ya want, but ya don't gotta."

Eyes narrow at him, she demanded, "Why?"

He heeled Traveler and got out of the way. "Looks like Ryta or whoever took your advice."

Jessica moved up, checked between the bushes and turned around, face pale. "That's horrible."

Gorias motioned with his left hand for her to fall in behind him and continue. "Guess she got to eat her sacrifice after all. I doubt the bandit had time to digest that little thing before he got dined on."

Hand to her mouth, Jessica shook her head. "That was monstrous. It tore his stomach out...."

"Probably ate it out, but it doesn't matter."

"I suppose not."

"Be careful what ya say to spirits. There's a lesson for ya."

Jessica looked back and winced, a tear escaping her left eye.

"And stop looking back. That's a bad habit."

CHAPTER SIX
Bones in Eryx

They rode until after noon time when the forest started to peel away and a deeper valley extended out like wings opening unto the world. Just as this vast panorama of beauty appeared, to their left Gorias pointed.

"There's the temple, where I'm headed, run by the priests here at Eryx."

"It's not what I expected," Jessica confessed, hands out and dropping to slap her thighs. "The stone dens beyond their dwellings look like those I've seen near Mount Ararata, but without the elaborate animal carvings etched in."

"Yeah, the stone slabs arranged in circles by the brick walls and mounds of skulls? That's the old religion still around, where man figured out he was better than everything else." Gorias wheeled Traveler around and scanned the area where the forest petered out and revealed the rambling complex of the priests of Eryx. "They aren't so flashy, these monks, but this place up here looks in bad repair since last year."

"I expected a mighty stone temple, all sacred and sleek set back in the woods, not a series of long ranches, log buildings and barns hemmed in by corrals." Her nose wrinkled as she looked beyond, toward the empty stone circles. "I wouldn't have thought I'd see a Soul Den out here so far from home. By the skulls, they believe the soul is in the head too?"

"Maybe. I see some of them monks diggin' over yonder in that flat patch. I wonder if it's head harvest day?" Gorias' right hand stroked his beard as he studied the ruined edge of the corral and then the damaged barn door. He relaxed when a man clad in a brown robe walked out of one of the ranch-style buildings and threw a chamber pot out into the field of trees that started a recession in the forest.

"Head harvest…" she mouthed quietly, then shuddered.

"Ya know what that means, huh?"

She didn't answer.

Gorias continued, "That's the old practice, bury 'em, let 'em age a bit, then retrieve the head for a remembrance thing or whatever. They are still around, it seems. Some religions never die or lumber on in another form. And there's a stone temple in back, kinda down into the ground a bit before the Soul Dens."

"Who do they worship here?"

"From what I gather, the same one back east. I think just the one true God or whoever they see as that God. They have great honor and respect for all so they have few enemies." He cleared his throat and studied the damage to the barns. "Which makes me curious about this here. See all of the axe marks? I don't think they got drunk and mistook the barn for a tree. This was done by some outsiders, see how wide the wedge mark digs?"

Jessica squinted and confessed, "Age has done nothing to your sight."

From out of the brush near the waste slope came a grunt and a snort. Gorias drew out his right sword. From the brush emerged a small animal Jessica mistook for a hog at first, but she soon saw it was a different animal.

"Is it a miniature hippo?"

Gorias didn't lower his sword but nodded once. "That it is, heh, they used to breed like rats around this area, but they've mostly died out." The small animal made a fierce showing, spooked Jessica's horse some, but the beast wandered closer to the edge of the forest and snapped at something in the tall grasses.

At his voice the nearest monk looked up and set down his pot. He called into the barn. In moments, a series of chimes echoed out and doors began to open all over the buildings. A dozen monks walked out into the sunlight, all clad in brown robes cinched at the belly by black leather straps. Not a one held a weapon and only one pulled his hood back, showing his black long hair and bushy beard, but no mustache.

"I expected them to be bald," Jessica whispered.

Gorias gave her a vinegary look and waved with his blade casually, "Good day. Melvin is it?"

"You remember me?" The bearded man blinked. "I greet you, Gorias La Gaul. It's too bad you didn't come by here yesterday."

"It's been a rough journey," Gorias admitted and looked casually in the direction the miniature Hippo wandered.

The monks seemed to sense his dismay and pulled long-handled hoes from beside the barn and started to direct the tiny Hippo back inside the ruined fence.

Jessica grinned. "You're afraid of such a tiny thing?"

Gorias returned his sword to the scabbard. "If you ever saw what a bunch of those little pricks can do to a horse's hoof, you'd change your tune."

Melvin coughed and agreed with Gorias. "He speaks the truth. We stampeded the Hippos and ridded ourselves of the interlopers who robbed us. The Hippos killed three of the Ballz brothers."

Gorias climbed off Traveler and waved at the rough state of the grounds. "The Ballz brothers did this?"

"Yes, but they didn't really count on us fighting back or the hippo herd."

"Yeah, the Ballz boys are sorta dim-witted save for their leader, Mondas. He's no scholar but he understands how to work his brothers."

Jessica slid from the saddle. "Who are these Ballz brothers?"

"Some fellas I had business with."

Jessica checked one of her scrolls and nodded fast. "You said you cut that witch's hand off because of them."

Melvin gave Gorias a brief look, but no judgment filled his eyes. Gorias said, "Yeah, in a manner of speaking."

Melvin motioned with his chin for them to tether up their horses. "We are preparing to eat. Water your mounts. Your affairs with anyone are not our concerns, La Gaul, but I fear that our usual business cannot be completed properly because of those very same Ballz brothers."

Gorias let Traveler drink at the trough and patted his mount's mane. "Excuse me?"

"What would we have to steal here?" Melvin asked, sarcastically.

Gorias eyed the barns and old temple again. "Even the Ballz brothers would know better than to think this place houses a storehouse of riches."

"We tend the dead and honor their bones, hence our

service for Gorias," Melvin said to Jessica, who looked at Gorias quizzically. "A certain rich man passed down from the great grasslands near Kemet."

At the mention of that name Gorias' mouth tightened and Jessica's look intensified. "What is it, Gorias?"

Gorias spoke but didn't unclench his teeth. "Go on."

Melvin said, "He willed his body be interred here rather than burned or buried elsewhere, thus many wondered after his estate. Rightfully, his children divided his riches and properties, but I think the idea is that his very person would be a strewn with precious stones." Melvin chuckled and then added, "The thought that men will kill for shiny rocks always amazes me."

"Yeah," Gorias agreed, mouth loosening up a bit. "They came for the body of this rich fella?"

"Yes. I think there is something significant about a certain jewel on his person. They gutted the body and found what they came for, but one of the brothers took a few more items before we ejected them from our presence." He swallowed, but faced Gorias with confidence. "I'm sorry, Gorias, they took several satchels of bones. One of them contained the bones of Althea."

"No," Gorias snarled and turned about so fast a half-dozen of the monks drew back in fear. He turned about again, his sudden anger steady. "I guess I'll just have to find those pricks. What in the hell would they want the bone bags for?"

"One of the Ballz boys is a necromancer in training, but they know they can sell off such bones to tradesmen or other wizards."

Jessica approached Gorias but gave him a yard of distance. "Who was this Althea?"

Gorias' seething face tore from her and he faced the monk. "I know the Ballz brothers have a base in the next town over from Eryx, but is that the direction they headed?"

"Yes. Gorias, we did try to stop them but stealing the bones was madness."

Angered still, Gorias walked in a circle and agreed. "Sure screwy."

Jessica offered, "Perhaps they knew of these bones and the importance of Althea to you."

"Who said she was important to me?" Gorias raged, fists tight but to his sides.

Calm, Jessica stated, "She seems important."

Gorias stomped to the edge of the corral where more tiny Hippos meandered. "Once, she was everything." Gorias bowed his head and said quietly, "But that was years ago."

"I'm sorry you cannot pay your respects," Jessica said and then stopped talking for a moment when all of the monks shared a communal giggle at her words. They straightened up fast and she went on to say, "How many Ballz brothers are there?"

"Five, now, I guess."

"You intend to fight and kill them all over stealing these bones? That's quite chivalrous, but…"

"I'm not gonna kill them," Gorias said, head still bowed. "They will be a means to an end." He raised his head. "I told you I got something from the witch because of them. I'll find them." He turned to face her. "I'll be heading out soon, sweetheart, and this won't end well."

"I'm staying with you. I have to."

"All right, if ya wanna go on through it all. Later on, don't cry and say I didn't warn ya."

Jessica blinked. "I wouldn't dream of it."

"Ya say that now. I think you'll be useful."

She frowned. "You didn't use me as bait when trapping the treetop rapist."

"Did I say you'd be bait now?"

"I don't like that look in your eyes."

Gorias frowned. "I need to work on my bluffing face then."

"What is it you are thinking?"

"I'll ride over there to the next town and see what happens, really. I need them alive." He looked into the faces of the monks, but each turned from his gaze, suddenly busy. "Ya'll know five *others* that'd like to visit the Oracle of Wodan with me?"

All of the monks sputtered negative words.

Jessica touched Gorias' forearm. "Why take the Ballz brothers to see this Oracle of Wodan?"

Gorias patted her small hand and smirked. "To have them meet God." He faced Melvin, who also looked at the ground. "Chief, ya wanna get us some food? We had a rough breakfast. We won't tarry further." He stretched, making sure to force Jessica to let go of him. "Where's the pisser?"

*****

Jessica wiped her mouth and then dipped her hand in the bowl of water the monks left by her plate. She nodded with a sigh of approval.

Melvin watched her across the vast room lit only by a series of candles on the table. "You like the frog's legs?"

"They are excellent, the wine as well."

"Gorias only sampled his," Melvin said with

disappointment in his voice, looking at the plate full of food by the empty chair opposite Jessica. "Not to his taste?"

Jessica wiped her hands on the cloth napkin provided. "I can't speak for his taste, but I wondered if he thought the food poisoned."

Melvin tilted his head and his eyes flared. "And yet he let you eat?"

"I have an immunity to poisoning brought on by taking a degree of a venom distilled back home every day. It's a trick from my professor. If you poisoned Gorias La Gaul, you better hope he dies fast."

"And what will come of you if he does fall over dead?"

She sipped the wine again and winked. "You think me a frail flower?"

"You have naught to fear from me, but I see you seething with the great thing that empowers folk more than steel, swords and poisons. You have knowledge. With that you are dangerous."

She ignored his words. "Who was this Althea? Why was she important to Gorias?"

"That isn't for me to say. Ask Lord La Gaul."

"He's evasive. You know, don't you?"

Melvin gathered up the food and stuffed the folded napkin in his tunic pocket.

Jessica pressed him. "Why does he seek to go to the Oracle of Wodan with these five brothers? I've heard of the Oracle in my studies, and it's not a pretty tale."

Again, Melvin was silent.

Jessica sighed loudly. "You didn't seem eager for that trip yourself."

"No."

"You don't want to see God?"

"No. At least not yet."

She got up, went to the shutters and opened them. Gorias sat out in the pasture, laughing with a skinny monk who brushed down Traveler. "I wonder why he didn't fight me harder when I asked to come along?"

"You fear his desires for you?"

"Certainly not that kind of desire. I feel I might be set up for some other task."

Melvin chuckled. "You'll offer him that all in due time."

"Unlikely. Our ages and lives are so different."

The monk nodded and grinned. "He has a way of charming women."

"I'm not attracted to men centuries older than me."

"He's more than just an old lecher."

"He's hardly a lecher." Jessica blinked and looked down. "He does have a rugged handsome quality, granted, and I'm not so silly that I can't see his method, letting his legend envelope someone and all." Eyes up, she sighed. "It is tough not to be swept up in the wake of his very being. I'm awfully resistant to such advances though."

Melvin's eyebrows raised. "Are you a celibate?"

"No, but it just seems like an unlikely activity with him."

"Then you are one of the first women to think such a thing about him."

Jessica exited the stone chambers and ascended the steps back to the surface. She wouldn't admit it, but a great peace washed over her being outside rather than confined below. While the monks treated her well, she would feel better in the company of the old killer. But Gorias wasn't by the skinny monk any longer. Perplexed, she scanned the ground and held up both hands to the monk.

The skinny man looked to a gap in the woods and said, "Please leave him be. He'll be along shortly."

Arms folded, she watched the monk re-saddle her roan. "He out caring care of a daily necessity?"

"One might say that. Please give him peace."

She turned and wandered away from the barn, eyes lingering on the gap the monk pointed to. Jessica grew bored quickly and walked over to the fence Gorias surely had climbed over and ducked under the bars. She glanced back at the monk, who stared at her, but quickly went about his business when she noted him.

Jessica stepped into the woods and saw a small path before her. A silence reigned all around and no wind disturbed the leaves. After a few steps, she heard the murmur of words. A few more steps and Jessica stopped, seeing Gorias' overcloak hanging over the branches. She then saw his armlets on the ground, then the dragon plates that covered his midsection. Also his leggings and boots before the forest cleared out. She stopped and crouched, seeing Gorias, naked, on his knees in the grass. She half expected an altar or stone slabs in a circle, but no such objects were with him.

She saw his scarred body, a network of lean muscle, scrapes, re-healed wounds and toughness. He didn't look 700 years old naked, she pondered, nor have any traits of a man with advanced age. But this revelation wasn't what amazed her.

On his knees, Gorias bowed his head over full, his long hair splayed about, his voice barely audible as his hands clutched the grass.

"I believe that you have made me and all creatures. You have given me my body and soul, eyes, ears and all of my senses. You preserve this body of mine." Gorias sat back, face up to the sky and Jessica jumped back. "You alone defend me against all danger, guard and protect me against all evil. I have done nothing to merit this. I see my duty to obey and serve you. I believe that on that last day, you will raise me and others all up from the dead and give me eternal life. Guide me, if it be your will, to live another day."

Jessica turned, swallowed hard and didn't run, but walked very fast back to the paddock.

*****

The skinny monk saddled up Traveler when Jessica sat down and waited.

"Ashamed at what you saw?" the monk asked, not looking at her.

"He shames me that I seldom call on my own goddess much."

In a few minutes, Gorias appeared in the yard, clad in his armor again. She blinked hard, thinking it impossible for him to return clad as such so fast.

"What's yer problem, sister? Get fed good?"

"It was very good. The monks seem to think you are out to kill them if you don't get the Ballz brothers."

Gorias petted Traveler's mane. "They're right." His eyes met the monk who brushed the horse and Gorias added, "Every damned one of them will die if I don't get those bones back. I wasn't asking them to raise a kid for me, I asked them to maintain a bag of bones."

"Althea meant that much to you?"

Gorias face tightened again. "Yes."

"You must have really loved her."

"Oh, that I did." Gorias exhaled and secured the saddlebags in tight.

"Will you show me the story with the Eyes of the Dragon?"

Gorias looked back at the gap in the trees he came from. "No."

She almost gagged. "Gorias! How could you leave such a mystery?"

"It's no mystery, not to me. That is the only one who matters. Let's go."

Jessica climbed up into the saddle and said no more.

"Don't pout, sister. It doesn't become the shape of yer face."

She thought of making a comment about his face on the ground but decided to stay silent.

*****

They rode on for several hours before they stopped at a creek to water their horses. They dismounted and Jessica told him, "I am enjoying all the tales you have shared, via the jewels or the spoken word."

Gorias knelt and splashed water on his face. "Glad I'm entertaining." He stood, glanced around the woods, reached out and grabbed Jessica by the wrist.

"What?" she yelped, stunned that he suddenly pulled her close to his body and wrapped his arms about her. "Stop it!" She screamed, punching him, trying to knee his groin.

"Hold still," he grunted, one arm grappling her and pulling his helmet down over his face.

It took her only a few more moments to understand his actions, that they weren't amorous, but to guard her from the arrows that flew at them. Jessica couldn't count how many missiles struck Gorias' armor and broke while he clutched her tight. She sucked air and tried to breathe but it was difficult in his grip.

"Fun to be me, huh?"

"I'm glad to be with you," she said with rasping voice as the arrows ceased.

Still holding her covered, Gorias raised his head and called out, "Hello to you too, ya fuckin' pricks. Now show yourselves."

While the forest rustled, no bodies emerged.

"Nobody huh? A bunch of gutless twats just like I suspected."

Another arrow flew and struck Gorias in the left side of his helmet. He laughed at the shot.

"Ya ain't gonna rob and waylay me, ya fucks. Just go on while ya can still breathe."

A voice hissed, "It's just one big dummy and a little girl. Let's rush him."

From out of the brush appeared a dozen ruddy-skinned men dressed in crudely-sewn buckskin pants and ponchos. Each held a crossbow made with high quality artisanship, but they also pulled tomahawks with edges that the sun glinted off.

Gorias laughed once and threw Jessica to the ground. "I expected midgets." He never drew his swords as the first came near to him, but all soon would surround him.

Tomahawk back and ready to strike, the first man was stopped by Gorias in his striking motion. A roaring shout spouted from the old warrior that made Jessica draw her breath. The bandit stood, frozen in place as Gorias grabbed him by the hand holding the crude axe and twisted, throwing him behind at two of the oncoming men. They pulled up fast, not catching their fellow in buckskin but being bowled over and dropping to the ground.

The nine others in from the forest formed a near-to-orderly semicircle but soon made a fatal mistake. They paused as one of their number became airborne, tossed into two others farther back from the hands of the old man when he moved too far ahead. All grew very close to Gorias and Jessica, not two yards away when the old warrior sprang.

His right shoulder leading the way, Gorias smashed into and over one of the smaller men and his outspread limbs clocked two more. His momentum continuing, his shoulder plummeted, rolling to the ground, but he came up onto his haunches quick. Three came at him from both directions, their axes swinging. His arms came up, heavy forearms nailing one on each side in the groin. Gorias' arms inverted somewhat and the back swipe up caught the next two with the dew nails, gutting each ruddy-skinned attacker from belly to sternum. When he rose up, the third attack on each side impacted on him, the men hardly noting their comrades as they screamed, guts unraveling onto Gorias' boots.

Almost simultaneously, two stone axes struck Gorias' helmet. The stone heads shattered on the dragon skin, and Gorias pushed each man off in separate directions, but staggered a little. Shaking the cobwebs from his head, Gorias turned and saw the two he clotheslined starting to rise. He reached out, grabbed a handful of guts from each of the flayed men, still screaming, and jammed these loopy ropes into the faces of the fresh attackers. Revolted and stunned, they wailed at the assault from La Gaul. This brief moment was all he needed to grab each by the skull and ram the two together.

"Gorias!" Jessica had called out, making it to her mount and crossbow. She aimed at one attacker as her cry made them all look away. Her target laughed at her and charged. He was wrong to laugh, for she shot him through the chest. He looked at the arrow, surprised, no longer laughing as he fell to his knees, not comprehending his oncoming death.

Gorias pulled a dirk from his belt, reared back and stabbed one of the attackers in the back so hard the air exploded from his lungs in a violent wretch.

Jessica notched another arrow and as sudden as it started, they were alone. The remaining attackers scattered, leaving their dead fellows behind.

"Yeah, run, ya fucks," Gorias yelled, cleaning off his knife on buckskin and putting it away. He drew out his larger blades at last, going to the couple stunned wretches who still clung to life and delivering a shot to their hearts.

"Who were they?"

"Doesn't matter."

"Just bandits? Not men from the Ballz brothers?"

Gorias cleaned his swords, holstered them again and knelt by one of the bodies. He opened the ruddy man's pouch and threw it to one side. He grabbed the side purse of another, searched it and swore.

"What?"

"Just a happy band of idiots, not mercenaries sent to kill us, nothing."

"Are you so sure the Ballz brothers didn't send them? Are you so sure they didn't take those bones on purpose?"

He looked down at her indignantly. "Yeah, I am. I know what I'm doing."

"I sincerely hope so."

"We better get going. Nice shooting, little sister."

Jessica shrugged. "You don't have to sound so amazed."

"I'm not so much, but telling ya nice shooting. I do value a spirited woman, ya know."

"Yes?"

"Sure. They are like a spirited horse. Who wants to ride a lame, submissive one?"

CHAPTER SEVEN
Showdown with the Ballz Brothers

Horses tethered back in a small thicket, Jessica and Gorias crept up a hill, then crawled as the small rise crested. Each showed caution as sounds of horses and activity bustled beyond the ridge.

Just before they raised their heads, Gorias cautioned her, "Careful."

"I am careful," she sniped.

He reached out, clutched her shoulder and stopped her from peering over the ridge. "This is a shitty time to get sassy, little girl."

"She struggled to get out of his grip and failed. "I'm not being sassy, damn you."

"What's up yer ass then?"

Her eyes snapped to him at these words. "Ever the charmer."

Gorias let her go and shrugged, focusing on the ridge again. "I try."

"Did you have to do that to the bandits? Ripping their guts out and stuffing them into the faces of their comrades?"

"It worked. It usually does."

"That's barbaric."

"I'm kind of a barbarian, many times removed, sister."

Jessica glanced at him and remarked, "I'm starting to see that, no matter how much you try to cover it in armor and wise words."

His left knee sinking in the loose dirt, Gorias twisted around, let his rump rest in the dirt and thumbed up toward the top of the cover. "Have a look. I trust you." He took a few breaths as if very tired all of a sudden. As Jessica rose up and peeked over the ridge, he muttered, "Don't confuse wisdom with frank bullshit, darlin' girl. That never works out well."

"Well…" Jessica said, her voice non-committal.

"What do ya see?"

"Cats."

"Huh?"

"Lots of cats. The place you think the Ballz brothers are in is crawling with them."

Gorias grunted loud, cursed himself silently for the noise and then struggled to join her looking over the ridge.

On the other side of the incline a valley dipped in front of them, but beyond a tree line of evergreens extended out, like they walled up the small community on purpose. Within these green walls lay dozens of small homes, but none of these were of bricks. Instead they were mostly primitive leanings on poles and skins. At the edge of the community stood stables, a barn and a one-story brick structure shaped like a horse shoe. A crude attempt had been made to put a better roof on this crumbling brick structure, but the thatch and boards were sliding off to ruin. From the revelry inside, anyone could tell it was a tavern.

Around this building and stables ran many a feline, of all

colors and breeds.

"Huh, like lice on a vagrant."

Jessica nodded. "That's almost so thick it'd be annoying."

"That entire community isn't much of a town more than a shebang paradise, a campsite."

"Why there?"

Gorias tilted his head and coughed quietly. "There must be a helluva well or spring feeding those horse troughs and spouts over yonder. Ya got good water, folks will stop. I've passed by here in years past, but not seen fit to stop."

"Why?"

"Seems a place for bandits and outlaws, not my ilk. I've stayed alive by being smart, not careless. Running into that morass of outlaws and kitty cats, that stinks of stupidity."

"Even for Gorias La Gaul?"

"Specially for me. Lots of headhunters down there."

"And yet you plan to go there."

"Well, now I do, sure. Kinda gotta."

"How do we know if the Ballz brothers really hold court there or are even there at all?"

Gorias rubbed his chin and pointed over at the stables. "Plenty of horses over there. Guess we can just go down and ask." He made no move to jump up and do so, though.

"Aren't you the bold one."

"I was thinking about sending you down there to ask, really. Guys will tell a woman a lot they won't tell a big fucker like me."

"I can see that."

"Plus, well, hell, I dunno how many are in there for real. There are about a half-dozen Ballz brothers, but them kinda guys will cloak themselves in other men's muscle."

"What kinda guys?"

"The kind that steal bones from a temple."

Her small hand lay gentle on his armlet of dragon armor, her tone softer as she told him, "If you told me what was so special about those bones, maybe it would make it easier to comprehend your passion."

His face an oblong ruin of defiance, Gorias slowly relaxed his jaw. "Later, I promise."

Her hand gripped the dew nail on the armlet and she smiled. "You're just figuring I'll get killed in whatever you have planned and you won't have to tell me."

He winked his left eye. "Aside from that, sister, ya got alotta gall figuring I have a real plan. I'm making this shit up as I go."

"So, what are you, or we, going to do?"

"I gotta get those bones back. I doubt them fucks have had time to do much of anything with them. From the look of the brothel over there and the road dust on the horses, them fuckers have been here a day or so and are getting ready for the next trip. The bones don't mean shit to them other than as part of the spell for the brother that thinks himself a necromancer."

"So what are you going to do? You said you wanted them alive?"

"I'm fulla shit sometimes, but I'd like them alive or deadish."

"What if the brother is a wizard?"

"His name is Mondas, by the way. What if he is?"

"Can your sword or manhood best a wizard?"

"I've done it before. If Ballz brother Mondas was a proper wizard, I'd maybe have heard tell of it from the monks. No dice, they weren't so impressed, 'specially if a miniature hippo stampede set him to light. No, I doubt he's much more than a novice."

"What if he's a mage?"

"Ya worry too much."

"I'm cautious."

Gorias chuckled and moved his head for her to follow him back to the horses. "Me, too." Once back at Traveler, Gorias opened the right saddlebag and started to dig inside it. He withdrew a small bundle wrapped in a dark cloth that'd seen some use. Once the wrap was removed, Jessica's eyes widened.

"You still have the hand in there?"

Gorias held up the thin digits of the severed hand and said, "Not just any hand, m'dear, but the right hand of a witch."

Her eyes darted around them but soon locked on Gorias' face again. "The witch at the bar in Segesta? The one clutching her hand to herself that you beheaded fighting that monster?"

"Yeah. Ya think I was just there for a drink and to kill them brothers?"

"That would be a full enough day. You cut off her hand and were going to leave her alive?"

"She double-crossed me and was lucky I left her maimed. She was supposed to give me a few tablets the monks back there like to use, ya know, kind of as a payment for watching the bag of bones. She screwed me around, thought that creature would get me. Nope." He rewrapped the hand and added, "I don't play games like that."

"What are you going to use it for? An exchange with the Ballz brothers for the bones?"

An indignant look spread on his face. "Ya know, this is why I like to travel alone. I don't have to post it in the public square each time I wanna wipe my ass."

"You need to tell me what you plan if I'm to help, or should I just wait here and shave my legs?"

He blinked. "Ya shave yer legs?"

Jessica nodded once. "What of it?"

Gorias shrugged. "Nothin', I like that, but it's rare in the world. Cheers to ya for that."

"I'm glad my high academic achievement has impressed you as much as my hygiene."

Gorias drew out his left sword, right hand still holding the witch's hand, and slapped her on the rump with flat of the blade as he eyed Traveler's saddle horn. "Help me with this and you'll really impress me."

"What can I do?"

"Get each of the brothers to swallow one of these fingers and thus, make them paralyzed and easy pickings."

Jessica frowned as Gorias waved the hand bundle in front of her face. "Seriously?"

"Naw, I'm just fuckin' with ya. Ain't no way we can work that one. From what I hear, ya grind up one of these witch fingers to a powder and then slip it into their drinks. Otherwise, stick one of them up their backsides, the paralysis lasts for a week."

"My…" Jessica mock gasped.

"But, we ain't got time for rational acts like that. Naw, this hand will serve only as a barter tool to get me inside. I'll make sure a lot of them fucks run outside, ya copy?"

Eyes closed a moment, Jessica nodded fast.

"Good," Gorias cleared his throat and put the hand in his belt pouch. He knelt some, facing her, "Ya got plenty of arrows?"

She nodded again.

Gorias had both his hands on her shoulders, squeezing lightly as he said, "That's my smart girl. I flush 'em out, shoot to maim, ya got me?"

"How will I know if those running are members of the Ballz family?"

"Ya won't." He turned and drew the scope from Traveler's saddlebags before climbing into the saddle. She followed him around the ridge until he edged into the open, looking at the tavern and stables through the scope. "Gods."

"What is it?"

"The sign outside the tavern reads 'The Wayward Pussy Inn,' heh." He gazed down on her. "I shit you not."

"Goodness." Jessica rolled her eyes and adjusted the quiver strap on her shoulder.

Sliding the scope back to its smaller size, Gorias said, "Goodness ain't got nuthin' to do with it, hon. Remember, shoot 'em down, but I need five alive." He heeled Traveler and the huge horse bolted.

Jessica started to work her way around the ridge and peered into a raw thicket down the base of the hill. This area looked to have been put to the torch months ago and remained relatively bare. Leaving her mount back where they first stopped, Jessica slipped into the thicket, hoping it provided her with enough cover to get in proper range of the door.

From what Jessica saw, she'd be able to hit those near the entrance as she eyed Gorias through her sights, the big blowhard riding up like he owned the world. Many got out of his way, oblivious to who he was, but not wanting a draft horse like Traveler to step on them. Her chest fluttered at the sight of the old hero, though, swinging a leg down, dismounting like he'd done a million times before, spine erect and his head up, mane of hair trailing. Confident, cocky and powerful. It was tough not to watch him, as even the dolts running around the Wayward Pussy Inn discovered. A few shaggy felines gave him notice if only to hop out of his way as he stepped toward the doorway.

The door opened inward and a figure much smaller than Gorias filled the frame. Though smaller, he didn't look intimidated to Jessica, who had a good view via her scope. From the way Gorias rested back on his right hip, he wasn't threatening anyway, but he did reach for the witch's hand and unwrapped it for the guy at the door. The man stepped out of sight for a moment, perhaps drawing away, but Gorias then disappeared inside the Wayward Pussy Inn and Jessica ground her teeth.

As she settled in, a grubby man, middle aged by the look of him, spotted her in the thicket. By his togs, she labeled him a stable hand, but wasn't certain. He blinked and shook his head, as if doubting his eyes. He made no sudden move, looking over his shoulder a few times as he staggered toward the stables. Jessica pondered if he were drunk or injured, but hoped he didn't take too much interest.

"Come along, Gorias," she whispered. "Let's be done with this."

*****

Gorias found the interior of the Wayward Pussy Inn lit by a few cracked windows, a couple lanterns and various fireplaces that didn't radiate much light or heat, yet smoldered anyway. The tavern wasn't a huge room, either, but a series of chambers, each relatively large, shifting from side to side in their order, in a myriad layout like a drunk designed it or the place got added to every so often.

The man at the door, a bearded youth clad in a dirty pair of trousers and a dirtier hooded tunic, led Gorias to a chamber just off the main bar, then bade him to stop while he stepped into the room. After he left, Gorias went along to the main bar and asked what they had to drink.

A youth not old enough to fight in a war, much less drink, tended the bar. "We have a run on beet-based wine today."

Elbow on the bar, back to the wall viewing the bored drinkers within, Gorias said, "Yeah? Why is that?"

"That's what Seth Ballz stole the most of."

"Guess I'll have some."

The youth nodded and reached to the wall for one of the hanging skins. "It's not so great, but it's wet."

"Sometimes that's all that counts, son."

Just as the bartender placed the metallic tankard in front of Gorias, the hooded man from the door popped out into the room, suddenly. He looked both ways and wore a look of shock that Gorias wasn't waiting outside.

"C'mere." The bearded man waved at Gorias.

Sipping the wine, elbow still resting on the bar, Gorias mumbled, "No, you come here."

Indignant, hands on his hips, the man stomped over to Gorias. "Mondas will see you, but don't get so smart, stranger."

Gorias drank more and his face soured. "Damn kid, yer not jerkin' me, this stuff ain't so good." He stood taller, eyes on the bearded man. "You mind yer elders, snot-nose."

Not flinching, the kid remarked, "What are you going to do? Kill us all?"

"That had occurred to me."

"You're surrounded."

Tankard onto the bar with some force, Gorias squared his shoulders to him. "Yer under a black cloud, punk. Ya just can't feel the rain yet." His cloak opened and his hands rested on the pommels of his swords. "Now, if ya don't wanna wear yer balls as earrings, you'll get the hell outta the way."

Still, the youth didn't back down.

A deep, gravel-filled voice called out, "Step away from the stranger, Seth." Out of the corner of his eye, Gorias saw a large shadow extract itself from the left side of the fireplace. A man nearly as big as himself, sporting a mane of filthy blonde locks parted in the middle and a face as raw as his voice, stepped across the expanse of the bar. Dressed in woolen trousers and a deerskin, sleeveless shirt, the other man sauntered over.

Gorias' head turned slightly, but his body remained convicting the youth. "Is he yours?"

The big man shrugged. "He might be. I've left a trail of bastards across this countryside." He cleared a phlegmy throat and rubbed his pockmarked, sunburnt cheek. "Enoch Ballz." He didn't extend his hand.

"Gorias La Gaul."

Chuckles rippled about the bar and Enoch grinned. "That so?"

"I don't give a flying fuck if ya believe me. I came to barter with yer wizard brother, Mondas. Little shit here said I could see him."

Enoch's rough face returned and he gave Seth a sober look. "He says a lot that isn't wise. Come talk to me. Bring yer drink."

"I've had enough of this piss water, but we can talk."

As they stepped away from the bar and toward the fireplace, Enoch looked Gorias over. "That's some getup under your cloak, stranger. You might be old Gorias for real, huh?"

"Does it matter if I am?"

Enoch flopped down on a cushioned bench affixed by the fireplace, a seat that looked to be his regular throne by the wear on the armrest nearest him. "No. Hell, we had Gilgamesh in last week. Crazy as a coon with no legs." When Gorias sat down across from him, positioning himself so that he had his back to the wall, Enoch took a long look at the hand Gorias left flat on the table between them. His eyes tracing the scars on the big paw, Enoch swallowed and said, "La Gaul, huh? Ya got stones walkin' right in here."

"Take it easy, junior. If I wanted yer head, ya'd be bleeding already."

No fear in his face, but a mild case of wonderment as he shifted on the box-like bench, Enoch asked, "Still a soldier for money? I'm glad you don't take my business actions personal."

"Don't give a damn how a man makes a living, Enoch. Just passin' through."

"With a witch's hand?"

While that surprised Gorias he knew such a thing so fast in the labyrinth of a tavern, he didn't show it. "One never knows when such an article might come in handy, don't ya know?"

"You decided to barter it for something Mondas can help you with?"

"Sure, we'll call it that."

"Something tells me you didn't ride all this way to do that."

"Is it really important to you why I'm nearby?"

Enoch looked him in the eyes for a long time. "You're trying to be kind, aren't you?"

"Trying to give ya a chance to let this drop. It doesn't have to end the way I figure it will, Enoch." Though Enoch's mouth opened, Gorias continued to speak. "You feel strong here, surrounded by your brothers, bastards and hired men, right? You feel pretty confident that you will be all right no matter who I might be. I gotta ask, is your pride worth dyin' over?"

"You aim to kill us all? If you are La Gaul, you are very good no matter your age, but I doubt you can slay a small army." Enoch gazed round the tavern, and while many walked the halls and rooms, none acknowledged a threat nor brandished a weapon. However, there were dozens of men nearby.

"See, that's where ya aren't thinkin' clear, sparky." Gorias leaned a bit closer. "I'm gonna kill you, first. No matter what else happens, you, Enoch Ballz, will die, really painfully. All of these little pricks who are too drunk to notice my words now will shit green when you die, so, I might just make it out of here alive. But I didn't come to kill you. I came for a bag of bones. Any price on yer head hasn't been assigned to me, so I don't care. Mondas can have the hand for his mummery, I take the bones and that is that. No problems."

Enoch's eyes narrowed at Gorias for a few moments. Then he looked away, relaxed back and motioned for his tall cup to be refilled. The waiter brushed a cat off the table as he poured a red liquid into Enoch's container. Once the waiter receded, Enoch leaned back further, tilting his head some to the left.

Gorias exhaled loud, turned a bit in his relaxed position at the table and said, "This is the part where you do something really stupid."

"Why do you say that?" Enoch asked without looking at him, still staring into space.

"Because its human nature to be ignorant, to let yer pride get the best of ya when it'd be a damn sight better to just let it go. I'm seven hundred years old, too. Ya think I've never sat in a tavern with a guy thinkin' his hard on will save his life against my swords? Yer gonna ask me why I want the bones so bad, aren't ya?"

Enoch's head turned to face Gorias. "How…?"

"Some things ya guess at, others ya just know. While yer a reasonable guy, ya can't stand not being in charge. Ya can't stand that I thought up an easy out in this without threats or further bartering." Gorias shifted his weight only a few inches and suddenly he drew a blade from his backpack holster and laid it on the table between them with his left hand. His fingertips remained on the pommel as Enoch's eyes flared at the blade.

"Why did you do that?"

Gorias exhaled and glanced around the room. No one really was paying attention to them. "Where's the bag of her bones?"

Enoch stiffened. "I asked you a question."

"This isn't worth dying over, not for you." Gorias started to spread his hand across the pommel.

Fast as a lightning strike, Enoch leapt off the bench, standing, pinning Gorias' hand to the pommel with his meaty left hand. "You think I'm afraid of you? How many men do you think I've killed?"

Not acknowledging the power of the hold on his wrist, Gorias answered, "You aren't going to kill anyone anymore."

"Yeah?" Enoch grinned as a few started to note the two

men grappling and talking louder.

Gorias gave a single nod. "You're only gonna tell me where the bones and that bag are." With a slight move to rise, Gorias' hand swung out and around from his belt, which Enoch leaned back to avoid, still holding Gorias' hand down. This is what the old warrior counted on, as the dagger from his belt drove through Enoch's wrist, pinning his forearm to the table.

Once the dirk nailed Enoch in place, Gorias pulled his left hand back and drew out his right blade. However, he didn't swing the blade down, but rather the heavy ball on the end of the pommel, hammering the forearm of Enoch Ballz hard. Enoch cried out, a crack echoing in the bar as bones broke.

"Where are they?" Gorias hissed, arm up and dropping again before Enoch could answer. The pommel fell again, this time striking the hairy forearm of Enoch about an inch from where Gorias struck before. Again, an audible crunch sounded and now, many in the bar stopped their talk and stared their way.

A third time the handle fell and broke something else in Enoch's forearm. Gorias' left hand held Enoch's hand down and the dagger still kept the wrist secure to the table. When he tried to push off on him, Gorias slammed his forehead into Enoch's, sending him nearly off his feet. Enoch's hand secured kept him from falling but didn't keep Gorias from striking a fourth time.

"Where is she?" Gorias grunted, rearing back to strike a fifth time. "Where are the bones of Althea?"

"Hey, stop!" the bearded youth Seth exclaimed, running over to the scene, fumbling for the weapon on his hip.

Seth overran the spot on the hardwood floor where he

could've drawn and attacked, such is the clumsiness of youth. Gorias raised the blade in his right hand, lashed out, took out the Adam's apple and jugular vein of Seth. He then brought the pommel down a sixth time on Enoch.

"Sonofabitch," Enoch wailed as Gorias slammed the weapon again on his turned forearm, shattering his elbow. "Mondas has them!"

"Where?" Gorias asked calmly, starting to strike further up Enoch's arm.

"In his den out back, that's where all of his crazy shit is... damn...."

Gorias paused. "Hurts, doesn't it?"

Enoch's bleary eyes riveted on Gorias and he cursed him.

"I'd take the pain away, but piss on you," Gorias muttered and turned the sword fast, chopping Enoch's arm off at the elbow. Enoch flew from the table and back to the bench as Gorias took the dagger from the wrist, having a bit of trouble getting the flesh to drop off. Boots stomped through the tavern as Gorias told him, "Sit there and bleed." He turned about and swished his swords together. As the band of a half-dozen men crowded into the cramped spot, Gorias faced them and said, "Deliverance will come."

*****

The minutes seemed like hours to Jessica, but when the door yanked inward and men began to run out, a new problem presented itself to her. Ready to shoot the men down, Jessica hadn't counted on so many running out at once.

Not a quitter, Jessica took aim and nailed one of the fleeing men in the kneecap. Howling as he clutched his right knee, he fell, causing a nearby cat to screech as he trod on its tail. This howling man had bigger concerns than a cat scratching him, for two men trampled right over him as they fled. A second man took an arrow from Jessica's bow in his pelvis, stumbled and stared down at the missile. As he reached for the offending shaft, another man ran out behind him, crashing into him. This new fellow in a buckskin tunic screamed…but not from the impact. He ran wild because he no longer bore a right hand, and held it up for all to see as he scrambled.

Jessica reloaded and whispered, "I know your touch, Gorias." When blood spurted from the cracks around a shuttered window, and then the window flew open to reveal a headless torso pawing at the frame, she really appreciated his work.

She kept reloading and firing, hitting a few of them in the head by accident, piercing one in the nose and perforating his brain into the open mouth of the man behind him. Although the first man took a few steps, confused over his new state of being dead, the man behind him gave him a shove and started vomiting. Hands on his knees, he lost whatever he had inside and wiped his mouth on his right sleeve. He stood tall, sighed, glad it was over…and got shot in left hip. When he reached for it, another arrow pierced his right hand, stapling it to his wounded hip. He cried out and went to the ground.

Gorias La Gaul filled the door and Jessica shot him in the right calf. The arrow glanced off his armor and he looked at where she hid, giving her an annoyed look.

She raised up a little, waved and smiled. He returned a grin, then motioned her to follow him around to the back of the building.

Jessica reloaded and left her perch, running amongst the fleeing cats and many men who paid her no mind, all just trying to stay alive. She wanted to shout out and ask Gorias where they were going, but figured his answer wouldn't be very serious. Rolling with his ways, Jessica kept jogging, watching him clothesline a man who'd escaped from the rear of the tavern. Not missing a step, Gorias kept on walking and she kept her distance, seeking a new spot to shoot from.

Behind the inn stood more stables, but one building differed in that it was made of logs and had a roof with a wide-open chimney, as if the thatch had been spun to let more smoke out. Indeed, clouds puffed above, but the smoke billowed black.

Gorias gave her a wink before he pounded on the door with the pommel of a sword. When the door opened, Gorias thrust both his swords in low, then raised them high. He stepped back, a flailing man clad only in a kilt skewered through the midsection, lifted on the blades. Gorias turned to one side, and threw the man off his swords, leaving him to clutch at his guts and bawl, rolling away.

"Got the servant," Jessica observed. "Now who are you after?"

More men and a few women ran from the inn. Gorias focused on the old smokehouse, or at least that's what Jessica called it in her head. Suddenly, he stared at her from her perch by the troughs. "I didn't say stop shooting people."

Although she wagered about a dozen or more lay maimed and bleeding, she complied and started to wound more as they popped out of the inn. However, the numbers were less and less.

Before Gorias turned his head back to face whoever resided in the smokehouse, a glob of a gelatinous matter struck his beard. Immediately, he jerked his head around, but didn't drop his sword as he raised his hand to get the mass free. Gorias swore and then shouted, "And yer a shitty wizard, kid! That didn't even break open on impact! Gimme those bones ya stole from the monks and I might just kill you fast."

Jessica sighed, "Ever the charmer."

The big man moved out of her sight into the smokehouse, then stumbled back out, arms flailing. She felt a bit of distress for him, as a larger glob of jelly struck Gorias and he fended it off. Still, whatever it was didn't break and impede him much, but it did succeed in pissing him off.

A screech loud enough to get their attention echoed, and with no other warning dozens of the felines darted toward Gorias and jumped on him. Jessica nearly laughed as in a moment, Gorias' armor and mane of hair wasn't visible beneath a layer of cats. Gorias threw himself into the side of the smokehouse, rubbing off many, though he dropped both swords. Hands protecting his face as the crazed cats flooded over him, even his angry shouts were lost in the fur. On his all fours, Gorias suddenly bolted into the smokehouse, faster than she'd have thought him capable. Worried, she left her perch and ran for the door to the log building.

Jessica trained her loaded crossbow inside, seeing the well-lit interior plainly. Many candles and a few lanterns illuminated the smokehouse, which had an eerie look of a dungeon. The chains on the walls, dangling hands and legs, some half rotted, others burnt and still a few mummified, but Gorias dominated her view. Between two tables holding bowls and braziers, he struggled on the floor.

Cats fell off his back, suddenly losing interest in him, but the legend was more concerned with another form almost out of her sight. Jessica could see a sandaled foot on either side of Gorias and a hand clutching handfuls of his cloak, but she couldn't guess what transpired beyond. Cautiously, Jessica stepped forward as she heard retching and gagging sounds. Sure to what she figured, Gorias strangled a man clad in a hooded cloak, a man younger than her by the looks of him. Jessica assumed this was Mondas Ballz. The fight left him and he broke wind, but Gorias kept strangling him as the cats slipped away out the door.

"Damn him," Gorias grunted as he lifted Mondas' head off the floor and then let his neck go, the skull thudding on the hardwood surface.

Jessica glanced about the big room. "Yes, indeed, I don't see a bag of bones anywhere."

Gorias stood up and raged loud, "That fuckstick Enoch Ballz. He fuckin' lied to me!"

"He couldn't have used them up by now, surely?" She waved a hand at the braziers and bowls on the tables, simmering. "I don't think his spice rack converted to a wizard's supply shelf is really full."

Gorias' face twisted, his beard moving as his mean mug expression soured. "Goddamit! If those monks lied to me..."

Looking up into his face, Jessica said curtly, "Look, he might just hide his things. I can search around here. Are they not in the inn?"

Arms stabbing at the ceiling for a moment, Gorias roared, "I dunno...damn." She thought he was going to add, *I handled this really well, huh?* But no such words came out.

As Jessica started to give the starkly furnished room the once over again, she admitted, "If they decide to find their balls, no pun intended, and regroup, we might be in trouble."

He went outside, picked up his swords, filled the doorway

again and stared at her. "That's quite a mouth yer developing, young lady."

"Learning from the best," she chided him as she joined him near the exit.

Gorias turned around to let her outside, looked from side to side and jerked slightly to his left. His bitter expression faced that direction as he barked, "Real nice. You'll have to do better than that, little pricks. Yeah, run!" As he moved, she saw broken-headed arrows tumble over his boots.

Using him for cover a little, Jessica exited the log house the rest of the way and asked, "Do we search the inn or stables? Where else would he hide things like that?"

"Can't believe the damned wizard wannabe didn't have them...." His voice trailed off and then he started stalking toward the rear of the inn.

Jessica checked from side to side, seeing forms off by the stables draw back and lose their will to fight. She ran quick, keeping up with Gorias, but he already tramped far ahead of her, single-minded on where he was bound. A few times, she stopped in her boots, stunned at the gore inside the tavern rooms. Her mind tried to write off the dismembered bodies and, at first, even tried to count them. Jessica soon abandoned both things, squinted her eyes shut to try and force it all out, and then opened them to pursue Gorias.

She stopped across the room from the big fireplace and Gorias, who gripped the neck of a dead man sitting on a boxy bench beside it.

"Wanna see what a lyin' asshole looks like?"

Although quite familiar with what one of those looked like, she noted the man briefly as Gorias threw him to the floor and took his left sword to swipe the cushions from the bench.

He swore again as he stabbed badly at the locks on the long bench. "Bastard Enoch," was about all she got out of it as Gorias crudely gouged the locks free from the bench latches. He threw down his sword on the table and pulled up the top of the bench, revealing several canvas bags inside. Gorias took a knee, patted a few from right to left.

"Coins, gems, ah, bones…not my bones…." He pulled two of the gem bags out and threw them beside himself before reaching in again. He slowly drew out a dusty burlap sack, very old and worn. "There you are," Gorias said in a voice so gentle Jessica's mouth opened. He cooed at the bag like a man trying to coax sex from a virgin. His moment of sweetness passed and he opened the bag, nodded and sealed it again. His voice, gruff again, barked, "Let's go."

"Should I take these bags?" Jessica wondered, pointing at the ones he named as money or gems.

Holstering his swords, Gorias nodded. "Sure. Why not?"

Confused at his cavalier attitude toward monetary gain, Jessica armed up two heavy bags and followed him out.

Once they'd secured the new bags to their horses, Gorias faced the inn once again. "All right, now go to the stables, get me five good horses and bring them around. I'm gonna tie up five of these sorry sonsofbitches you wounded for our trip to see the Oracle of Wodan."

Her crossbow at the ready, still fighting off the lurid images of the innards of the tavern, Jessica jogged to the stables and started to free up horses. For a moment, Jessica thought of objecting to his command, as she wasn't his slave girl. However, she found herself obeying, falling in line effortlessly in his adventure.

She encountered no trouble, but realized a small number watched her from a distance. Jessica heard a few talking, perhaps gathering their courage to attack. However many watched her and Gorias, though, they couldn't pool a pair of testes between them enough to attack in full. She dutifully led the five horses out one at a time and hitched them, all the while seeing Gorias tying up and gagging bleeding men she'd shot before.

Jessica tried to help Gorias lift the prone men onto the horses, throwing them over the saddles or blankets like bags of wheat, but he did most of the work. The old warrior, spry as ever, breathed heavier as the task went on but didn't lack in power to perform the labor. At the end, though, he led the horses away from the hitching posts and stopped, hands to his knees, sucking air in huge breaths. She didn't worry for him, as he seemed to recover quickly, but noted how weary he was as Gorias went to Traveler.

Forehead pressed to the saddle, breaths coming in slow, he asked, "Now, be a dear and go burn that damned place to the ground."

"What?" Jessica answered, surprised.

Gorias didn't look back as he thumbed over his shoulder. "Go in there, loosen up a few lanterns, burn that inn and the stables to the ground. Ya can let the horses out if ya want, but we need to get the hell outta here."

She paused and then asked, "Why the stables?"

Tired, his eyes shut as he leaned on Traveler's saddle. "I guess the horses didn't do us any harm. Stop arguing and go burn the fucking inn down."

She smiled. "You could say please, you know?"

"I could say I'll hamstrung ya and leave yer little ass here, too. Now get going."

Jessica burned down the Wayward Pussy Inn using only two lanterns. The men hiding in the stables didn't try to stop her. After all of their comrades she'd maimed, they decided against it.

As the flames started to course about the inn, Jessica mounted up and looked to Gorias. He took a long draw on a skin of wine and threw it at her suddenly. She caught it and wiped the end before upending it herself.

"Off to see the Oracle of Wodan?"

"Yeah," Gorias nodded, pulling a fresh skin of wine from his saddlebags. He let his left hand rest on the bag of bones, secured tight to his bedroll. "Keep that one and finish it off. It'll tickle yer innards good for the trip."

She drank and observed the long lines connecting the horses of the men they brought along. Jessica swallowed hard, eyes shut, contemplating why he needed them alive, why he needed the bones and what exactly she got herself into.

CHAPTER EIGHT
Return of Mondas and the Oracle of Wodan

Jessica couldn't sleep. Fingers intertwined behind her head, she stared at the stars, breathing through her nose.

From what looked like a mound of blankets nearby, Gorias' rough voice said, "You all right?"

"Of course," came her brusque words.

"Liar."

"You talk to me of lies?"

His voice cleared out and a cough or two later, Gorias asked, "What are ya thinkin' 'bout?"

"The stars, the patterns and how they don't look right."

"I reckon not."

"I'm wondering if I'll see them right again, back home, you know?"

"I understand. They look screwy the more ya travel. Ya should go way up north and see the lights the sky gives off, really somethin' at night."

"I've heard about those. They speculate about why the sky does it back at the university."

He took a deep breath. "Ya miss the university?"

"Kind of. This isn't so bad, living all raw like you do."

"Then why are ya sucking wind through yer nose like ya wanna kill me in my sleep?"

Jessica smiled. "Aren't you attentive."

"I get dead if I'm not."

"It's the five on the horses, and the witch's hand and all."

Gorias rolled over, looked in the direction of the tethered up mounts and the five men still tied up on them. "What about 'em?"

"I'm not complaining that they are so docile...."

Gorias yawned and turned over. "Why are we talkin' again?"

"You're so vague on why we need them for the Oracle, but I have a vivid imagination."

"Don't go soft on me now, sweetheart."

"I'm not your sweetheart."

Gorias let out a loud sigh and Traveler stirred from his standing sleep. "So you tell me. What is yer issue, sister? The way I used the witch hand on them to make them paralyzed? Did ya wanna hear them yap all the way to Ivor's abode?"

Eyes closed for a moment, trying to blot out how Gorias placed a finger of each witch in the five injured men in the most severe manner, Jessica soon said, "No, I don't care that you violated them to shut them up or plan to trade them to the Oracle for something."

"Then what's yer problem?"

"That you aren't being forthright with me."

"Other than what lurks in the night..." Gorias said quietly as Traveler stirred again, this time turning in a circle, "you have nothing to worry on for yer own self. I'll give you a good view with an Eye of the Dragon in due course." He then cleared his throat and whispered, "But first, I gotta deal with this asshole."

Jessica frowned and turned her head in time to see a shadow rise up as if out of the earth itself and fall on Gorias. Even in the night, when Gorias struck him and his hood fell back, she could see it was Mondas Ballz. Unsure if this was his twin, he was undead or just lucky, Jessica was off her bed mat in a moment and reaching for her crossbow. The two men struggled before her and she couldn't get a bead on Mondas.

Gorias' fingers sank into Mondas' ears as he shrugged off the first attack. When the Mondas tried to pull his head back from the big man's grip, Gorias' forehead smashed into his mouth. Black goatee spattered with scarlet, Mondas convulsed and fell back, yanking at Gorias' shoulders. La Gaul rose up to his feet. Mondas tried to stab a dagger into Gorias' heart, but the curved blade became hung up in the warrior's armor. Since Mondas refused to give up his bejeweled knife in the dragon scales, Gorias stumbled, feet skidding in the dirt. Even though he weighed twice as much as his opponent, his uneasy footing betrayed Gorias and he fell...atop the wizard.

They rolled in the dust, cursing, biting, bouncing heads off the ground, but neither ever landing a square shot. Mondas uttered eldritch curses as folds of his gray robe waved in the plumes of dust. Eyes afire, he rolled and came up sitting astraddle the bigger man. Gorias' left hand grabbed Mondas' throat before the wizard could raise the dagger. Mondas sported a bloody mouth from the headbutt, so Gorias aimed his right fist, connecting with his chin. Mondas' head wobbled on its root and he coughed deep in his chest. A stunned expression spread on the wizard's face before he vomited on Gorias. The stream of blood, wine, bile, biscuits and loose teeth that bathed

Gorias' bearded face didn't improve his demeanor.

A primal roar echoed in the night, filling in the spaces between tethered horses. Jessica nearly thought of moving to a better hiding place.

The wizard went airborne and flew against the nearby line of withered shrubs they had tied the horses to. Up in an instant, Gorias planted his feet, reached down beside his bed mat and drew the swords lying there. Hands gripping the pommels, looking through the crossed blades at the wizard, Gorias opened his mouth to call on the tribal deity of his youth.

Then he stopped. "Piss on Wodan. May as well call on the death god Balor, better use for this one now."

Jessica swallowed, thinking of adages she heard as a girl, like, *Death is easy, but life is hard.* She wondered mildly if Gorias' father ever told him this axiom.

The act of capturing someone alive proved difficult for any man used to dealing death or, at least, disfiguring blows. Gorias stood over the man splayed beside the brush and cursed. He stabbed his swords into the earth near the hitching spots and frowned at the man, then shook his head as Mondas' legs twitched. One struck his left foot. Abruptly, Gorias jumped back at the touch and dropped to his knees. A huge hand to the convulsing wizard's throat, Gorias swore again.

"Damned fool, broke your neck on the way down." Eyes tracing the bloody smear staining stark on the bushes, Gorias sighed. "Wodan jests with me. I thought I strangled him at the inn and he follows me all this way to break his own neck." He smiled at Jessica. "Ain't life a kick in the balls?"

"Terrible luck, at least," she replied, lowering her crossbow.

Gorias stared into her face. "Jessica, there is no such thing as luck. What does your home goddess think of luck? No luck involved. Fate, however, is a whore I should've banged into submission by now. This is the trouble one gets when trying to deal with workers of magic."

Jessica sighed and then looked down. "But don't they have to be alive for the Oracle?"

Gorias shot her a grim look as she soothed back her hair. He spat on the dead man. "More is the pity."

"We don't need six, right?" Jessica offered as Gorias took up his weapons.

"Damn, I'm getting too old for this duty."

"You mean your visit to the Oracle of Wodan?"

"No, dammit, for gathering up men alive for him."

"Living souls?"

Irritation in his voice, Gorias fired back, "I know the drill. Consider yourself lucky I dragged your ass halfway across the world for this exercise."

Jessica's gaze wandered away from him and to the paralyzed men tied up on the horses. "Oh, I feel quite lucky."

"You oughta," Gorias said quietly, pulling a flask from his saddlebag and removing the plug.

"How many girls before their twenty-first birthday get to travel with Gorias La Gaul and learn from his ways?"

Gorias drank deep, wiped his mouth on his blood-stained armlet, then spat at the ground. In the bloody spittle was a small tooth, not his own. "Damned wormy wizard. Anyway, we'll arrive tomorrow." Gorias stowed his flask, then placed a finger on his left nostril and cleared the other. "You've learned not to throw a necromancer down too hard this evening, right?"

Jessica nodded and then slung the bow up as if to place it

on her back. Instead she swung the bow out, like she meant to playfully strike Gorias with it. However, when Jessica brought the bow back across her body with a laugh, a small dart stuck just above the handgrip.

The motion of Jessica leveling the bow at where the missile originated moved as a blur, as was her aim to strike at the attacker in the shadows. Men ran in all directions from her shot in the dark, but one stumbled into the dim starlight, an arrow's shaft protruding from his throat.

"Glad to see your talents are still with you," Gorias said, not imparting thanks.

Jessica grinned, happy with her shot, but never taking glory in the accuracy. "No different than striking down a squirrel in the timber, save for this one smells worse."

Nostrils flaring, Gorias watched them run. "Figures that pussy wouldn't come alone. Glad we will get there tomorrow. I'm about out of whiskey."

She reloaded her crossbow and asked, "You still feel like sleeping?"

Gorias smirked down at her. "Let's ride on a few hours before resting again. I'd put some space between this shithole and my slumber."

Jessica looked back in the general direction of the inn. "Should we have not burned the inn? They are a pack of dogs now."

"I can't afford to be gracious, even if these little pricks followed us. We better get going." His smirk faded. "I once spared a town when I was the Regent for the King of Transalpina, and those ungrateful bastards rose up and fought me the next year. That's what I got for being genial." Gorias turned to Jessica as the youth lowered her bow. "You think me harsh?"

"You are you. I've heard tales of your life. I know the extent of your mercy on those near to you."

Gorias spat and then said, "Nothing emboldens sin so much as mercy. You saw what those bastards did. I spared their town back then and they came to kill us again. Believe you me, little sister, they won't trouble anyone else again."

*****

"You want to cut their throats, warrior, or should I?"

Gorias blinked at the old man beside him. From her position at the entrance to the lower level, Jessica thought the old man, Ivor, rather casual standing in the stone chamber. A hand on the hip of his slate-colored garnache, Ivor let a grim smirk play on his weathered face. Gorias let little or no emotion show while the elderly one started to pace under the five bodies affixed to the ceiling, a mane of white hair and pointed long beard wavering as he twisted and turned.

"I'll do it, Oracle," Gorias said as he looked south again through the small doorway, past Jessica. Out in the sunlight, a half-dozen women in hooded gowns gathered up the horses of the five men they'd brought. Jessica meandered away from the door, sipped from her water canteen and felt so unwelcome in the domain of the Oracle of Wodan.

Gorias raised his right hand and beaconed her to come on in. "Watch and learn, Jessica."

Ivor offered Gorias a slender blade from his waist-belt, not unlike an ornamental misericorde. Still, the large man made no move toward the five bodies suspended over their heads. Gorias swept back his hair and stared at the thin blade.

Ivor then stopped and glanced up into Gorias' forbidding

face. He looked south as well. "You know, staring that direction won't make Kemet fall off the world. Even a fighter from Zenghaus Mountains would know that."

While he raised an eyebrow, Gorias faced the smaller man, saying, "For all of your magic, and for all that comes with being the Oracle of Wodan, even I know the task you mention is beyond any power on Earth. If the gods willed that this damned world were cast into the sun or drowned in the waters of space, perhaps I could rest easy about Kemet and what's there." A meaty hand rubbed his thick beard as Gorias spoke.

"Well?" Ivor prompted him again, glancing at the five bodies suspended over a tiny pit in the stone cavity. The ropes creaked as they swayed; yet no sound escaped from their mouths.

The sunlight cast a small beam off the thin blade in Gorias' paw. Without looking up, he ordered, "Place her head in the pivot spot."

Never moving, Ivor replied, "I have. The invocation will begin as soon as one of us acts."

Gorias nodded, shot Jessica a glance, and looked at the bundle spread out on the curved floor of the chamber. A pile of bones lay on a woolen sack and seemed harmless, if ghoulish. Slight and sleek, the bones neatly arranged by the female acolytes of Ivor waited. These ladies of Ivor stood off out of the way of the depressed center of the chamber. One by one, they then filed out, faces partly obscured by thin veils, their eyes riveted to Gorias.

Ivor said gently, "Tell me, Ingaevoneos man, do you look forward to seeing her again?"

Only his eyes snapped up to face the wizard as Gorias

replied, "Yes. My blood races to see my old love. Let us begin."

Of the five men hanging upside down, only two were awake. The others succumbed to unconsciousness and would miss the main show. Gorias carefully stepped across the basin-shaped sandstone floor and grabbed the first man by the scalp. A grubby cloth gag restricted this man's mouth and his eyes pleaded with Gorias, practically screaming for mercy.

"They are men from across the land bridge of Bosporus, not from around here," Gorias murmured to the Oracle of Wodan.

Ivor folded his arms and sighed. "I don't care."

The misericorde slashed, rending open the suspended man's neck at the jugular going straight across. Blood gouted as he convulsed from the brutal wound made by an elegant weapon. The victim did what men do when they are opened... he gushed blood, shuddered and soon died. Gorias repeated this action on each of the imprisoned men, making sure to sever the correct areas, but showing no purity in his harsh moves. One of the sleeping men woke up as Gorias performed this function, but the others would only awake in the realm of death.

Five crimson floods splashed down onto the bones on the floor and the Oracle chanted, making his spell. Rattling a pair of iron-tipped canes on the stone floor, the old man threw back his head and roared at the ceiling.

Gorias grabbed a skin of wine offered by Jessica and sat down to wait beside the entrance. Jessica said nothing, but didn't look away from the pit. Gorias sighed. One hand on the knee guard of his armor, the warrior drank as the fresh blood congealed over the bones and started to give off a glow not unlike embers in a dying fire. Jessica blinked her eyes hard, but the radiance increased.

Ivor's bony hands rose, casting off the canes, and his arms slashed the air. The female servants of the old man glanced into the chamber from the doorway, but kept their backs to the opening.

The five swaying bodies smoldered an emerald green and drew in on themselves. Unimpressed by this act of great magic that sucked the innards of the bodies tighter, Gorias drank more. Jessica understood the corpses really couldn't inhale. By the time Gorias drank half his wineskin, the bodies had transformed into a gelatinous jade substance. In a few more seconds, they fell free of their bonds and into the basin, landing on top of the bones. Most of this material seemed to scatter away into nothingness like a nest of disturbed mice, but every time some plopped on the bones, the red light around the basin increased. Beams of the scarlet light touched his eyes but Gorias never blinked. Every so often, Jessica sipped from a small flask. Never once did the she look away.

Ivor took deep breaths and said quickly, "She's coming back fast. Donar, the son of Wodan, must be feeling gregarious this day."

After he wiped his mouth with the back of his hand, Gorias reached into a pouch on his belt and nodded. "Good. Perhaps I can make the whorehouse by Tybar tonight if the Thunder God hurries."

Ivor ignored Gorias' remark and dropped his arms. He stepped back from his labors. Somewhat winded, the mage sat down beside Gorias. "It won't be long now."

"Thanks Ivor," Gorias said emotionlessly, eyes focused on the growing burgundy radiance. He upended the wine hide and stared ahead, seeming to look on past the event.

Ivor nodded in response to his words. "For the son of Ambiorix, anything, my boy." The silver eyes of Ivor squinted at the blades on Gorias' back. "Your father make those or did they really come from the wings of an angel?"

"No," Gorias muttered, the red hues from the basin dancing across his hairy face. "I stole them from a whore in Jericho. Someone else's father made them."

As the lumps before them formed grooves and attached to the bones, transforming into muscles before their eyes, Ivor asked, "Are you heading back to the mountains or to the west?"

"Neither," Gorias replied, not looking at the wizard, all the while staring at the massive gobbet of muscles and bones, then tendons and veins appearing in the basin. "There's a war brewing in the east. I'll probably take up arms to get my grandson out alive."

"Oh?" Ivor responded, slightly surprised at his words as the mass before them became more tubular.

"Those in Albion pay better, but I have to save Maddox La Gaul and return this young lady home to Nineveh." Gorias snorted, watching a series of knots poke up through the middle of the mass. These protuberances formed a column leading to the skull. In another moment, the skull raised and trembled. In rapid motion, blood flowed across the bones, running over thin tissues swiftly encased by skin…then a forest of hair shot up from the scalp.

From the pouch in her blouse, Gorias brandished a jewel, an Eye of the Dragon, and turned it over a few times before putting it to his forehead. Jessica gasped a little as he yanked the jewel out but calmed quickly. Gorias' eyes closed only an instant, he handed it to Jessica and then looked to the mass on the floor again.

She gaped at the jewel. "Now?"

Gorias instructed, "Wait a minute."

Jessica's eyes widened as the upper torso started to take on the shape of a humanoid in full, for in moments the skin ceased to be scarlet and turned bronze. While the legs never seemed to form beyond meaty stumps, the thin, willowy arms of the woman tried to make the torso rise up, not dissimilar to actions of a new colt. Falling back down to her small breasts, the being continued to attempt to rise. The face fashioned fast and with great suddenness, the eyes popped open. Though at first the whites ran crimson, they soon grew lighter in color and her violet eyes stared forward.

Gorias stood up, recognizing the beautiful woman enough to name her as, "Althea."

The eyes looked at Gorias and her mouth parted. The thin lips became fuller and her dry mouth croaked, "I see you, by all that is unholy...." Struggling to get a breath, she stammered, "Gorias...I can see you again...."

Hands on his midriff belt, Gorias peered down at her and said, "Yes, what do you remember?"

Eyes blinking, shaking on her spindly limbs, Althea's face registered horror as she said, "You have dragged my spirit back here by the magicks of this elder man of your creed." Her words grew stronger, but still arid and halting. "You cannot believe the torment...the utter despair...away from the gods...which you have pulled me from...." Choking, vomiting clear fluids and then blood, Althea muttered, "The journey out of the gates of rusted blood was long and nearly as bad as the place within...the god Seker was nowhere to be seen...."

"Look at me," Gorias said with a strong tone in his voice and Jessica wanted to run.

Althea fixed her eyes on him and she blinked once.

Jessica thought her eyes were stunning.

Gorias smiled and motioned for Jessica to put the jewel to her head. He said, "It will be a very long story, be ready."

"All right." Slowly, she lifted the jewel to her forehead.

He recalled, "I remember the first time I ever saw those ovals of violet...and then the time they looked the most beautiful...."

Jessica closed her eyes and the rest was history.

BOOK TWO

Beyond Good and Evil

"I know indeed what evil I intend to do,
but stronger than all my afterthoughts is my fury,
fury that brings upon mortals the greatest evils."
Euripides

CHAPTER ONE
Fighting the Bantu

In Gorias' memory, Althea never looked more beautiful than just before he went to war against the Bantu warriors, when he was a few years past twenty. She stood on the reviewing stand before the arrival of her father, the King of all Kemet, with many of his advisors and family. With an army of paid barbarian warriors as well as those soldiers from her own homeland, she didn't fear the mass of Bantu gathering in the distance across the sandy plain. The sunlight glinted off the jewels of her necklace. These minuscule stones were placed in-between tiny bones, making it almost appear as if she smiled from her breast at the brash young Gorias from Thule.

He turned his attention from her gorgeous shape and to the lines in the expanse between the enemy and their army. Gorias heard the chants of his adversaries, the Bantu. These mighty, if primitive folk threatened to overrun the southern land of Kemet. Though from Thule, the land of the ice and snow, Gorias joined the thousands of foreign mercenaries paid in gold by the leader of Kemet, Akhensobek. Gold was plentiful in Kemet and driving out the alien forces proved hard, but amusing work for various foreign-born mercenaries. Gorias understood tactics and learned over time to fight on a grander scale from Ingaevoneos raids into afar off Shynar. Thus, when the mercenaries gathered to supplement the army of Akhensobek, Gorias stepped forward to lead the mongrelized foreigners against the Bantu savages.

One of the burly fighters riding a red roan near Gorias drank from a skin of wine. He let the ruby liquid run into his long, blonde beard before observing, "What a task for us lowlifes, aye? To expel Bantu forces invading a land King Akhensobek stole from them in the first place."

Gorias pulled the long reins of his war chariot, a thing Akhensobek commanded he drive to lead the first line of forces, and said to the drinking barbarian, "It's an ironic world, Holskar."

The burly rider put away his wine and gripped the handle of his flail before joining his brothers in making obscene gestures at the Bantu. He shouted at his enemies, "Yeah, in a dog's ass you will!" Holskar looked at the slave boy in the chariot with Gorias and laughed. "No offense, kid."

Though Gorias' eyes returned to Althea, his right hand rested on the shoulder of the skinny youth with him in the chariot. "Tend the spears, Dog," Gorias muttered a somewhat cheerful command to the one-armed youth.

Though missing his left arm, Dog reached into the quiver of slender lances behind Gorias and pulled out one with a shiny metallic tip. "Ready to help them all die, sir." Unlike the majority of the barbarian mercenaries and their charges, Dog wasn't Caucasian, but his skin ran deep bronze, almost like those who stole Kemet from the black Bantu.

Althea stood silhouetted against the vast grounds soon to become a battlefield. Her shimmering wrap dress left naught to Gorias' imagination in the morning's light. The crystal jewel of her necklace, nestled in an array mostly made up of tiny bones, glittered like a twinkling star. Though an army of warriors shuffled their boots or sat atop horses behind him, Gorias couldn't keep his blue eyes from the lithe form of Althea. The glow of the daybreak induced a halo on her trim frame.

"Look at that, Gorias," a redheaded Ingaevone in chain mail said as he gestured to the convoy of litters arriving behind them. "The King his own damned self and his family."

"I saw them, Rothwell," Gorias snorted, glancing from Althea and her violet eyes to the procession of litters borne by hulking men of Kemet. Also, borne on a smaller litter was a willowy woman in silken robes. Several women bore this woman and Gorias named her as, "Gizane, the Bastet priestess. Just what we didn't need was their gods on our side. If their gods were worth a shit, they wouldn't have paid us to fight with them."

The men laughed at Gorias' words.

Behind Gizane's litter walked several short men in tan robes. The leader of them sported a black goatee and beady eyes like a canine.

Rothwell winked at Gorias and said, "Those little ones are hardly the size of Ingaevone boys."

"Uylikla and his worshipers of Anubis," Gorias said of the short men. "More bloodsuckers on this plain today than if we fought a host of vampires."

Holskar coughed as he looked to the King and said, "By Wodan's sack, how many children does that shiny-headed prick have?"

Many of the Ingaevoneos fighters laughed at this jest, seeing that Akhensobek only had a long ponytail from the side of his shaven head. Gorias himself grinned and said, "I hear near to one hundred and fifty, some with his own daughters."

The stern, frightening King reviewed the troopers of the massive army. He either didn't note the stares from the foreigners or simply didn't care. Akhensobek's manner of supreme power remained firm, even if he had to pay a supplementary force to extend his kingdom.

As if sensing this feeling of supremacy from the King, Holskar ground his bludgeon in the dirt and muttered low, "That one must command great magic to have such balls, eh?"

Gorias gestured at the dais, filled with people disembarking from the litters, and remarked to his troopers, "If I had one hundred and fifty children, I'd wager my nuts work well enough. Piss on the wizards." He looked down at Dog, who winked at the Ingaevone.

Dog pointed at Uylikla and said to Gorias in a quiet voice, "I hear he can become jackal."

"Can he now?" Gorias said and suppressed a belly laugh. "Wonder what good it does him."

Holskar laughed deep in his gut. "What a country of freaks. From all of the obelisks and pillars erected to Akhensobek's honor we passed getting here, I think that prick is overcompensating."

The red-haired Rothwell adjusted armor over his broad chest and then asked Gorias, "We fight for gold and a bevy of whores, but you, Gorias, have other things in mind."

Gorias never acknowledged his friend's comment. He focused again on Althea, so elegant and lovely standing near King Akhensobek on the dais. The King still checked the lines of troopers before they readied for battle, many times talking to the archers and fighting men from his own domain.

With soft words to Rothwell, Gorias said, "Makes him feel like a man to see examples of what his prick can do. He should be lounging by the giant reclining idol to his feline god, Bastet, not here, slowing us down. His glorious valley of tribute is a better place for him to be." With a wave of his massive arm, Gorias motioned to the lines drawing closer to the King.

The black eyes of Akhensobek focused on Gorias, who pulled up near to him in the chariot drawn by two horses. "You will lead these combined forces against the worshipers of Damballah," the King intoned, his voice loud, deep, and as god-like as the tall leader fashioned himself. "Let them fall and be consumed by Seker and those of the undead that wait in the underworld. Let the souls of these usurpers feed Seker forevermore. The hawk will overcome the snake. You shall be the instruments of my will and create a victory of legend."

Gorias, though a man of twenty-five winters, eyed the imposing figure of Akhensobek bravely. True, he had served this egotistical leader of Kemet many times in the past few years so far from his homeland, but this time, it was personal.

Akhensobek stood nearly as tall as Gorias, but a leaner of muscle. Though probably into his middle age for the antediluvian era (anywhere from forty to five hundred years old) there appeared no sign of weakness in the intense King of Kemet. Renowned for how he cut a great farming community on the savannahs near the mighty river Nyle, the lush green land of Kemet slowly wrested under Akhensobek's wings, a section at a time, from the blacks. Indeed, the land name, Kemet, which meant "land of the blacks," would soon be obsolete.

Gorias said matter-of-factly to his men, not hiding his

words, "Akhensobek wants all of the land in Kemet for its gold and resources to prop up his enormous ego." Since Gorias cared little save for adventure, gold and women, a mass killing proved uncomplicated work.

The shadowy eyes of the King drilled into the Ingaevone. Akhensobek's mind surely burned with the same thoughts as Gorias. When he drew close to the King, he confirmed his theory.

"Lead them well, savage, and you will have your desire," Akhensobek said darkly, menace lurking in his baritone words. "You look at my daughter as if she's a prized harlot. It's bad enough you took her once before, a year ago."

Gorias replied calmly, "That's the only reason I'm here now, Akhensobek. What has come from her that's mine, I'll have."

"You'll not see your offspring until these mongrels are eradicated," Akhensobek declared, waving a hand at the desert area beyond the edge of the fertile, grassy lands. Though hardly visible to the naked eye, advanced pickets told the true tale of the massive force of Bantu awaiting the attack.

Eyes drinking in Althea again for a moment, Gorias then gave the King a wicked grin. Akhensobek stormed away from him and addressed his archers yet again.

When Gizane took to the ground, raised her skinny arms and started to chant to the sky, Uylikla and those men near him lay on the ground, face down.

Holskar remarked in a low voice, "Gorias plays a dangerous game, bedding one of the daughters of the force that hired him."

Rothwell answered, "Perhaps, but it's part of our nature to do as the will leads. Maybe if Gorias were older, he would have made a better choice. Still, he was beholden to Akhensobek to return to his land."

"You men worry too much," Gorias told them and reached back to grip the sword sheathed on his back. This action seemed to make his confidence grow. The slave boy Dog secured the long holster of the blade and looked obediently at his master.

Mindful of the ears of the Kemetish guardsmen near to him, Rothwell muttered to Gorias, "You have balls to enter this land of strange gods and weird men again, my friend. Akhensobek would have your sack on a stick for nailing one of his daughters if not for all of your brethren that surround you. It's just one kid, Gorias. You probably have many more spread over this world."

"It's my blood." Gorias said as the battle lines formed around them. "Bah, he has over a hundred children. What's one more to him?"

After he drank again, Holskar reflected, "Perhaps his arrogance for power is greater than his personal loss of a child to a barbarian."

With a laugh, Gorias said, "What do I care? She's a fine lover, but what of it? I want my blood. I want my daughter that Althea had. If Althea wants to come with me back to the lands of ice, so be it. I travel much. I shall raise the girl as I was raised in this world of struggle. Let that girl return to cut her grandsire's throat someday. They'll never see my hairy ass in Kemet again after this is over."

The mass of bodies opposing them made the first move, out of character for the Bantu, Gorias thought. Still, he motioned for his fighters in chariots to move forward. They advanced, but not in a fast attack mode. After several minutes, allowing the Bantu to proceed out into the open, Gorias held up a spear and howled. All of the chariots halted. Hundreds of the men of Kemet followed the chariots on foot. These men, dressed in light plate armor took a knee and trained their longbows to the sky. As the Bantu pressed forward in an impressive show of primal might, these men of Kemet released volley after volley of arrows. Soon, the low sky hazed with the glut of arrows arching heavenward and drooping to fall on the mass of charging black warriors.

While some of the primeval Bantu wore protective coverings made of reeds, bones or wound-up grass, most of them ran nude. They ran into the teeth of this attack showing no fear.

In the King's army, several foreigners astride horses assembled into longer lines, casting off their garments and helmets. At this sight, Holskar belched and said, "Crazy bastards from Avar. They think that fighting with armor on is unmanly. They're as foolish as those sons of bitches across the field from us."

Rothwell made sure the strap on his helm felt secure, and then reminded Holskar, "The Bantu believe that the magic of their high priest will protect them."

Gorias heard their words faintly. He felt their expressions true, but he also understood that steel forged from the knowledge of father Wodan would break flesh. Indeed, the Kemetish arrows tipped with Ingaevoneos steel fell like daggers into the soft tissue of numerous Bantu. Many of those that weren't struck halted in their advance, vexed. Still, hundreds of brave Bantu warriors persisted.

Gorias shouted the battle charge for those in chariots and to various foreign-born men on horseback. Warriors from

Larissa and as far south as the Erythrean Sea rode horses behind Gorias, paid to fight and not planning to die. Not all of these men stood as strapping giants like Gorias and his Ingaevoneos brethren, but all were knowledgeable fighters. Whether with curved bronze blades or heavy broadswords one needed to swing with two hands, these men of action dealt death for pay. Their chaotic charge looked too insane to succeed.

Yet, the scrambling force of the Bantu readily attacked with club, bone-sharpened knife and spear. Though larger and greater of muscle than most of the army of Akhensobek, the scattered lines of the Bantu bent badly as the war chariots unleashed their loads of lances. The archers retreated as the barbarian hordes on horseback followed the brunt of these spears. These men flooded past the war chariots, screaming the names of their bloody gods, charging into the jaws of war. The insane assault of hired warriors combined with Kemet regulars, smashed through the advancing Bantu braves, stomping many bodies to the ground.

The tiny slave boy Dog handed Gorias a new short lance every time the barbarian's hand emptied. Gorias heaved the spears, sometimes as cover, other times directly into the stomach or heart of a Bantu warrior. Every so often, they died close enough to hear a surprised grunt as the lance hit home.

After a few moments in the center of the fray, Gorias' horses turned to avoid the press of flesh. Dead bodies unbalanced his wheels, so he shouted, "Roll, Dog!" As Gorias drew his broadsword from the sheath on his back, the slave boy Dog dropped from view. After the barbarian grabbed up a small shield and leapt off the chariot and into the tussle of combat, the carrier crashed. Twisting and flipping over, the chariot served a purpose in its destruction and confused the immediate lines of Bantu. The black warriors soon ignored it, moved around it and went on, but Gorias had made a clean escape.

Wild in the midst of the fight, Gorias sliced and stabbed. Though he used his shield many times to block blows from attackers, this object soon became a bludgeon. Once he dashed the brains of one Bantu, then he swiftly used the shield to upper cut another, breaking the man's jaw. Swinging the heavy blade, he sliced into the kidneys of one warrior and brought down his shield sharp, ruining the knee of a different enemy.

A flood of bodies rushed against him and Gorias felt the shield slide away. However, this crush of humanity soon fell as the battle howl of Rothwell and his men sounded in Gorias' ears.

"Wodan deliver us!" Rothwell screamed as his battle-axe smashed one Bantu's head clean through. The blade arose and quickly lodged in another man's neck. Blood squirting into the mouth guard of his helmet, the Ingaevone swore.

Gorias laughed as he swung his sword, "If he does, I'll stop drinking."

Holskar cleared a path with his flail and sword, declaring, "Then I shall take up your leftovers." The flail sank into the abdomen of a Bantu and then ripped back, unraveling the many loops of his guts with it.

As Gorias' brethren ran forward, vanishing in the fight, he used the broken chariot as cover and rolled out of the way of more running Bantu. Near his shin, the slave boy Dog emerged from the wreckage from a chamber in the rear of the cart. The boy had easily slipped into this space that housed spare lances and now came forth to the air. He handed Gorias a tiny flask.

Gorias caught his breath and drank of the whiskey. He then arose and went back into the killing frenzy.

In the din, Holskar grabbed a passing horse and tried to ascend into the saddle. A Bantu seized his belt from behind and pulled him from the mount. When the big man hit the grassy ground, the Bantu brought an axe with a stone head down. Holskar's skull ruptured and Gorias smelled brains... just before he ran his sword through the gut of the Bantu warrior. Mouth agape, the savage appeared stunned at his death. Gorias pulled out his blade and removed the head to stop the scream. He never looked down at Holskar.

Gorias caught up to the horse and leapt onto its back. Kicking the alien mount, the young warrior roused his men and invited many to charge with him to the home lines of the Bantu. The force of savages grew more elongated as the skirmish wore on.

Only a dozen of the Ingaevones rode with Gorias, but many that hung back in the Bantu home lines fled at their attack. Hoping their enemies' back up forces scared and gone, the Ingaevones pressed on. Gorias zeroed his eyes in on a slender Bantu man sporting a long black cloak and a round-topped headdress. Around the neck of this elderly man curled a thick python. Gorias' heart raced the closer he came, watching the old one raise his arms.

Exhilaration seized the young Ingaevone and he gripped the hilt of his sword tight. So certain grew Gorias that victory was his, the image that appeared shook him. Just before he reached the old Bantu, a vision not unlike a python sprouted behind the conjuring man. Bat-like wings spread out of this reptilian beast. When Gorias swung his long weapon, it felt as if a tree trunk slapped him on the left side and the giant

Ingaevone left the horse. He tumbled free and was amazed that he didn't kill himself on the sword in landing. Wodan remained with him, for he landed on the flat of the heavy blade.

On all fours, Gorias leered at the conjuring man as more of his brethren fell from their mounts. Still, the power of this old man was shown finite and eventually there were too many warriors for him to resist. At last, an Ingaevone rode over the top of him. Gorias heard the hooves of the horse stab into the flesh of the slender conjure man. With a grunt, Gorias rose up and took his sword with him. Though he never got to kill the wizard magicking for the Bantu still sporting his winged avatar, Gorias settled for slicing the slithering serpent in half. The snake writhed on, so Gorias swung the blade a few more times, sectioning the creature up. He kicked the head away and looked to the field of battle. Soon, his attention turned behind him.

The Ingaevones and a few naked Avarians gazed beyond the lower land where a quantity of the Bantu fled. At first, Gorias thought the disturbance he saw was a horde of rats scuttling up from the makeshift ditch. No, his heart skipped when the forms running toward them, diminutive in size, took on a human shape.

"Children?" Rothwell asked no one in general as he discarded his helmet, ruined in his fall from the saddle.

Gorias shook his head from side to side. These beings looked like shrunken images of the Bantu, but were darker still of skin…all sporting miniature spears and a shield woven of flaxen plants.

"Run!" Gorias shouted as he sprinted for his horse. "There must be a thousand of those little pricks! We'll be overrun here!"

Like a nest of mice, the pygmy warriors flooded the mercenaries. A majority passed them by, making a an amusing, albeit deadly, charge into the open battlefield around them.

Like a swarm, they were on Gorias before he could make it to his horse. Two on each limb, and a few on his back, Gorias went to the dirt. Flailing, he rolled, cursing, "Get off me, you little bastards!" Over and over, they stabbed at him with their tiny spears, but they broke these points and many teeth against his chain mail armor.

Every time he punched at the air, Gorias threw off a body. He felt more of the minuscule men leap on him or tiny feet tread over his body. Terror seized him, knowing that soon they would find a vital spot in the links. He seized one by the ankles and swung the pygmy, impacting on soft flesh. Gorias smelt blood, but was unsure if his actions would save him.

Suddenly, more air flooded Gorias' face. Rothwell's curses became louder and the voices of more Ingaevones surrounded him.

Free of the pygmies, Gorias returned to his feet and said, "Many thanks. That's an auxiliary force I'll never forget."

Rothwell laughed, pointing at the swathe he cut in the tiny bodies with the aide of more Ingaevones on the scene. "Anything for a brother, Gorias. We remember our own. Let us mount up and join the fight."

Gorias trod on many fallen pygmies on his way to the conjure man's body. Those hooves and blades had caved in the chest of the aged wizard; Gorias saw that his brothers failed to do as they should. He gripped his sword handle, drew back and swung the blade, removing the old man's head. After scooping up his prize, he found an abandoned Bantu spear and shoved the head down on its tip. Warm brains ran over his hand and Gorias thought the head looked good enough for the coming task.

Back on horseback, Gorias said, "Let us see how much fight they have once they know mighty Damballah has left them."

The archers of Akhensobek met the rush of tiny warriors and took to picking them off. In time, the pygmies overwhelmed the archers or pushed them back to blend into the chaos of the battle.

Across the field bloodied by Bantu, Kemetite, and mercenary alike, Gorias rode. He carried the head triumphantly forward. The war whoop of the incoming horsemen caused many Bantu to glance their way. Many froze at the sight of their wizard's head, and were slain in their dumbfounded state by soldiers from Kemet. Afraid and disillusioned, the remaining Bantu fled.

Gorias gestured with the severed head, entreating the remaining longbowmen to come forward. They took careful aim and shot the fleeing Bantu in the back. Gorias' horse reared up and he cursed, trying to avoid the rush of the pygmy assault still determined to kill any they could.

Horses prancing, many stomped the brains and backs of the tiny fighters. A few men on horseback swung long bludgeons and swatted the pygmies into the air. In time, a few of the Ingaevones made sport of these little ones, swooping down, connecting, knocking them airborne and then another Ingaevone would slice the projectile pygmy in twain with a blade. A few Ingaevones cussed for the bodies became caught up in the threads of their Morning Stars.

Suddenly, the mass of pygmies noted that the Bantu

fled. This knowledge spread fast as if they all sported but one mind…and soon they acted like rats fleeing a vessel. The tiny ones scattered, but mostly to the west, not back south.

Rothwell laughed as a fresh force of Kemet archers jogged into view. He pointed at the scrambling pygmies and said, "Maybe they're a slave class, for they don't seem concerned with following the Bantu home."

Gorias directed the unsullied archers to run on and take position. These troops served as a line of defense in case the Kemetish army had to fall back. No longer in danger of a retreat, they came forward and shot at the fleeing Bantu unmolested.

Their flasks upended, the Ingaevoneos men regrouped. They caught their breath and watched as the archers launched arrows.

Rothwell asked Gorias, "Is it time to destroy their villages now?"

Gorias looked back at the men that jogged forth with lanterns bearing small flames. Beyond them, he saw Gizane, the priestess, writhing on the ground, giggling as if mad. Near her lay Uylikla, but he was nude and swimming over a mass of naked bodies…those of his followers.

The Ingaevone leader looked away from these people, sighed and nodded to Rothwell. "Spare no one in the Bantu camps," Gorias ordered. "This job will be complete before sundown."

And it was.

CHAPTER TWO
What the Gods Keep

The sun sank away as the funeral pyres lit. Hundreds of pinpricks of light spotted the tranquil waters of Lake Myrute near the city of Typosyris. Akhensobek, borne there on a litter along with many of his sons and daughters, watched the barbarians place their dead on rafts and set them alight.

Fresh from lighting Holskar afire, Gorias and Rothwell walked up the bank. They regarded the King lightly and turned to watch the embers rise over the lake. In time, the cinders joined with the ashes of the other Ingaevone warriors, forming a hazy cloud of the dead over the land of Kemet.

Gorias stepped back, eyeing Akhensobek. "Have you brought my daughter?"

"You'll have her in due time," the King promised, the flames dancing on his features. "I don't pretend to comprehend why you burn your dead, savage."

"Then don't try to, Akhensobek," Gorias snapped, saying the name like a curse word. "I don't jest with you for making idols of a cat. You waste human lives to create giant boxes to live in after your soul is gone and I could care less why."

The ash cloud dominating his dark eyes, Akhensobek

stated steadily, "The Ingaevones believe that this fire propels them to a god?"

Gorias shrugged. "If our gods choose to take them, yes. If they don't warrant the warrior's paradise, then they may suffer a dire providence."

"Such as?" the King inquired, holding his incredulity in check.

"Wodan and Donar could make them wander amongst your tombs and haunt your folk forever. That would really be a pain in the ass to an Ingaevone."

The Ingaevoneos forces gathering up weapons and possessions of the dead chuckled at this, but Akhensobek appeared to shrug it off. "So how will you now honor your dead?"

Rothwell roared, "Why, with drinking and some of the temple whores, Bastet and Wodan be willing!" The men cheered at their words and Akhensobek frowned.

The King said to Gorias, "You look at death so lightly."

"Is there another way to look at it? Unlike some, we're not afraid of it. I weep not for my brothers, for the women can do this task if they prefer. That's the way of my father. He taught me never to fear death. What's the old saying, one's father should be as to you, a god?"

"I find it unlikely your father was anything akin to a god, barbarian," Akhensobek said in an arrogant tone, arms folded. "However, my patron, he descended from the son of God himself, one of his own children, Seth. He endowed me with great vision and the understanding of the cosmos." When Gorias never answered him, Akhensobek asked, "Do you think me a bad man and yourself good?"

"If I were a good man, you wouldn't have hired me to

kill your enemies," Gorias said, reflectively. "I don't pretend to comprehend the will of the gods, or understand all things, and neither did my father."

"Why not?" Akhensobek demanded, hands on his hips.

"Because," Gorias admitted, "we're not assholes."

Cold, but hardly hiding his rage, the King returned to his litter and left the lake.

Rothwell pointed at the force of stout men carrying the King and his kindred away. "They are eunuchs?"

"They look like it," Gorias noted. "Ironic, men guarding him have no balls."

With a laugh, Rothwell wondered, "You know the difference between that caravan train of litters and a porcupine?"

"No."

"All the pricks are on the inside of that caravan."

*****

The King of Kemet walked through his valley, stepping lightly as his dreams arose from the fertile soil. Testaments to his desire took form in the shape of temples, images of gods and likenesses of his phallus. Since the hour ran late, the laborers had gone to rest for the night. Out beyond the borders of the valley, a few of the industry overlords laid out bodies on 'U'-shaped benches. Akhensobek never spent more than a moment on the corpses of those who perished working in the valley that day. After all, he surmised, even the jackals have to eat.

He glanced back, seeing those who bore him resting on their knees by the litter along with six of his sons. His blood kin stood near him, hands at their sides. One of them gazed at the basin and then back to his father.

"Yes," Akhensobek said to them all, but eying the boy who stared across the land. "A temple, replete with an altar, springs up for all of my children. My sons, for you and your sisters, for the eternal race from the Grandson of God, me, himself, I will go to any length to insure my dream."

The boy Akhensobek regarded raised his chin and The King bade him to speak with a wave of his right hand.

"Father, for this reason we cast out and kill the Bantu?"

"Not just for temples, my son. For blood and soil, any man should stand and fight. For your kindred, for the lives of my children, for the extension of my self, I will do anything."

The King turned and they walked the avenue between the temples. On each side, miniature versions of the reclining cat god Bastet flanked them. The boy spoke again, saying, "The gold that was mined the barbarians take home, it's worth it?"

"Gold is but a rock, a piece of the Earth the Great God of Heaven saw fit to make. It makes men do strange things, like leave their homeland to kill other men for strangers. The barbarians are mutts, savages not worthy of life. Yet, God made dogs and goddesses bred with them, thus, we have Ingaevones." The sons of the King shared a laugh and Akhensobek smirked at his own mirth. "Ingaevones are tools, similar to hammers or swords. They can serve their purpose and, in time, may break or dull with age."

The boy asked, "And what happens to them then?"

"They are cast away, sometimes into the fire. I've heard that the Ingaevones bury their broken swords, drop them in bogs." Akhensobek stared into a face carved on an obelisk, his own likeness. "Dolts. They get drunk and tell tall tales such as they say their smiths drop a spirit in each weapon." He turned, faced the boys and spread his arms wide as if to embrace the entire land. "They are fools, for I shall place my spirit not only in this land, but in hundreds of pairs of feet that march from my loins, I shall cover the entire world in my seed. There wouldn't be a bog big enough to cast my spirit into."

The young men nodded, agreeing with him vehemently.

He took a breath and his voice rose louder. "And then, when all life recognizes the face and power that is Akhensobek, they shall fear and love me." He crossed his arms across his chest and whispered, "Lord of this World."

As he walked further, the group of his sons dispersed. Once he'd read the writing on the nearest monument, he turned toward the bearers, still resting afar off. They comprehended his look and snapped to attention. In a minute, they bore the litter to their King, jogging at a steady pace.

Once aloft, Akhensobek spotted a party astride tan ponies near the entrance to the valley. From the regalia on their breasts, he recognized a few of them as his daughters. He couldn't tell which ones, save for the slender one riding sidesaddle in the lead. It was Althea, for even in the night the crystal about her throat glistened. Her violet eyes glowed across the expanse of land against the backdrop of the coming night. The girl never rode toward him, nor was he borne in their direction.

Akhensobek smiled.

*****

Gorias watched the pyres rage on the lakes. The illumination flickered off the hairy faces of his men and the stone idol gods of Kemet nearby. The flames licked at the bodies, consuming departed friends. Head back, his eyes followed the plumes of smoke belching up from the lake, then traced back to their origin points. Gorias thought he spied a ribcage in the flames, but never told his fellow fighters.

"The mind plays tricks," he muttered, boot resting on the back of a stone jackal by the lake's edge.

Rothwell gave him a sideways look. "What?"

Gorias shook his head, took his leg down off the idol and then looked back to the sky. "If I stare up there long enough, will I see God?"

Once he had swallowed a swig from a flask of whiskey, Rothwell postulated, "I asked my father that once."

"Yeah?"

"He made me see stars."

"As well he should," Gorias nodded. "I'm thinking about hitting you and we aren't even related."

"Piss in your saddlebags," Rothwell said with a grim smile. "At least their hurt is over."

Gorias' heard the fighters younger than him start to sing a dire tune from the battlefield.

"To the halls, the battle slain fly
Great warriors who this day have died.

Their ashes rise from the tide

Under Wodan's watchful eye.
For kin they have fallen

True to the eternal wheel

Life turns over again
For death should not be feared

We take this life under Wodan's wings
And trod the path of the warrior kind
For in the Heavens a better life waits
Beyond the eternal bloody sky.

So we take these gifts that Wodan brings
And to the Master of the world we sing

Swords and quivers sharp, aimed at the sky

The oath to our Fatherland is to DIE!"

"All for gold for tomorrow," Rothwell said and coughed, turning away from the sight.

Gorias said, "My father told me there was no tomorrow. This was the last day of the rest of my life, so live it to the fullest. He said never be a slave to sentiment."

Rothwell sighed, weary of Gorias' words. "Why are you here again?"

Fists at his sides, Gorias remembered the face of his father, well. He recalled Ambiorix's words and cursed himself for being weak. Still, a nagging voice told him for kin and blood, returning for your child wasn't weakness.

Something else nagged at his mind. He turned in the direction of Kemet's great valley of temples. In his fears, someone cursed him, tempted him, and reached out to strike at him from beyond. Eyes closed, Gorias could see strange shadows in his mind. He opened his eyes and his mind cleared. The shapes in his head didn't scare the Ingaevone.

"Goddamned idols," Gorias said and walked to the edge of the lake. He called on the name of his god and kicked the head of the stone jackal by the waters. The head of the wild dog flew out and the lake swallowed it.

*****

Gizane stripped off her robe as she walked around the forward area of her temple. Though attached to the hindquarters of the reclining cat god, the small stone structure proved near to invisible to the naked eye. Only the wizard Uylikla heard her chants and he wasn't about to interrupt. His hands and feet bound, drool ran from his mouth as he watched Gizane perform her incantation.

In the small chamber, Uylikla held his peace; sitting on his buttocks just below shelving that circled the room. As Gizane chanted and fluttered her fingers in the air, the wizard saw the jars that lined the shelves begin to pulse an orange color.

"Come to me," she entreated the ceiling and then slammed her hands on the rectangular stone dais in the center of the room. "Feed me."

The orange glow from the jars took up a regular rhythm, emitting every two seconds. Gizane held her hands up again and the dais itself started to radiate a yellow light. This brightness took the form of an oval, and then condensed into the shape of a man. The figure coalesced into a thuggish brute and Uylikla started to shake. From his angle, he saw the profile of the new creation and started to whine.

Gizane waved her arms over the shape of the man and then said to the bound up wizard, "Change if you like. The dogs in the pen outside won't be in heat for another day or two."

Sweat ran down Uylikla's visage as his eyes took on a canine glow. The face on the dais defined itself further, but it stayed a creation of light. Bonds holding him back, the small wizard gave out an inhuman howl and his head snapped back. Salvia ran from his mouth as hair started to grow from his knuckles.

Gizane giggled and said, "Be still, Uylikla, and mind your mistress." Her hands descended to the face on the dais and she said, "Welcome to Valhalla, Holskar."

Her long tongue protruded from her lips and ran down his face, from the forehead to his chin. When she looked at the face of Holskar again, a long stripe of nothingness divided his face, a divider one could see through. Slinking like the cats she prayed to, Gizane climbed on the dais and started to lick the spirit of Holskar all over. Bit by bit, inch by inch, she erased the spirit image of the Ingaevoneos warrior.

Once Holskar disappeared, she curled up on the dais and smiled. Suddenly, she leapt off the stone surface, grabbed one of the orange jars and held it to her mouth. Repeatedly, Gizane coughed until she hacked up a glowing yellow ball of light. Once it fell in the jar, a watery splash filled the room. Gizane laughed and took a deep breath.

"Akhensobek will appreciate his new power potion made from the remains of this warrior." She sniffed the jar and then gazed down at Uylikla.

All she saw was a jackal, bound up, licking his balls.

*****

The voice of King Akhensobek echoed in the dining hall of the palace as he said, "Killed nearly to the last man? This is an excellent happening indeed." He toasted an incredibly long table full of Ingaevoneos warriors and selected adult children of his one hundred and fifty brood. His words reminded everyone of what they knew, of course, but the King loved to relish the victory. "The slaughter yesterday will make sure they never return unto the land of Kemet."

Gorias and Rothwell, freshly washed, wearing only boots and trousers, drank from their own wine flasks. They nodded at his words. With a grunt, eyeing the fish on the plates in front of them, Rothwell muttered, "Kemet belonged to the Bantu in the first place, right? He speaks of this as if it were fresh news, not material for ballads already."

"Kemet means land of the blacks," Gorias whispered and took another swallow. "Not land of the shaven-headed jackasses. Then again, the Bantu had no use for gold save for decoration. That perfumed asshead can use the gold in the mines of Kemet to build his dreams. Let him play with himself here in this land. We know our homeland is too far for his borders to ever reach."

Akhensobek lauded the victory, oblivious to the comments of the men half a table away from himself. His interest was not even imparted unto the willowy woman, Gizane, beside him. Stunning in her sleek clothing, her eyes and manner remained catty to all.

Rothwell whispered, "Is that Gizane the Bastet priestess?"

Gorias nodded, rolling his eyes toward the ceiling. "She controls the temple whores, yes, yes."

His fellow Ingaevone grinned. "Stay focused on Althea, my friend. One more slut for me."

Althea ate politely, barely touching the thin breads on her plate. Her violet eyes stopping on Gorias briefly, but never resting there, she smiled politely at all in attendance. Once, she flittered long, painted nails over her necklace of jewels and bones.

Wiping his mouth, Rothwell then spoke again, a bit louder this time and said, "Lucky for us he is liberal with the riches, aye?"

The black eyes of Akhensobek glowed like an eclipse as he faced the barbarian. Fingers drumming on the table, the King said pointedly, "Quite a few of your hairy fellows have set off for their homes already, fortunes on mules or horses. I am glad you few came to dine with us this night. All of the magistrates of our outer providences and mayoral leaders can see the fighting men who preserved their territories in the flesh, warts and all."

Rothwell returned Akhensobek's look and he replied hotly, "I'll be leaving soon. Some of us have other reasons to hang back in your country. My ass can't wait to leave this realm."

Jaw tightening, Gorias assumed Akhensobek objected to Rothwell not addressing him as King, aside from the profane swipe. Yet, the ruler seemed placid, though oily as usual.

The King's eyes danced as he looked the barbarians over before asking, "You do not care for the wine of Kemet?"

Gorias drank from his own container and said, "I trust what we brought along more." The barbarians at the table all grunted and laughed, causing Akhensobek to purse his lips. It was no secret the foreign fighters refused wine and ate little food from those in Kemet, fearing to be poisoned before they could exit with their treasure.

"You insult me," Akhensobek grinned, oddly good-natured at the personal stab. "But I am gracious in victory to understand your foreign customs." Eyes on Althea, Akhensobek's feigned politeness dropped and he said hotly, "All manner of payment will soon be made. I would be done with you all as soon as is prudent."

Lowly, Rothwell murmured, "His balls grow greater the farther our brothers get from this land."

The King stood up straight abruptly and snapped, "It will be a fine morning, tomorrow, when you are all departed. I shall burn a sacrifice at the base of the Sphinx in honor of my father at your departure." The King sneered at Gorias. "How do you honor your father? Swilling more wine? Was he a drunken fighter as well?"

"I follow his example," Gorias stated, sweeping his long tresses of auburn hair over a bare shoulder. "No matter how long it takes for me to realize my father was right in his ways. He talked little. His traditions teach me truth."

"What is truth?" Akhensobek threw out and never waited for an answer. He then went on to ask an aged dignitary in hooped earrings about the breeding of hawks.

Gorias stared at Althea for a long time. She never returned his look, but once petted the crystal on her necklace of bones. He ignored her father and then said to Rothwell, "Perhaps you were right. We should've just razed this entire land and just took all the gold."

Fists on the table, Akhensobek spoke louder, saying to Gorias, "Speak words plainly to me, savage, if you so desire to gain my wrath. I cannot wait to see the last of you."

Slowly, Gorias arose. The unhurried rising made his superior size to Akhensobek all the more obvious, as if it took time to unfold his gigantic frame. The young man said to the King, "Give me what's mine and I'll be gone this night. I still haven't seen my blood. Where is she?"

Akhensobek looked at the woman that sat at his left hand, covered in white silks and arching her eyebrows. Though skeletal in her appearance, a great allure to her beauty oozed out. "Tonight is the sacrifice to Bastet. You can wait until the morn, can you not? Gizane invites you and your men to partake in the temple doings, if you are so inclined."

Realizing Akhensobek referred to the acolytes of Gizane, the temple prostitutes, Gorias eyed Rothwell…who gaped at Gizane.

"I have no interest in your whores," Gorias grumbled as he stretched casually. "Perhaps the men will participate before they leave. For me, I'll go unto our encampment for the night."

Gizane arose, moving like the feline god she worshipped. "You have pitched your tents toward the Temple of Bastet," she purred, her tiny, pointed breasts never moving save to indicate her direction of movement. "It would be a short walk."

Gorias' eyes shot spears at Akhensobek as he clutched a skin of wine on the table. He said, "At dawn, my daughter and her mother, Akhensobek."

Turning his boot heel, the looming barbarian exited the long hall. He never looked back into the tragic face of Althea or the grinning visage of her father.

*****

Once, the tent city of the visiting barbarian army seethed like a vast organism made up of men and animals. That night the plain near the pillared temple of Bastet was nearly devoid of life and the only thing that remained in abundance was the refuse left by the exiting army. Amid much of this rubble, Gorias tethered his horse and found peace in a small shebang of a tent. Knowing the slave boy Dog would look out for him, he drank from the skin he picked up off the table and tried to sleep. He could hear the few men near the river distant, trying to cook a crocodile. Weary and his mind drifting, Gorias thought they would end up using the skin and abandoning the labor of cooking the beast on the spit he beheld earlier.

Dog whispered to Gorias, "We must leave this land of the evil man Akhensobek."

"Every man must decide for himself what is good or evil, Dog. That prick, well, his good is evil to us. My happiness makes him sick."

"It's a bad world, Gorias," Dog informed him.

Gorias soon swam in his dreams to a place he visited a few years ago; the first time he bedded young Althea. After crushing a force of Bantu and their allies, the gray-skinned Dohilemans, Gorias and his men drank their full before visiting the temple of Bastet. Invited there by a different high priestess than Gizane, his men took the temple prostitutes with great relish. Gorias recalled the moment he was about to mount one of the lovely whores, and she had presented herself to him, oddly enough, doggy-style on the altar of the cat god Bastet.

As he dropped his breeches and worked himself into the whore, Gorias spotted Althea in the shadows. Though he drove himself into the temple prostitute for the greater good of his own body, he stared at the lithe daughter of Akhensobek in the dimness cast by the torches of the cat god. Althea, he knew her well from the reviewing stand before the first war with the Bantu and Dohilemans. After her father had departed the scene, she walked amongst the barbarian mercenaries, offering water.

Those violet eyes, they seemed to glow in the dark recesses of the temple. Gorias gripped the hips of the moaning woman on the altar and could only watch Althea…as she touched her small, pert breasts, and let her hands soothe over her body.

The temple whore pulled away from him and flipped over. Gorias climbed on her and entered her again. He nearly slipped on her cast-aside samite robe, but held firm in his footing. The small woman cried out as the weight of his frame collapsed on her. His turgid member entered her again and he grabbed the whore of Bastet under the shoulders. Still, his icy blue eyes were on Althea…and her exploring hands. Althea's tiny digits walked like graceful dancers all over her flesh.

Speeding up faster than he usually did in this position, Gorias prepared to arrive. The temple prostitute, an expert in her vocation by her gyrations and filthy talk Gorias surmised, grunted deep and demanded that he not spill his seed inside her. Confused by her words, Gorias registered astonishment at the whore pulling him from her, allowing him to explode all over her stomach and heaving breasts. The woman smiled and sighed, working his member as Gorias stared over at Althea. The daughter of Akhensobek quivered and gasped, her body trembling as she watched Gorias spray the whore in his seed.

Gorias wanted her, he could smell her, practically taste her….

Once off the altar, the chants of the temple prostitute started to echo throughout the temple. Gorias reached down for his pants. Althea slipped back further into the darkness as the shrine servant slid off the altar as well.

The whore stumbled a bit, and then walked closer to the burning censer before the mini version of the Sphinx. Wiping Gorias' seed from her belly, she slapped it into the fire, chanting as she did so. The flames brightened and she shook, as if in orgasm once more.

Rothwell, present in the dreamy recollection as well, approached Gorias with other men, all stunned at the behavior of the temple whores. He said to him, "By Wodan's beard, Gorias, she placed it in her mouth once I...."

"You need to travel more," Gorias said blithely as he directed them out of the temple. "Though I'm sure you are no stranger to whorehouses, it seems they get more open the farther south one travels."

One of the Ingaevones remarked, "Wodan knows what they will do in the jungles beyond Kemet."

Gorias eyed the walls of the temple as if they would close on them as he exited, saying, "Then go and find out. I have no longing to see them."

When they headed to their tethered horses, Gorias spotted a fading image in the night, a thin girl astride a small colt. Surely, even in the dim moonlight, he recognized Althea. While Gorias watched her grow fainter in the night, he barely heard his men talk.

"I want to get out of this land," Rothwell stated as he untied his mount. "I hear the slave classes talk too much of creatures and beasts in the earth hereabouts."

Many of the Ingaevones, heavily superstitious, remained afraid of the foreign gods once out of their safe homelands. Gorias heard another man talk of beasts in the sand.

"You can hear them screech and scrape in the night!"

"Fah, you're fucking drunk," Gorias snapped, eyes straining for Althea.

One of the younger men swore a salute at Bastet's temple and then said, "One of the slaves spoke of a creature called the hippogriffin and the Lord of the undead, Seker."

"To hell with slaves, and their talk. 'Tis a shame we ever use attendants in the war." Gorias snorted as he got in the saddle, eyes seeking Althea. "Hippogriffin my ass! There's no such beast. Seker? Who is that? The sheep Wodan wipes his ass on?"

The youth again persisted, saying, "They say it lives under the earth and one can hear its claws scrap under the stone giant Sphinx of Bastet!"

Rothwell clocked the boy on the head, hoping to knock sense into him. He then mounted up and looked over at Gorias, saying, "It's a combination of a horse, eagle and lion, a Hippogriffin."

"How the hell do you know that?" Gorias retorted, angry unto his loins that he could no longer see Althea.

"I used to screw a witch in Urak, south of the Caucasus Mountains." Rothwell nodded. "Even she never did the things to me these whores did. She told me things...."

Gorias gave him a mean look. "Was she a Hippogriffin in disguise or are you going to bore the shit out of me with this story?"

Laughing at Gorias' bash, Rothwell said, "Hold your water. She told me of many creatures and even showed me artists' renderings of them."

"Artists," Gorias spat as he kicked his horse. "They eat mushrooms and share their madness with us all."

The small tent city the barbarians occupied on the plain outside the capital was tended well by the servants of the mercs. Hundreds of tiny tents spotted the land. In the dream, Gorias saw the tiny, one-armed slave he had dubbed Dog waiting with a drink and a wet towel for him by his tent.

Gorias drank from the wine flask and then dropped his trousers. Dog held the towel and looked away as Gorias washed himself. The boy Dog said, "There's one inside your tent, Gorias."

He eyed the boy quizzically, then knelt and peered inside. From the scented smell of her and the glowing violet eyes, he knew it was Althea.

Dog shrugged and admitted, "I let her in, Gorias."

Nodding, Gorias said, "You did well."

He then crawled into paradise.

Before he could even make it to her face, her spread, silky legs caressed his muscled frame. Her long nails dug into his mane, forcing his face between her legs.

After the act finished, Gorias told her he'd never had a woman quite like her. He lied. In his mind, Gorias recalled the whores of Salema were warmer and far more active. The allure of Althea gripped him strong, he thought ruefully. It was as if her sex tugged at him and demanded her go inside her completely.

She giggled, telling him all of her hopes, dreams and fears. He listened, for Gorias was young then. Some of it, he even believed. She talked so long, one moment amazed he could perform with such vigor after an encounter in the temple…then prattling on about how she detested her father and wanted to see the world, Gorias nearly drifted to sleep.

Startled awake, Gorias knew not if he was back on the plain, still mentally thanking Dog that the boy proved his worth that night…or sleeping in a similar tent city after the extermination of the Bantu. While he recalled that he was in the latter time frame, Gorias soon figured out that he no longer lay on the plains of Kemet.

In fact, his limbs were immobile. By dim light, he could see a stone wall in front of him.

In the distance, he could hear the echo of scraping on rock.

CHAPTER THREE
In the Walls of Akhensobek

Groggy and nauseated, Gorias found that clarity came from a pail of water. The splash to his face didn't clear his bleary brain in full, but it helped Gorias focus on his surroundings. Though expecting sunlight and the interior of his rough tent, he awoke enclosed in gloomy, cold surroundings, pinned to stone blocks...barely able to discern shapes in the timid green light. His head abuzz, Gorias assumed he lived because of the pain in his limbs. When he saw a human shape, he felt relief at first.

Unfortunately, the face he beheld in this dim chamber was that of Akhensobek.

"Even poison cannot get you down, savage," the King sneered, his black eyes on fire. Finger wagging in Gorias' face, he said, "That's of no matter. This is your just payment for services rendered unto the King of Kemet. I hope that you enjoy it."

Gorias found himself spread eagle on the wall, his ankles and wrists secured in a gluey substance proving rock solid. Eyes cast down, he saw that behind the King stood Gizane, eyes flickering feline in the dim light.

"Bastard," Gorias swore, flailing himself from the wall,

but the bonds held fast. "You used news of my daughter to get me back into Kemet. Hell, I brought an army with me! If I knew of your dishonor...."

Hands on his hips, Akhensobek grinned. "But you did not. Your friends are gone, back toward the northern mountains, laden with gold. So easy are they bought to spill blood, they have left their blood behind."

"Wodan shits on you, ya bald prick," said Gorias, spit flying. "And on your goddess, too, bitch." Gizane turned away, hand to her mouth, giggling. "My kindred will return for me and cut every damned throat in Kemet. The Nyle will run red and the ground will be poisoned with crap from your bowels!"

"Unlikely," said Akhensobek with confidence, the coolness of the air causing gooseflesh to arise on the King's bare arms. He handed the small bucket to a servant, who then bowed and ran away. "You are a wayfaring fighter, no? You seldom go back to your homeland. For years, you have gleaned experience killing other men, isn't that how you sold yourself to us a few years back?"

Rage boiling, Gorias' voice dropped as he said, "Piss off."

"You are not expected back home, are you? Once your pockets are full of gold, your vaunted hairy kindred will think Gorias off, drunk and besotted in some whorehouse for months. They will not be looking for you. In time, your memory will fade from their minds. That is the way of the low people."

Looking all around his self, Gorias retorted, "I'd kill myself to see you die!"

Still calm, Akhensobek related, "Even Rothwell, your friend, left, listening to the entreaties of Althea. He believed her completely that you and her were going off together with the child." Akhensobek could barely finish his words due to the laughter in his chest. Almost convulsing at the idea, he wiped tears from his eyes and said, "You must forgive me, savage. I amuse myself so greatly in all of this."

"They will return..." Gorias promised, his chest heaving.

His face straightened to a look of seriousness, the King asked, "And they will find what? Nothing. No trace of you. Seker will soon pick the last bit of flesh from your bones. You will beg that god of yours that does not exist for mercy. It will not come. Besides, if anyone returns, we will say you took your whelp and left. My daughter, jilted over her mistaken love for a barbarian, remains in mourning."

"You said she told Rothwell...."

Cold rage burned low in his words as Akhensobek snarled, "You still cling to her supposed love of you? Go on, take that unto your death." In the distance, again, the scraping echoed but this time accompanied by an otherworldly howl.

Gorias glanced around in the emerald glow. "Where are we?"

"Beneath the Great Sphinx, the tribute to the great god Bastet," the King affirmed. "There was a great complex built underground here, a sandstone maze, if you will, before our slaves and artisans cut the idol above from the grand stone. It was probably some primeval or Atlantean wizard or some such worker in magic who left himself in these tombs. All of those men lay long dead before the blacks claimed Kemet. I don't know who created these walls and maze, nor do I care, for they are mine now. Nothing ever escapes what we loose into the labyrinth from the breeding ground."

"Am I supposed to be impressed? Suck your own, ya bastard!"

"Take to your pathetic afterlife the idea that you were bricked up alive in the walls of Akhensobek. The creatures that are trapped in the netherworld below scout the tunnels every so often. There is no escape, savage. The slaves made the tunnels secure years ago. If you travel far enough down, Hell is no release point. There is barely enough room for the beast to walk free. Trust me, we will not meet again."

The King and Gizane turned and walked several paces; Gorias looked after them and saw that they slipped in-between a gap in a jagged brick wall. Soon, more bricks were placed on the breach, slapped together with mortar and other mixes.

Once he allowed his body to calm for a few moments, Gorias flexed his arms and legs. He then threw himself away from the wall. Repeatedly, he tried this move. Gorias struggled against his rubbery bonds to no avail. The dim phosphorescence in the tunnel never ceased.

Suddenly, Akhensobek stuck his head through the small gap remaining in the wall break and said, "What? No boasts? No threats of revenge? No melodramatic promises like you will kill me like no man has ever died? Come along! You disappoint me again! You fell so easily in your sleep from the venomous powder in the wine. We switched skins when you stared at Althea. So sick with love, you never noted it. Come along, tell me how I will die."

"Nothing like that," Gorias replied, ears tracing the regularity of the sounds far away from him. "You will die like many others have died."

The last bricks slid into place and Gorias, son of Ambiorix, was walled up beneath the great Sphinx.

Taking deep breaths, refusing to concentrate on the words of Althea's betrayal....

Lying bastard!

Gorias bowed his back out and tried to extract himself from the wall. Like a fly in a web, he convulsed and worked, at first in standard intervals, then like a madman. As his hopes of freedom dwindled, he sucked air in gulps. Gorias thought if he pulled free, he could kick out the mortar before it dried. He then wagered the troops of Akhensobek would fill him with arrows before he escaped.

Still, he refused to give up. Unsure of the time or hour, he continued to work until his limbs felt afire. He let them rest and tried again. Bullheaded to the core, Gorias worked himself wet with sweat...and until his mouth ran dry. It seemed as if many hours passed, but he was unsure.

Angry and weary, Gorias drifted off to sleep. The sounds in the tunnels faded as well.

*****

Gorias felt his body slump down and this snapped him back into reality. Confused over how long he slept, the sudden feeling of freedom in his legs caused glee in his mind. This feeling swiftly passed for the pain in his shoulders became the focus of his exhausted mind. Muscles flexed and he pulled himself up toward the gelatinous bonds that bound him fast.

When he looked down, he saw a tiny figure in the green glow. Unsure of the identity of this individual, his mind brought forth olden tales of dwarves, sprites and fairies residing in the earth.

"By Wodan's ass, if it isn't my Dog," Gorias said, a gush of laughter spewing from his bearded face.

"Glad you can laugh at death, Gorias," Dog replied. He held a small Kemetish dirk in his hands, gilded with gold on the edges. "It took me an hour each to cut your feet loose. You still snore."

Gorias stared down at him. "Then climb up me and cut my hands loose."

Thinking himself stupid for telling a one-armed boy to do this feat, Dog quickly proved his assumption wrong. Dog placed the dagger in his mouth and leapt up onto Gorias' leg. Balanced on Gorias' boot, Dog climbed fast. He soon reached Gorias' thick midriff belt by using wiry muscles and curved toes. When Dog balanced on the buckle and started to climb out onto one of his arms, he winked at Gorias.

"How the hell did you get in here?"

Like a squirrel in a tree, Dog slithered up Gorias' muscled right arm. He started to saw on the gelatinous substance with the knife and said, "The slave class knows where every gap is in this maze. None of the breaks are large enough for a man to fit down here. I took a chance. I made it. There's no way out for you that way, I fear."

"You should have run away, saved yourself," Gorias said bitterly. "Stupid boy."

"My life is yours, Gorias. If not for you, I'd not be alive."

"I didn't want you to throw that existence away. You should have run away, dammit. Your life won't be worth spit now."

"It never was or my mother wouldn't have tried to terminate me," Dog said calmly as he worked. "If you hadn't arrived to collect jewels from that barber turned abortionist, I'd be dead all the way, and not just maimed."

Dog referred to a fatal incident years ago. The barber had grabbed the unborn baby, Dog, with a metallic device to forcibly extract him from his mother at eight months. The arm this tool clutched sliced off as Gorias thundered into the barber's house. He'd not soon forget how it looked in profile on the end of the hook in the firelight. Gorias was a boy then, just fifteen when he slew Dog's abortionist. Just fifteen when he watched the child partially emerge, then performed an emergency cut to get the baby free. Just fifteen when he slew Dog's mother and kicked her head against the wall.

"You must escape from here and run away," Gorias informed Dog. "You must make it back to the mountains, see if you can catch up with the forces...."

"Perhaps there's a way out. If there is indeed a beast down below, he must have a way to escape."

"Whatever lurks below lives in the earth."

"It has to eat and get air from somewhere, Gorias. That and I have heard tales of tunnels one of the forefathers of Kemet installed when wanting to dupe his followers. He left himself a false route out to feign resurrection from the dead."

Looking around them, Gorias shook his head to clear his mind. "Did he escape?"

"Er, no, that's the drawback. Story was that his coffin got sealed and thus, the old magus couldn't escape his tomb."

His strength pressing on the bond, Gorias ripped the limb free with a grunt. Dog flew to the floor, but the nimble youth flipped and landed like a cat.

Gorias extended his hand and Dog gave the blade to him. Inserting the blade into the clear mass, Gorias muttered, "Some concoction of Akhensobek's priests?"

"I think it came from that priestess of Bastet. She makes odd traps and spells from her own body fluids." The boy grinned and said, "Gorias, a slave to pussy as always."

At last, Gorias fell from the wall. Crouching, recoiling

from being on a solid surface, Gorias gave the dagger back.

"Perhaps, if I go to where they just laid the bricks I can push them back?"

Dog reminded him, "Into the face of guards? That tunnel will be guarded for some time. It terminated in an avenue of crypts. You would never get out that way. I think I can locate the gate to heaven itself."

Gorias stared at Dog indignantly. "Are you determined to get me eaten by that beast in the distance? What are you babbling about?"

Dog motioned Gorias to follow him. "I think I know of another spot where a tunnel passes close to the crypt of that magus. There was a peculiar race of men that lived in this land even before the blacks. They built these tunnels and crypts, but Akhensobek added to them and closed many exits. He couldn't destroy the mind of every slave who saw it happen. Perhaps there's something in that tomb to help us escape."

Hunched over, Gorias swore as he followed the boy through the glowing walls. "Why do the walls cast off light?"

"They are phosphorescent," Dog explained.

"What does that mean?"

"It means they cast off light."

Gorias groaned. "Why did I save your ass again?"

Dog giggled as he sniffed the air. "It was an accident, remember?"

"There are no accidents," Gorias said, wishing he had a sword to face whatever horror screamed in the expanse. "Wodan's wisdom saw to it you were saved when I slew that barber, elsewise I would've been trapped on the wall there forever."

"Life is full of lessons," Dog said, waving at many of the

reliefs on the walls.

Gorias squinted, seeing abominable creatures carved in the rock, mating with humans. "Wodan help us." He saw a rendering of a humanoid creature with a tentacle for a head and his memory burned of creatures he fought once, not long ago in a land not far away.

Dog smiled as he cocked his head to the right. Again, they heard a distant echo, like the scuff of metal on stone. "I think that's getting closer."

Impatiently, Gorias snapped, "You're full of great tidings, Dog. Is this place, the gate of heaven, any closer?"

"Yes," Dog nodded and jogged down the network of tunnels. Gorias reached out and took hold of his left shoulder so he didn't lose Dog in the dim light. The boy paused, looked down at Gorias' feet and said, "Your boots are making too much noise."

"So will you when I choke the life out of you, dammit!"

Gorias and Dog crept for a long time until they beheld a huge breach in the hallways. The sounds of howls and scraping grew more distant, but clearly, they originated from deeper in that opening.

"To hell with that way," Gorias said and turned.

Dog touched his arm. "You should see what's below."

"What say you, Dog? Have you been below this place?"

Dog nodded. "I'm small and my scent faint, so the creatures never noticed me."

"You're mad if you think I'm climbing down into that darkness."

"Don't be afraid, Gorias."

"Only a fool isn't afraid."

The boy took his wrist and coaxed him into the darkness.

Gorias took a few steps, prepared to protest, but a glow caught his attention. It was golden brown and gained in radiance the further they walked. The slope they walked down grew steeper and Dog warned him to go over to one side. His boots found steps and enough light emitting from the earth's gut to guide them.

"What is it?" Gorias whispered to Dog.

"The abode of the gods."

"Stop screwing with me."

Dog half laughed and said, "There's a safe place to observe or I'd never bring you down here."

"Why in the hell are you taking me here? We need to get out!"

As the glow increased, they stepped into a larger subterranean chamber. Flowing out before them, and delving deep, was the abode of the gods.

Or, it looked like it.

The rock gave way to a glittering surface and all around gold gleamed from the walls amidst the green hues. Gorias understood gold needed refining after mining, but it surged from the walls. He expected to see many men mining this great find, but what he saw was much different.

A large, spongy floor spread out below them, not colored gold. It seethed, breathed, and resembled a starfish Gorias saw once on the coastline to the south. His heart rumbled in his chest as it occurred to him that the floor was alive…and the long legs or tendrils of this thing oozed golden bile…coating the walls.

"You wanted me to see this?" Gorias spat at Dog.

"I wanted you to see where the King's gold comes from."

"A curse be on him for such a travesty of nature."

When the screams and scrapes resounded louder, they hurried away and back down the tunnels. To Gorias it seemed they rose up higher in the complex of tunnels.

Dog stopped, glanced in the direction of the scraping sounds and then pressed on the wall. The place where the boy ran his only hand looked no different than the other walls. The boy pointed and said, "Throw your weight into this, Gorias."

"I'll have both shoulders on one side if I do that."

The screech of the creature sounded out louder, so Gorias braced himself and gave the wall a blocking blow with his right shoulder. The attempt wasn't his best, as he feared hitting an unforgiving surface. However, Dog proved correct in his search. The wall gave a little under Gorias' push. After a few more body blows, the wall cracked and Gorias saw that piece of slate, not a half-inch think, covered a wooden barrier. The wood, rotten and falling to pieces, provided him hope. He drew back and kicked a boot through. Profanity joined the noisy screeches as Gorias became stuck in the wall. He tried to pull back and hopped on one foot. Dog tried to help him balance as the wail of the beast increased.

"Wodan, I need a drink," said Gorias before he swore more.

"Me, too," Dog agreed, then suddenly pushed Gorias' buttocks.

Off-balance, surprised, the Ingaevone lurched forward. The weight shift sent him through the rotten wooden barrier and Gorias fell through the breach into the next chamber.

Gorias rolled over and laughed, looking around the room, lit again by the green glow on the walls. He struggled to his feet as Dog slipped into the opening. He glanced back the way they came and then followed Gorias.

There wasn't far to go, for the room was a fifteen-by-twenty-foot box. The place held only a rectangular container and a line of cylindrical clay urns.

Gorias pointed at a doorway opposite the way they entered. "This is bricked shut." His shoulder block on that entrance showed that it wouldn't cave easily.

Nose close to the bricked doorway, Dog frowned. "Yes. The priests sealed him in, thinking this persona dead." He pointed at the long box. "I fear the tales are true and that he never escaped like he planned."

Gorias kicked at one of the long urns. It broke apart like thin ice and a roll of parchment fell out. Angrily, he stomped on it, fragmenting the stiff document.

He said ruefully, "Then there's no way out in here, dammit!" He peered at the remains of the roll of paper as the scream of the creature became deafening. Gorias couldn't decipher the characters. He faced Dog and said, "How is it the slaves knew of this spot?"

The boy shrugged, wandering near the way they entered. "I think they robbed his sepulcher, Gorias. That's why his escape route is wooden and fragile. From the look of the sarcophagus, the old boy got nailed in there by his priests."

Gorias spat at the few urns left and grunted. "I guess they saw this stuff as pointless to steal?"

Suddenly, the scraping sound ceased and a large hunk of the thick outer wall gave way. Under the touch of pointed claws twice the size of a man's hands, the creature announced its presence.

Gorias grabbed Dog by his only arm and pulled him away from the opening as the shape of the creature blotted out glowing walls. When two bird-like talons gripped the edges of the jagged opening, Dog murmured, "It is a hippogriffin?"

Once he stowed the boy behind himself, Gorias backed away and desperately eyed the chamber for a weapon of any sort. Gorias muttered, "I don't think so."

In the dim light, they could see the glittering talons, a sheen off many dark feathers and a slender head. The creature found them, yet didn't reach out to them immediately, thus giving them scant hope.

His nostrils smelling the creature, Gorias reached down and grabbed one of the clay urns. These few objects interned with the unknown forefather of Kemet were his only projectiles.

When the creature opened its pointed maw, Gorias thought it indeed a Hippogriffin, the bizarre beast depicted on the reliefs as a combination of a lion, horse and eagle. However, the hooked beak, glowing eyes, and rustling wings that shone inky black from the glow of the walls made Gorias think it more bird-like throughout the entire body. This fact never stopped him from heaving the urn at the open mouth of the giant beast.

Out of raw instinct, the beast snapped at the incoming shell, smashing the clay tube to bits. However, inside this urn no parchment fell. These actions heartened Gorias. First, that the creature reacted in such a way, leading him to believe that it was nothing supernatural. Secondly, that out of the urn fell a long metallic object. Unsure if the object that clattered to the stone floor was a weapon or not, Gorias threw Dog on the other side of the coffin and started to kick at all of the remaining urns.

Dog screamed at the monster, "Seker!" before the creature extended its neck into the chamber. The boy flattened on the wall behind the coffin and Gorias did likewise as the beak of the creature, akin to that of a raven or hawk, smashed into the stone cover of the coffin. After taking a clean bite from the sarcophagus, the head of the beast arose. Its neck then stretched further, stabbing at Gorias, missing.

Gorias was so stunned at his latest discovery from the shattered urns, a bronze tomahawk, that he failed to notice the hawkish snout stab toward his side. The blunt edge of the beak jabbed him hard. He reeled and went to the floor. On all fours, gaping at the tomahawk, he then faced Dog, cowering against the wall and vulnerable.

"Seker," said Gorias as the creature thrashed at the opening, unable to get in farther due to its wings. Seker, the god of the undead in Kemet, Gorias ruminated. However, he saw the giant hawk writhe its tongue and suck in air before it smashed into the coffin again. If it could breathe, it could die, he surmised.

He turned and seized a piece of the coffin lid in-between Seker's attacks. Gorias tipped it up and let the beak smash into the piece he held. As the beast struggled to get free of this mild annoyance, Gorias rolled across the coffin and dropped to where he had smashed the urns earlier. The tomahawk tight in his fist, Gorias briefly eyed Dog as the boy slithered closer to him beside the coffin.

Up on his haunches, Gorias tried to formulate a plan of attack.

Seker strained against the opening that Gorias guessed would break in due course. The beast couldn't quite reach them, so it settled on destroying the rest of the coffin. In the dim light, Gorias could see a humanoid shape in the casket, and several small jars as well. The beak of the great hawk inserted into one of these jars and for a moment, was stuck.

Just as it parted its beak and broke the jar, Gorias acted.

Forearm across the beak, Gorias reached back and swung the tomahawk down between Seker's eyes. Expecting a mighty crushing blow, but only managing to break the head off the old weapon, Gorias filled with anger.

Seker reared its head and connected with Gorias' sternum, throwing him back against the far wall. The hawk screeched and then tried to reach in with one of its claws. Again, it failed to snatch them.

Dog, still covering his head, looked up at Gorias and said, "A buried weapon would have been miraculous if it worked. It was meant to work in the next life."

"Piss on that," Gorias spat, looking at the handle of the tomahawk he still held. "There's no tomorrow."

Though Gorias wrote off the cloud of dust in the air as displacement from the raging beast, his eyes were soon drawn to the coffin. Truly, an ejecta of fine dust arose from the sarcophagus. At first, Gorias doubted his eyes, but the dust truly emanated from the broken coffin like a cloud that never dissipated. Then he didn't trust his ears for in the chamber echoed a pulsing sound like a colossal heart beating. Even Seker paused and blinked red eyes at this sound. Suddenly, a tall form unfolded itself from the coffin. Standing nearly as tall as Gorias, the occupant of the sarcophagus stretched and looked at its coal-black hands. This being peered at Dog, then at Gorias.

"At last I am free," the arising man said. "Again, the great magician Ra-Horakhty, man-god of the rising sun, walks the Earth!"

Gorias and Dog exchanged a look.

The arisen magus went on to say, "At last I can facilitate

the will of the Elder Gods and call up the spirit of he who shall not be named!"

Gorias said, "You're just what I need."

Fingers fluttering as if they swam in the rising powder from the coffin, Ra-Horakhty blinked, squinted, focusing eyes on him and said, "What?"

Gorias bellowed and kicked the arisen man-god in the belly, knocking him askew and back toward the twitching talons of Seker. With no hesitation, Seker snatched Ra-Horakhty by the left thigh, ripping corded muscle loose before burying its beak in the arisen mage's throat. Ra-Horakhty's mouth opened wide, but he couldn't scream, for his voice drowned in blood, robbed by the thrashing beast. The leg tumbled off and his head hit the floor as a spray of crimson gouted into the slick feathers over the head of Seker.

However, once Seker grew occupied with ripping the arisen mage to pieces, Gorias jumped. The bowed head of the blood-doused hawk, busy with splitting the rib cage of Ra-Horakhty apart, never rose as Gorias closed his left armpit over the beak...just before he drove the handle of the tomahawk deep into the left eye socket of Seker. The stunted weapon submerged deep, causing the creature to explode in a new frenzy that sent Gorias flying to the far wall again. This wrath made Seker drop the mage and bust through the walls further into the burial chamber. Head up and screaming, Seker's huge form shook. After a whiplash spasm that sent particles ejecting from its jaws, grisly bits of Ra-Horakhty splattered Dog and Gorias.

Eyes wiped clear, Gorias scooped up Dog by the waist and looked at the widened doorway with hunger. When the enormous hawk tried to raise its head in another fit of anger, it connected with the low ceiling. The head stuck there, so Gorias ran across the room and pitched the boy into the hallway. He reached down to grab a piece of the newly shattered ceiling. The jagged hunk of slim slate felt good in his hands. Dirt and further pieces of stone fell down from above, pouring over the creature.

Gorias stepped onto one of the hawk's claws and tried to plant his other foot on the floor to gain greater leverage to strike. Unfortunately, his right boot slipped in more gruel from Ra-Horakhty, and this action made the warrior miss his slashing blow. Trying to gain his footing, the wings of the beast wreathed Gorias as the head of Seker popped free of the ceiling. More dirt blinded the Ingaevone and his boots fumbled over the dead arms of Ra-Horakhty and the shifting claws of Seker. With a primal roar, Gorias slashed up, driving the jagged hunk into the main body of the hawk. He felt that he struck through flesh, if not very deep, so Gorias jumped up, tackling the right wing of Seker. All of the man's weight bearing down on the appendage, Seker extended his wing to shake off the aggressor. The hawk tried to bite at him as well. Gorias' legs intertwined through the long feathers and his body swung low like a hammock. The beak just missed him, but his weight, the move and the flail of the hawk's mass snapped the wing.

More ferocity and pain enflamed the creature as Gorias twisted his limbs, trying to rip the wing loose. Seker, though, refused to be beaten and almost casually snapped Gorias' mane of hair in his beak and threw the Ingaevone off himself. Back slamming the far wall, Gorias knew his demise drew nigh. Up on his feet, Gorias shouted the name of his god and decided to charge into his death.

Before Gorias reached him, the ceiling caved in, covering

Seker in immense amounts of dirt and rock. The thrashing creature fought, drowning in the debris, and ultimately, it fell under the weight of the earth.

Legs partially buried as the room filled with a pyramid of dirt, Gorias still shouted the name of his god as if he were heard. Not used to such an outcome once he prepared to die, Gorias stared, perplexed for a moment.

"Gorias?" the voice of Dog called into the burial chamber. "Can you get free?"

Fresh, cool air bathing his bearded face, Gorias chuckled in spite of his situation. "Yeah, I think we both can." His legs shifted and Gorias thought he found a stone to balance on. Pulling his one boot up, his other leg twisted on the object. "Son of a bitch," he swore.

Crawling over the pyramid of dirt, Dog blinked. "What is it?"

"I think it was the skull of that damned Ra-Horakhty I just slipped on. Damn, he was a gift from the gods when he showed up, but the old mage has been a pain in the ass ever since."

Dog looked up at the ceiling, saw the light and said, "That's quite a way up there, but I think even you can fit."

"I sure as hell hope so."

"Better let me go up there first, though," Dog told him as he scrambled up the debris toward the opening. "I'm just a slave. They won't think anything of me popping out of a hole in the ground."

"But you were my slave, or servant boy," Gorias reminded him as he pulled his legs up. "I'm shocked they just absorbed you into their culture."

Dog shrugged his better shoulder. "What's one more

slave to these people?"

The small boy scurried up the opening, obscuring the light at times. Gorias cursed as the child kicked more dirt down into his face, but never complained as he freed himself from the room. Not wanting to wait to see if Seker really happened to be crushed to death by the collapse, Gorias started up the tunnel.

His head peeking above ground, Dog glanced around and then down at Gorias. "It looks to be just after dawn. I thought as much. We can escape easily enough, Gorias."

"Indeed," said Gorias, anger boiling in his words.

CHAPTER FOUR
Escape, Priestess and Love Hurts

Far from the gap in the earth, Dog and Gorias made their way from the shadow of the Sphinx. Gorias carried Dog much of the trip on his back to make better time. They traveled for most of the day, keeping away from any crude roads or well-traveled field passages. In time, they arrived at a tributary of the Nyle River. They washed off, minding the territory for any crocodiles, and then they rested for hours.

By scavenging the banks, Dog produced wild onions, roots and a couple scarabs they could consume. While he munched the butt end of the bug, Dog watched Gorias, who stared north. The blue eyes of the Ingaevone wandered in the direction of the capital city as if he could see it.

"Better just forget it, Gorias," said Dog as he chewed. "Akhensobek is surrounded by guards and his own little army."

"Piss on them," replied Gorias as he snorted, still looking the way of the city. "The King hired us out to do his dirty work, Dog. One Ingaevone against them...."

"Yet, he holds a large force of his own folk who are his guards and military," Dog reminded him gently as he wiped his mouth with the back of his forearm. "Your brothers are long gone back to the mountains and your sword is gone. It isn't worth dying over."

"It? Huh. It. You say so, Dog," Gorias reflected, his voice composed. "My brothers...I shall steal a horse and catch up to them then."

Dog sighed. "Perhaps we can. I don't think they'll be keen to turn back and fight, though."

Testy with his words, Gorias reminded Dog, "I'm one of them, boy."

"Granted," Dog agreed as he discarded a leg of the scarab. "But they warned you to not be so thickheaded, no? Your desire for Althea enraged the King and gave you a bloody nose. Your folk are apt to bloody your nose further and tell you to count yourself very lucky. The Ingaevones are barbarians, not dumbasses."

"I just can't believe..." Gorias snarled, and then his voice faded.

Dog blinked. "Believe in what I just said?"

Gorias waved him off. "No, dammit, I can't accept that Althea agrees with her father. The lying damned prick, his ego is such that he thinks no one can exist without him."

With a moan deeper than a boy his age should exude, Dog said, "Gorias, you take many whores in every city you travel to. What's so different about this Althea? Was she that good performing on the bed mat? Why believe her words out of all of the ones you have heard?"

With a swallow, Gorias' voice remained tranquil as he answered, "I thought she really...gave a damn. My...I...." His manner stiffened and he said curtly, "If she doesn't want me, then that's that. However, I'll not let my daughter be raised by these devilish folk. I'll not have any with my blood pray to gods like Seker for deliverance, nor venerate Akhensobek and his brood as gods."

"You don't know where she is, your daughter," Dog offered. "I've never even heard the slaves tell of her."

"She'll be in the complex of Akhensobek and his one hundred and fifty children," Gorias nodded with assurance.

Dog sighed again. "And I am certain there's nothing I can do to dissuade you from invading such a well guarded place?"

"You don't have to come along. You were never really my slave. That's a word these swine in Kemet use to control minds and bodies. You know that your freedom is always there."

Dog nodded. "I came along on this venture when you stopped by my home city for supplies. I've known you my entire life and owe you my life."

"Shut up with that talk," Gorias said bitterly. "Your existence isn't a mishap."

Dog looked at the stump of his left arm, sliced at the bicep. "How many are really wanted in this world? The gods dropped me in your arms alive for some cause."

Gorias thought that if it weren't for the boy, he would still be a prisoner in the walls of Akhensobek, or eaten by Seker. "I have no choice, Dog. I have just one life. I must do for my kindred the best I can. I must save my blood wherever it lies."

Drumming his heels in the dirt, Dog smiled and related, "Well, in the dark, you may need a distraction."

"True."

"Remember, I'm a slave to them. Most guards or aristocrats won't even look into the face of a slave. I know the alleys and streets used by the servants."

Hand to his beard, Gorias pondered it all and prayed to

the son of Wodan, Donar, for deliverance, because he knew Wodan really didn't give a damn.

"It's as good a day to die as any."

*****

The act of obtaining a horse and riding to the luxury city of Typosyris by Lake Myrute proved an easy job for a killer like Gorias. Dog commented that it was almost like shopping in the marketplace when going into private estates with Gorias. The big man just took what he desired and killed anyone who objected. Those of Kemet were much smaller folk than the Ingaevones and Gorias' hands crushed two necks of simple farmers that tried to stop them. Unfortunately, Gorias found the food they had wasn't to his liking. Not wanting to take the time to slaughter or cook anything in a small cage, Gorias swallowed dates and nuts, but bitched most of the time.

The darkness proved an excellent cover for Gorias and Dog. They stealthily lost themselves amongst the obelisks and stone tributes to Akhensobek around the fringes of the vacation spot. Gorias led the horse as if it were packed with goods, not just bundles of cloth to aide in their deception. Many of the guards never batted an eye at the pair of travelers in slave cloaks, stinking of the raw lands.

What startled them was the howl of many dogs. The repeated yipping made Gorias divert from the path to the home of the King and wander near a high spite fence, made of boards.

Dog whispered, "Gorias, we don't have time for all this!"

In a gap between the boards, Gorias squinted and then blinked.

Inside the fence, he saw several dogs restrained in a small

pen. He also spotted the priestess Gizane and his anger boiled. With her stood the skinny wizard Uylikla. Gizane held a small rider's crop in her right hand and beat the wizard on the back. Uylikla was nude and shaking.

Amid the dogs howling, Gorias heard her scream, "Transform! Become the jackal that you are and do what you desire!"

Uylikla fell to the ground and started to froth at the mouth. His limbs trembled and he screamed more than the animals in heat.

Gorias glanced down at Dog, who also peeked through a different crack in the fence. They exchanged a look and peered back inside.

Roaring like a beast, Uylikla was up on his legs and dived over the inner pen fence. He grabbed the nearest dog and wrestled her to the ground. As he howled and fought to enter the animal, Gizane giggled like a hyena and walked away, back into the abode.

Gorias and Dog stepped away and again looked at each other. Gorias said, "And I am a barbarian?"

Dog shrugged. "It wouldn't have been so bad if he really turned into a jackal." He looked back at the fence but not through it, and shook his head. "He's still a guy acting like a wild dog. I don't understand…."

With fiery eyes, Gorias turned to the house. "You don't have to, Dog. Come with me. I'll see an end to that bitch once and for all."

They left their horse and snuck along, low to the ground until they reached an open window in the rear of this home. Gorias could taste blood and smell the scent of the priestess. The air crackled as Gorias started to rise up, Dog beside him.

Inside the room they saw Gizane, topless, her *three* breasts bounding near the edge of a wall of light…and inside the light barrier under a six-sided star on the floor, at the base was an image in scarlet. Truly, the cloven-footed, horned beast she kept in this star was her demon…and the thing shot out a forked, snake-like tongue, lapping at the teat in the center of her chest. Though scaly-skinned like a reptile, the demon bore a humanoid shape, hairless, yet had no belly button.

Gorias and Dog sank to their backsides and each took a breath. The Ingaevone whispered to the boy, "I think I'll kill her later."

Dog nodded. "Good choice."

Carrying a heavy bundle liberated from the man Gorias strangled for the horse, Dog walked to the pantry entrance of the long, complex home of Akhensobek. A series of interlocking rectangular stone buildings, only one guard reclined at the back servant entrance. A one-armed child never made him nervous.

Gorias watched the boy disappear into the home and then observed the guard sit back down, half asleep. Stunned that the palace was so lightly guarded, Gorias' hands were hungry. The men he killed weren't enough for his thirst. The King was so conceited, he expected no attack, Gorias mused. Then again, why would he? All of his enemies were dead and only a Bantu assassin would be crazy enough to seek Akhensobek out. How likely was it that a lean Bantu would make it through the city to this point?

Behind the hedge line, looking at the guard lean back to regain some sleep, Gorias gripped the two weapons he had been able to find up to that point: a heavy iron sledge with a spiked backside and a curved dagger. When the guard closed his eyes and started to head off to slumber, Gorias squeezed the handles of his weapons. Though not made by a skilled artisan, and certainly not intended for slaying, Gorias found himself excited about burying them in the bodies of anyone who opposed him.

Though Dog learned Akhensobek resided in the city that night, resting, Gorias doubted he would have a chance for revenge on the King. He tried to convince himself that attaining his daughter was enough. *Another day*, Gorias told himself, *I'll cut out Akhensobek's heart…with fine Ingaevoneos steel…and eat the soul of the damned King of Kemet.*

As the night deepened, Gorias left his cover and moved across the yard of obelisks closer to the pantry entrance. He placed the knife in his belt and gripped the handle of the sledge with both hands. The guard failed to stir until Gorias stood nearly atop him. When he did move forward, Gorias swung the hammer with great speed. He struck down lower than he planned, hitting the guard's throat. The strike of the hammerhead through the neck went so hard Gorias laughed that the guard's head didn't topple off. His opponent died, arms out, searching for air, his blood exiting fast in a brutal crimson burst. Gorias sat the guard back down, as casually as if the watcher were disturbed from his sleep and decided to rest again. Gorias slapped the sledge toward the earth, whipping off a crimson covering, and then adjusted the dead guard even more on his chair.

Once he pushed open the door, Gorias stepped into the kitchen area. Near the enormous hearth, big enough to cook many meals, lay the bodies of two serving women and one man. Gorias smirked at the orderly fashion they'd been laid out in, for he doubted they lay back in a row for Dog to cut their throats.

The boy traveled quickly across the room, waving hard for Gorias to follow him. When Gorias joined him, Dog said with no malice for those he slew, "They were loyal servants."

"I like them better this way," Gorias muttered and looked down the hallway. "If the guards are roused, run. They'll execute me, but I'll drag as many to Hell with my sorry ass as I can. Disappear, Dog, understand?"

The boy nodded, pointing with his scarlet-tipped blade down the left side of the hall. "Althea's chamber is the fifth one down. I've been here before carrying messages. I wish it weren't in the middle of the other rooms of his children."

Gorias ground his teeth together and then gripped the dagger on his belt. Still holding the hammer as if he were about to drive in fence posts, Gorias stalked down the hallway.

He stopped at the door where Dog indicated Althea resided. He paused, listening for signs of life. Gorias' heart raced as he got what he wanted, for he heard a female yelp in ecstasy. The rhythm of her breathing and the creaking of furniture told Gorias all he needed to know. Unsure if his baby girl lay inside and more interested in the truth from Althea's lips, he shoved the door open, snapping the primitive bar on the inside.

Immediately, the figure mounting Althea in the dim moonlight rolled off her and scooted across the floor. Gorias' eyes ignored this person and focused on Althea, Her identity revealed by the moonlight on her profile and pointed breasts. He took a few halting steps toward her, stunned that she never bothered to cover her nakedness.

"Althea," he whispered, searching for the words to say.

Abruptly, his world turned, for the carpet under his feet was yanked away by the man from the bed. Gorias stumbled backwards, backpedaling, hitting the open door. He bounced off it and never had a chance to dodge the one blow the man delivered. A glittering object clenched in both hands, his assailant swung and nailed Gorias on the forehead. Dazed, the Ingaevone slashed with the hammer, but found the floor coming up to meet him.

He rolled over, swooning and wished the world would stop spinning; he couldn't make his arms work. Eyes up, Gorias knew he must be dreaming, for the naked man standing over him was Akhensobek.

Then, darkness reigned.

*****

When the spit hit Gorias' left eyelid, both of his eyes fluttered open. Immediately, reality returned to the hulking man, but his rage couldn't flow. Bound up with rope, Gorias lay back in a rectangular wooden case, shortly blinded by the noonday sun overhead. After so much time underground, Gorias still felt liberated by the outdoors reaching in to embrace him. Yet, there were closer bonds hugging him back, denying him freedom.

"Awake, savage," came the cruel tones of Akhensobek. "I want you conscious for the end."

The King of Kemet leaned into the path of the sunlight, looking like a smug man-god. Surrounded in this halo of dazzling light, the black eyes of the King glowed like a solar eclipse. Gorias' heart sped up, just as emboldened by the portents of this eerie sighting.

He tried to move in the box and failed, feeling the bite of ropes on his ankles, wrists and across his chest. He could smell water and could hear the river, though the walls of the box obscured all else. He could sense people, smell them, yet only the King could he see.

Akhensobek patted the sides of the container and said, "The slaves know how to make an ark, no? They are good to their master, for they had better be. They have fastened this ark with enough pitch on the bottom to carry you out into the river. However, this pitch will degenerate in time and you will slowly sink."

A few of the slaves, their forearms filthy with blood and pitch, stepped into view. Soon, they hid their faces from the piercing eyes of Gorias. He reckoned they didn't care to see an animal die badly, much less a human. However, he felt certain they'd seen it before.

"Why not just kill me with a public spearing or arrows, you cowardly prick?"

"Because," the King said steadily, clouds starting to roll behind his head, "I want you to suffer."

Gorias gave out a single chuckle. "By drowning?"

"I have no doubt you will break your bonds in time. I also have no qualms that you will be smart enough to escape the ark." He paused as Gorias felt movement on the outside of the box. Akhensobek questioned him, asking, "Do you feel that? They are painting this ark with blood. The crocodiles will be near as soon as you stick that revolting maw out of the box. Eaten alive by dozens of crocodiles, what a delight to endure, aye? My guards and my new army of marauders from the south wanted a grander death for you, one with great sport. However, never let it be said that Akhensobek is unmerciful."

Into Gorias' view stepped Althea, tall, beautiful and emotionless.

Gorias gritted his teeth and then managed to say,

"Akhensobek, you damned pig. You banished me to the walls because I bedded your daughter and she produced an heir? A real man would have fought me."

The King thought for a moment as thunder echoed in the distance and then said, "Don't be so dramatic, savage, but yes, that was it. Oh, I could not stop Althea from her passions, nor prevent the gods from making a child come forth from your seed in her. I comprehend the will of those above and below, Gorias. However, I have decrees of my own. I needed you to overpower the barbaric Bantu forces of the south. In that, you served me quite well, better than the raiders from the south I usually employ. Nevertheless, a son-in-law or heir you will not be, nor will the product of her belly be on my throne."

Gorias looked at her with pleading eyes, but his heart fell when he saw her smile. In fact, Althea's silly grin made his heartbreak transform into confusion and then burning fury.

"Piss on your kingdom of Kemet. I never wanted it."

The King went on, saying, "Do you think she would give up her position and a life of comfort to be your consort in the world abroad? Don't be the dumb stooge you look like, dirty mountain man. Of course, you infected her with a child, but surely you understand what happens in a case like this?"

"Go to Hell."

"If one owned a canine of pure lineage, then a wayfaring mutt humped upon her, what would you do with the offspring? Yes, put them in a sack and drown them in the river. In this case, an ark? Not quite the same application...." Akhensobek reached out to his daughter and his fingertips touched her necklace of tiny bones and jewels. Abruptly, he snatched them from her neck. The girl made no objection. In fact, she smiled wider when her father slipped off the crystals on the ends and returned them to her. The King held up this string of tiny bones. "Too late to drown her properly like an unwanted cur, for she has been bled for Bastet, the day she was born."

"You--" Gorias choked, a terrible reality of the petite bones suddenly clear in his mind.

Akhensobek laughed and threw the necklace into the ark. "A further means for your slow death, barbarian. Take what remains of your daughter with you. Contemplate that on your way into the afterlife. I have over one hundred and fifty children, but I would not give one of my daughters to you."

"You...you sonofabitch," Gorias stammered, body trying to burst the bonds as he felt the bones of his dead daughter on his sweaty skin. "I'll do worse than kill you! For the life of my daughter...." His eyes, streaming with tears, stared at the tiny bones on the necklace. They seemed to burn against this flesh.

With a bored voice and an exaggerated, weary manner to his body, Akhensobek declared, "Cease the threats, cretin. You survived the walls under the Sphinx, and the master of the maze leading to the gold mines, Seker. Do you know how long it takes to breed one of those guardians? However, this will be your undoing." He looked to the skies, which darkened in tune with the distant thunder. "The slaves have stirred up the crocs. They are gathering already."

Althea looked at Gorias, hardly blinking. The barbarian glared at her, looking for a bit of hope, that she was forced into this eventuality...that she didn't willingly bear his daughter only to sacrifice the babe's soul to Bastet...just to gain his service in the war. Gorias found nothing in her face to convince him that she was anything more than a projection of her twisted father. Suddenly, his rage against him shifted.

The servants brought the wooden lid of the ark near to

covering Gorias, but Akhensobek stopped them. "Wait! You have forgotten someone. Never let it be said that I am unjust or uncaring." A servant girl brought forth the body of the small, deformed boy who aided Gorias in the war. She dropped the one-armed boy into the coffin. When Dog tumbled over on Gorias' stomach, the Ingaevoneos man saw the child was dead.

Gorias looked to Akhensobek but no words came.

The King smiled, then this look faded. One of contempt filled his visage as he said, "You disappoint me, Ingaevone. I expected far more bragging and intimidation. Let this freak accompany you into the hereafter. Heaven knows it has no soul."

"You shouldn't have killed my daughter," Gorias growled through clenched teeth as a deep boom of thunder rolled overhead. "You shouldn't have killed my Dog."

"Nail it down," Akhensobek said with an uninterested sigh. "Pour more blood on it. The crocs will benefit from my sacrifice to the goddess of the waters." He leaned over and said, "Fare you unwell, Gorias. You will never see the face of Akhensobek this side of Hell again."

Stern-faced, Gorias replied, "If I have to rise from the dead, my shadow will follow you *and* her for all eternity."

Akhensobek put his arms around his daughter from behind. Althea kissed her father's jaw as his hands squeezed her hips.

Then the world of dark clouds was sealed over Gorias' head. He breathed deep, smelling the river, the land of Kemet, and the cold flesh of the dead boy on his chest.

When he felt the box lift into the air and then forward movement, Gorias expelled all of the air from his body. Once his frame relaxed, he hoped there would be some slack, however slight, in the bonds about his chest. The ropes moved a fraction. He kept repeating the move.

Suddenly, a great jarring of the box, followed by a brief stillness made him realize the obvious. He had only a moment to contemplate that fact that the slaves had heaved him into the river.

The shift of the box disoriented him at first, but Gorias again started to work at his bonds. Truly, the box wasn't built to last long in the river. Just as Gorias thought he had moved the ropes on his wrists down a bit, a heavy object struck the side of the container. The body of the boy Dog tumbled over as the ark spiraled in the water. Now the corpse lodged over Gorias' neck, pushing up to the lid.

Unsure if a croc broadsided them or if they struck a rock in the tributary, Gorias felt the box pick up speed. The rushing current in the Nyle River gripped them and they sailed away from the home of Akhensobek.

Gorias thrashed his legs as another object collided with the floating box. Outside, he could hear the faint sound of thunder. Head wrenching to avoid contact with the dead body, it dawned on Gorias what he must do.

"Be a good servant, Dog," Gorias rasped, breathing deep again. "One more time for me, kid."

Never uttering a shout or a prayer, for Gorias knew he dwelt on his own; the Ingaevone thrust his head and neck toward the lid. He pushed up with his elbows, his body pressed against the one tiny thing between him and the outside world. The lifeless body of Dog wedged tighter to the cover of the box, the stunted left arm ramming itself in the corner. Almost laughing at the idea that the dead boy really planned to make that move, Gorias roared in his throat and gathered all his strength into one push.

This move shoved Dog's tiny limb into the nailed breach, shredding some of the skin, but making the daylight spill into the container. Water also splashed Gorias' face, reminding him of his peril.

He raged anew as the liquid bathed his beard, but he felt the bonds about his chest slacken and his wrist attachments come undone. Hands free, they grabbed the flesh of the dead body and rammed it hard into the gap of the coffin. With all of his strength directed at one spot, the lid flew off.

Up on his haunches, Gorias pawed at the ropes on his boots. He looked from side to side at the furious river, attempted to get his bearings. Through the churning waters and spray around him, he could see that they drifted out in the wider portion of the waterway and no cities lay nearby. Swimming to either side would be a chore, he reasoned, aside from the numerous dark shapes in the water. Rain started to fall, and this wasn't apparent at first in the spew of the river. A proper storm brewed overhead and lightning flashed, stabbing across the sky.

Free at last, but weaponless, Gorias then noticed water seeping into the bottom of the box. In a moment, he had no more time to decide. An enormous croc splayed itself onto the end of the box, nearly flipping it over. Gorias almost tumbled into its gaping mouth, but wedged both legs and arms to the sides of the ark to stop his progress.

However, Dog fell to the mouth of the croc. The jaws snapped as Gorias reached out to save the body. As the box slapped back down level into the river, Gorias regained his footing and realized he held the boy's lower torso, snapped off at the waist.

He dropped what remained of Dog into the water.

He turned his back on where he cast the remains. An enormous set of jaws smashed a section of the box free. Gorias wrenched off a section of the hard wood and used the last bit of solid force left in the sinking box to propel himself into the air. He landed on the back of the enormous crocodile, much as a man would sit astride a horse. The mighty jaws opened in a bellow and Gorias stabbed the jagged hunk of wood into the roof of its mouth.

Punctuated by a crack of thunder, Gorias dived off this howling beast and started to swim. The current proved violent and he felt as if he carried two men on his back. He made long strokes in the current and saw his reptilian foes making plans. They pursued him like a pack of wolves, but fought the vile current as well.

Like a spear flying toward him, a croc set itself to strike at Gorias. When the creature knifed at him, Gorias dropped lower in the water, curled and embraced the crocodile as it missed him. Seeing a few of the reptile's brethren nearby, Gorias twisted with the beast, much smaller than the monster he sat on earlier, and aimed its flailing jaws at them. The current, Gorias' enemy before, now pushed these creatures into the mouth of their brother. He released the beast and dived down into the water again. His breath held still, he saw the creatures start to fight, confused at the violence thrust on them, enamored by the blood in the water.

He took great strokes under water and swam as long as he could before desire for air forced him to rise.

Just as he cleared the surface, spying the bank closer than before, one of the crocs attacked again. This one was smaller, younger. Its mouth just opening as Gorias' legs kicked on the surface, one under its jaw, and his other boot stabbed down on the top of its head. Gorias grabbed for the tail of the beast as it thrashed, but suddenly, it darted away from him. Indeed, so did the rest of the crocs.

Gorias treaded water and sucked air, trying to comprehend why they broke off the assault. His senses afire, fearing the worst, he turned and tried to head for the shore. Out of the corner of his eye, he noted that some of the crocs made a line for the shore. Something told him it wasn't to head him off.

The storm worsened as he fought for nearly an hour to reach the edge of the river. Time and again, he was swept down the channel, closer to the edge, but still in the embrace of the current. Quite a few crocodiles were out, but many retreated due to the storm. At last, Gorias brushed the mud under his boots. The sensation rushed over him felt as fantastic as sex. Like a drunk, he staggered through the waves and fell on the shoreline. The rain assailed him and the lightning struck the water afar off.

Never did he ask his gods for aid in this venture. Even now, he still refused to bother Donar and Wodan. In their wisdom, they gave him the storm. Donar sent his lightning to frighten the beasts. That was enough. God was all right. Sometimes.

On the shore, he stood, limbs shaking like a newborn colt. His eyes faced Kemet.

Gorias then turned his back, faced north and knew what he must do.

CHAPTER FIVE
How Not to Slay a Dragon

In a vast savannah, many would see little in the way of food, but Gorias had a full belly. He wandered, though, like the days before, living off the rabbits, squirrels and field mice of the area. This great field of grasses full of critters to be plucked was mildly familiar to him, having crossed it weeks before with the great army of warriors from Thule. At times, Gorias convinced himself he saw evidence of their first travels, mashed down tall grasses created at mass stops, but he was more intent on looking for their recent markers, signs that he still followed in their wake after being left behind in Kemet. While he wandered in the general direction of home, Gorias understood the scorn waiting him there wouldn't cure the pain Kemet incurred behind. When the enormous grasslands ended and the mountain ranges of serrated cliffs jutted up before him, he greeted them with no real emotion.

Miserable and not even able to get drunk over it, Gorias continued on, unsure of the place he stopped to sleep, other than it was a cave and cool at night.

When the great shadows passed over the mouth of the cave, disrupting the morning sunlight, he snapped awake, his mind alert for danger. The shadow clued him in, but the scent in the air proved a great confirmation of menace.

Scrambling on his knees to the mouth of cave, he shrank back some. Once he beheld the fantastic creature that passed him by, he doubted his sanity for a moment, but quickly shrank even further down to the rocky surface, hoping the eyes of the monster wouldn't spy him.

A magnificent beast, surely worshiped by stupider men, he thought, the dragon moved in the sky with more elegance than one might first imagine. Then again, he frowned at his own thoughts, how would one really think a dragon would fly? The wings moved fast, like a bat or a hummingbird, not flapping with grace like a great raven or eagle. Those animals stretched out and swam in the air, while this dragon looked to have a grudge against the sky, slapping at it violently.

He observed the creature until it came near to the series of cliffs not far from where he hid. Gorias wagered at the velocity it flew, the dragon would crash into the cliff and he'd view an interesting death fall. However, the creature pulled up at the last possible moment, the momentum carrying its tail to strike the cliffs lazily, but the lower set of legs extended claws to grip ahold of a rocky shelf, while the upper arms stabbed into the rocks.

"Blue dragon," Gorias mumbled, afraid to speak that the thing would hear him, even if it was so far away. The sun glanced off the blue plates and added to the incredible beauty of the dragon.

The upper arms dug into the rocks like a child sifting sand, then disappeared from sight. Though Gorias figured it burrowed holes, he soon came to see the creature broke up a stone covering of caves…no…tombs. This revelation came as the beast pulled wrapped up bodies from the slots it created.

It collected four corpses, one wrapped in red-dyed linen. The beast pondered this one but was making a good showing of holding the bodies in-between the fingers of its right claw like a gambler would do with cards or chips.

Satisfied, the creature flew off, shooting up skyward, but quickly rolling over and heading toward Gorias, who flattened, face to the rock, afraid he was next. The dragon passed him by and he relaxed, but in a few moments he heard a distant sound not unlike the playful chirping of birds, but it was also like a hissing of vipers. Rolling to his back, Gorias' eyes shut tight as the sound was punctuated with weird cracks. The chirping hisses returned and the dragon rumbled, cracking sounds echoed and soon, abated the cries.

"Feeding her young," Gorias said to no one and sat up, then quickly looked to the cave's entrance. His hand to the grooves on the edges, he laughed, not having noticed in the previous evening light that the cave he slept in had been broken open by claws just as he'd seen.

He got up and walked deeper into the tomb, seeing certain articles left, a broach, a broken vial, a face scarf full of dust, probably worn by the deceased to shade the awaking in the afterlife.

"Stupid, shoulda burned them," he said, not understanding why anyone would bury a body. "Couldn't have been a warrior king, huh?" No weapons, and wanting one since he'd been reduced to using a makeshift sling to get his food, Gorias searched on. He saw nothing of use and assumed the grave had been cleaned out of anything valuable already. Down to one knee, he did find a few shredded smocks, and felt something metal. He pulled up a curved object, rusted and discarded by anyone seeking valuables. "Sickle?" Gorias pondered the old tool, and shrugged at the small handheld reaper. "Guess that's better than nothing." He looked at the empty shelf carved out of the side of the rock wall. He'd mistaken it for a natural formation until the idea of a tomb sank in. "Thanks, ya farmer."

The sounds of the baby dragons feeding faded, so Gorias stepped from the mouth of the defiled tomb, but recoiled again. Up the side of the cliffs he spotted a couple figures walking along a trail very near where the dragon had just dug.

"Huh, hadn't seen any walkway up there," Gorias sighed. "Guess they had to get up there somehow to entomb them."

Armed with only a rusty sickle, Gorias started to follow interconnecting paths toward the places the dragon raided.

Up through a series of narrow paths that hadn't been apparent when he chose his resting spot for the night, Gorias quickly ascended the side of the rocks. He stopped, crouching cautiously as a gruff voice barked out orders, belched, then laughed. He went forward, slowly slinking up to the mouth of the opened tombs hidden in the caves.

"Hurry it up, Davin, we don't have all day."

From deeper in the cave Gorias heard a voice reply, "What else do we have to do? Cash in these trinkets at the next village?"

Gorias heard a loud swallow closer to the mouth of the tomb. "Good point, but I'd rather be out of here before the pissed villagers show up to fix the holes of their dead folks as best they can."

"I want to get going, too. I heard what they did to Nogtromsa and his brother when they came scavenging up here."

"Yeah, I'd rather be fed to the dragon than be crucified and fed alive to the pigs before I passed. They were two cowardly, backstabbing brothers, though."

"I'm hurrying."

"Good. We'd best get out to the south and around to avoid that damned group of ruffians bivouacked to the north."

The voice grew louder and a loud belch punctuated his appearance on the ledge outside the cave. Flat against the wall, Gorias saw the speaker, a huge fellow much bigger than even himself. But this slob didn't spot him, and seemed only concerned with fumbling in his kilt for his manhood. Gorias didn't breathe as the man pissed over the ledge.

However, when the yawning man did turn his head and lock eyes with Gorias, the young warrior sprang, left hand on the man's beard, swiping down the sickle. Gorias really tried to chop off or injure the man's right hand, but inadvertently sent his manhood flying down the side of the cliff. Urine and blood jetted on the rusted sickle as Gorias pulled up the beard, bringing his weapon up to his target's neck. The old tool did its job and sank in deep enough. When Gorias pulled back, the gouge left in the slob's neck stopped any screams and started a gush of blood.

Mouth open, the slob put his hands up and the kilt fell, mercifully hiding the brutalized lower portion of his self. Cutting a comical figure as he tried to scream, hands in the air, blood running down his legs, the slob teetered and Gorias shoved him with a single poke of the sickle's butt in his chest. The dying man fell, only making noise when his body scraped on the cliffs on the way down and ultimately flopped at the bottom. Down below, legs broken, the man floundered a little before growing still.

"Rubandell?" the voice inside the tomb called out, just as Gorias squared his shoulders with the opening of the tomb carved out by the blue dragon.

"Ya won't be taking orders from Rubandell any more," Gorias snapped, bloody and piss-soaked sickle slapping the side of the tomb. "Give up your weapons or any found here and it may go better for you."

A short man stepped from the shadows, a lantern fueled by wax and wicks near to his side. He blinked, looked down at the smaller bar in his right hand and then the tiny gold dagger in his left hand, and extended his hands to Gorias. Each hand trembled. His knees quivered as he came near to falling to them.

"I...I...." he stammered, not dropping the tiny knife.

"You're a grave robber and I don't care." Gorias stepped forward, hand briefly up to the necklace of bones on his chest.

Tears springing to his eyes, the man dropped the articles in his hands and pressed his face to the floor of the tomb. "Spare me, slayer, and I've serve you."

"I'm no slave master," Gorias told him. "Who the hell are you?"

"Davin," the man muttered, face still to the floor.

Sickle handle to his hip, Gorias said, "Get up."

Davin peeked up at Gorias, his dark features still mostly hidden in the shadows.

"Yer not from around here, huh?"

Clearing his throat a bit, but not looking up, Davin replied, "You, either."

Gorias stomped forward one pace and Davin cowered lower, shaking.

"Aw, knock it off. I'd have killed ya by now if I was gonna. Get up." Gorias walked past him and scanned the tomb, freshly destroyed by the dragon. "Not a warrior buried here either?

Fate pisses on me."

Davin peeked up and then started to rise as Gorias sat on the slab meant for the body. "How did you know I was an outlander?"

Gorias' eyes traced the walls, bland and only marred by a random dragon claw mark. "You're darker of skin, reddish like those far south of Jericho. You dress like that folk, too, unless ya stole them clothes."

Davin shook a little as he stood, but not out of fear. He reminded Gorias of a dog awaking from a nap or fresh out of water, shaking out the kinks as he set his feet in surprisingly brand-new sandals. Not too surprising, Gorias thought. *He prolly stole them someplace.*

"You are not from here, either, slayer."

Not setting his eyes on him, Gorias exhaled and focused on the opening in the cave. "Brilliant as well as a grave robber."

"Are you from the others?"

Gorias then glared at him. "What others?"

Davin pointed at the stone wall, north, as if he was citing an object clearly visible outside. "The army from the north. They're traveling through Blackstone territory and are camped beyond, by the great string of brothels outside Leonore."

Leonore, the complex of brothels and whorehouses on the trade route down off the Bospurus land bridge. Gorias knew of it and his great force from Thule had passed by on the way to Kemet weeks before, but only had time for oral oblations, not a full-scale service call.

"Do I look like these men?"

Davin nodded fast. "No one is that tall, has hair that colored or a beard so thick in these parts, slayer. However, you do look different."

"Call me Gorias, and how am I so different than the others?"

"You have no armor or weapons. Those men are weighted down with swords and knives, mail armor and the like."

Gorias confessed lowly, "I've had a few bad days." He then spoke up and stood up, saying, "Ya must show me where they are."

Davin gave the entrance a worried glance and wrung his hands.

Gorias asked, "Yer a wanted man?"

"Not by name but my master was. "

"Your master is dead. Change your clothes, shave your face and wash your ass, no one will know it's you."

"I hope you are right."

Gorias figured killing him wasn't worth the effort as Davin would end up getting himself killed easily enough.

As they walked the cliffs, cautious of the dragon, Davin wondered, "Do you have any food?"

"Do I look weighed down with provisions?"

"I'm starving."

With Davin in tow, Gorias headed down the cliffs, heeding some of the shaky words of the grave robber. He saw no point of tempting fate in walking through the town, even if they were backwater folks. No, a dozen of them armed could kill him or worse, and being crucified or sat out as dragon bait didn't appeal to him. While they couldn't stop a dragon from defiling their graves, he was certain they would take out their anger on a couple of foreigners for that.

Gorias found himself following Davin's lead around the community, which proved a tad larger than he first thought. Though the usual small village could live off the nearby river if enough sanitation holes existed, Gorias felt shock that large pens stretched for goats, cows and pigs. There were even breaking corrals for horses.

"That's crazy," Gorias said, stopping, but quickly feeling Davin prod him on to keep going around it all.

"Whatever you say, keep going."

In no real hurry, Gorias kept stepping. "Why would a dragon eat the dead when all this livestock is out here in the open?"

"Maybe the dragon is mad," Davin suggested.

"Maybe the dragon is drunk," Gorias mumbled, then looked to the sky. Not far off to the east he spotted the dragon in the air, or at least he hoped there was only one. The creature hovered with the grace of a hummingbird at times, wings not beating as fast as such a bird, though.

Davin spotted the beast as well and quickly dove into the tall grasses of the savannah.

Gorias didn't move, stopping dead. He heard something else in the distance, beyond the area he saw, more by the whorehouses of Leonore. Elephants, perhaps the trumpets of mastodons.

Davin covered his head with his arms and peeked up at Gorias. "Run!"

After a sigh, Gorias said, "Your arms won't stop it."

"What are you going to do?"

Gorias replied, "Get under a bull and pray for rain. Get yer ass up." He grabbed the forearm of the cowering man and lifted him off the grasses. "She isn't interested, see?" He pointed where the dragon ceased to fly.

Once Davin had shuffled his feet and brushed himself off, he stared at the hovering dragon, a few miles off. "He's right over the camp."

"She," Gorias corrected him and then wondered, "What camp indeed?"

"She? Uh, well. The barbarian army bivouacked to the north."

Gorias' heart jumped as he felt his folk nearby at last. "Wonder what the dragon wants?"

When Gorias started to jog directly at the scene, Davin shouted, "Are you crazy?"

"I don't think it likes live people to eat," Gorias yelled over his shoulder, still running.

Davin ran to keep up with Gorias, yelling, "How can you tell it is a she? Markings?"

"Male dragons don't lay eggs, dumbass."

Starting to breathe heavier, Davin agreed. "All right, good point. But why are you…we…running at this thing?"

Gorias took several more strides across the grass, seeing a lower dip in the land spread out and away from the nearby town of Blackstone. "It looks to be thinking something over, look."

The grasses Gorias and Davin traipsed through grew longer as they left the edge of the village and drew nearer to where the dragon floated in the air. Gorias saw the beast clearer, became certain it was the same creature he'd seen eating the dead bodies. He also perceived projectiles striking it.

He stopped and Davin fell at his calf, panting, thanking a god Gorias had never heard of for the rest stop.

"Someone is trying to give it trouble," Gorias muttered and looked down at Davin. "How did you live this long in life with such courage?"

Ignoring his words, Davin said, "The tribesmen who

passed by, they are wild men or crazy enough to think they can slay such a thing."

Gorias started to walk again, more cautious this time. "C'mon."

"We're in the open," Davin wailed, not moving.

"I don't think this dragon likes the living or she'd really fuck up the tribesmen as you call them." For the life of him, he couldn't fathom why the monster hadn't crushed whatever attacked it.

The dragon kept dipping its legs down, trying to grasp at something or someone below Gorias' line of vision. He assumed this in response to the missiles thrown its way. As Gorias crested over the hill, he saw the valley spread out below him and the reason the dragon hesitated.

On a section of the grassy valley, a rectangle of greenery didn't quite match up with the savannahs. He could see it, Davin could, too..., Hell, the fucking dragon could see it, Gorias guessed...which is why the beast didn't land on the area to get the obvious bait...three dead human bodies.

"You guys are bright," Gorias groaned, speaking of his comrades down around the area, hundreds of armed warriors from Thule, all out in the open, their trap not sprung, their ruse not successful.

Davin rubbed his eyes and said, "Tiger trap under the brush cover, not a bad plan for killing that thing."

"Not really, but I doubt they have anything sharp enough in the pit to penetrate that skin. Not a bad idea," Gorias declared and motioned for Davin to follow him into the open. When the smaller man recoiled, Gorias shouted, "Don't be such a damned pussy, grave robber. That thing ain't gonna freakin' kill us. It'll eat these asshead cousins of mine first."

At his loud shouts, a few of the warriors that focused on the dragon looked their way. A couple gasped Gorias' name, but soon returned their attention to the task at hand.

"They wanted him to land there and fall in the big trap." Gorias started walking, not caring if Davin followed, seeing some of the brush cover caved in a bit. In a moment, Davin did catch up to him. Gorias spoke louder so the other Thulites could hear him. "Good idea, shitty execution."

The dragon ascended, bleating loud, making all hold their ears. Everyone stood and watched the beast soar. Within seconds a huge man stepped from their midst and shouted Gorias' name.

"Rothwell," Gorias shouted back. "I hope you have some wine left, ya sonofabitch."

"We all thought you taken to big family living with the daughter of that king." After a rude embrace, the two huge men separated. Their smiles faded. "What happened?"

"I will tell all, but give me a sword and some food."

Rothwell chuckled and then pointed to Davin. "Who is that mutt?"

"Davin, a grave robber from up the cliffs over yonder. We met by accident and I think I know why this trap of yours didn't work."

"It's a sound idea."

Hands in the air for a moment, Gorias agreed. "Damn straight it is, but that thing doesn't care for fresh or even rotten meat."

Rothwell leaned on his spear, then pointed at the areas where the grass cover continued to fall into the pit. "Yeah, we thought about that too. How do you know?"

"I saw it feed on dead bodies, nothing new, either. It must

have a taste for that."

"That's fucked up."

"And a flying lizard isn't?"

"So we need some long-dead bodies to kill it?"

"I reckon."

Rothwell nodded and glanced at Davin. "That cowering twat know of any places to get some?"

Gorias turned to Davin. "He's talking to you, twat."

Davin swallowed hard and stood up straight. "The tombs beyond are but one place, but there are dirt graves down by the edge of the savannah where the great desert begins. The ground is dry and folks figure no animal digs too deep for a fresh meal in all that."

Rothwell coughed but didn't address Davin. "I'll send off a half-dozen men to dig up some bodies where he says. Let's eat and drink a bit. You look like you could use both, Gorias."

Once they had sent Davin off with several stout men, Gorias and Rothwell reclined in a tent far from the dragon death trap pit to eat.

"God, pork chops," Gorias said of the meat fresh from the spit, his eyes watching the crack in the tent flap where several youngsters were peeking in.

Rothwell grunted. "These fools around here won't eat swine, but raise them for their poop."

"Huh?"

"Their crap. I think they put it on crops."

"What a bunch they are."

"And they say we are barbarians."

Gorias chewed and scratched the skin under the necklace of bones he wore. "Yeah."

"So what happened to you?"

Gorias told him the tale and left nothing out.

Rothwell listened, eating a snout and drinking from a wineskin. After the long story ended, he said, "Well, fuck a duck, man. That's something."

"Enough to really make me angry. That's about all of my story," Gorias drank his full of a wineskin and threw it to one side. "Fool that I am."

"These things happen," Rothwell said quietly, shrugging a little, looking for words on the tent ceiling that were not there. "Hate to be obvious, but if I were you, I'd be mad as hell."

Gorias didn't look over at him. "Yeah. But I'm one man against a lot of guards and mercs he might have employed since we took off. I was stupid to go back to his complex alone once already."

"And you aren't thinking too clear," Rothwell assessed. "Blind rage can make a man stupid, as you learned. Killing that King is one thing, maybe easy enough if you can get through his defenses, and his magic folks, but...I doubt killing that prick is good enough for you."

"Yer right there." Gorias lay back, forearm over his eyes, exhausted. "And I'm angrier at her than him, really."

"Who else do you want dead in Kemet?"

Horses thundered up outside the tent as Gorias mumbled, "All of them." He yawned and fell into an impossibly deep sleep as the voices of his brothers from Thule told Rothwell they'd found the graveyard and started getting bodies out.

He though he heard Rothwell say to set the trap again and prepare for another go at the dragon, but sleep gripped Gorias tight.

Born of Swords

*****

Startled awake, Gorias sat up, unsure how long he'd slept, but seeing that darkness swallowed the interior of the tent, he wagered all day. He saw Davin sitting, legs crossed, hands on his knees, peeking out the tent flap.

"I'm not surprised to see you there, strongman," Gorias yawned and stood. "What is the ruckus outside?"

Trembling, Davin replied, "How can you sleep with such things going on!"

Gorias yawned, went to the flap and threw it open, causing Davin to shrink back on his knees. Gorias scowled. "Ya think the tent is gonna protect you against that dragon?"

The dragon in question flapped above the pit area out beyond the camp, once again.

Davin drew close to Gorias and said, "Something crashed loud a bit ago, their plan must've failed."

"Seeing as the dragon is flying away, yer a bright one."

When they went to the pit, they saw it missing the fresh cover the Thulites had spread out. Down in the pit were dozens of broken shafts, many spears and sharpened branches.

Rothwell walked by the edge of it, cursing.

Gorias called out, "Dragon got away again, huh?"

Rothwell made an obscene gesture, but said nothing.

"Better give up that idea."

His anger proof that he refused such an idea, Rothwell let out a stream of salted curses and then said, "Damned flints and regular metal can't penetrate the scales on that big blue bitch."

Gorias looked back toward the hills above the cliffs. "Prolly need something stronger to get through the plates."

Rothwell kicked a dusty skull, probably a leftover of bait

used to lure the dragon in. "We'd need the help of all the gods and a few devils to kill that thing."

"We are lucky it doesn't decide to attack us, huh?"

"We?" Rothwell glared at Gorias. "You are one of us again?"

Gorias' look fixed on Rothwell, but he quickly looked away, south.

Rothwell half smiled. "They cut one of you balls off in Kemet? You left some of your nerve there by the look of you."

"What?"

"Years ago, I'd be wearing my ass for a helmet if I said such a thing to you."

"Perhaps I'm getting older."

Rothwell spit on the skull at his feet. "But no wiser."

"There was no blood rite to tie me or anyone else to Thule forever. I was free to roam if I chose."

"Want to impress me? Kill that fuckin' dragon."

Hand scratching the chin of his beard, Gorias looked to the sky. "Don't whine like a bitch, Rothwell. It isn't becoming of you."

"Yeah, yeah…."

In a low voice, Gorias said, "I cannot do this alone…."

"No joke? I thought that…." Rothwell stopped speaking as he stared at Gorias again. After a few breaths, he said, "Not talkin' about the dragon, are you?"

Eyes from the skies, Gorias faced him. "I cannot do it alone."

"What is your desire?"

Gorias told him.

Rothwell nodded softly and ran both hands through his mane of hair. "That goes beyond the ability of one man, not to say further than common revenge."

"So refuse?"

Rothwell breathed two full breaths before saying, "I didn't say we couldn't, just said it was a helluva idea."

As if on cue, the dragon howled out in the distance. Both men turned to face the vile screech. On the cool wind came a fainter sound, an echo of a similar vein, only weaker.

"Even the babies of that fuckin' thing mock us," Rothwell mumbled.

"Mock us or you?" Gorias posed to him. "How about I solve your problem?"

Rothwell laughed. "You do that."

"Strike up the forges."

"Are you daft? Not a weapon can pierce it."

Gorias turned away from him. "I'm not going to bring you back a sword to refine."

CHAPTER SIX
Armor

Gorias adjusted the sword on his back as the climb became steeper. Every so often, he gripped the sword handle on his hip, as if it really steadied him on his ascent to the dragon's nest. It felt good, nonetheless, even if it couldn't pierce the dragon's hide. *It isn't supposed to....*

Under his left arm, he gripped a large cloak folded up and took care not to drop it. What did surprise him was the composure of the little ones trailing him. They didn't giggle and chatter as all children are want to do. Yes, they were typical kids, albeit Thulite boys and girls, until they neared the sloping hills. They understood what was at stake. Hell, they'd already been up this mountain once already. This time, it was dark and the trek timed out to be negotiated near dawn. They understood to keep their mouths shut. As it was them the dragon would want.

"Dead people and kids, what an appetite," Gorias muttered to no one, for even Davin had refused to shadow him on his venture. No, he didn't take the children as a sacrifice, but as bait. Near to man-making age, the boys were always brave or silly enough to crave adventure. The girls, too, or they wouldn't be much as Thulite women. Gorias didn't know any of their names, didn't want to…save for the girl with red hair and her face painted blue. Her grin as she threw another nine-year-old into the dirt until he cried…Keyra, that was her name.

Not worried in their ability to distract the dragon, as they'd led it back to the camp a few times already, Gorias focused on his task.

The place where the dragon nested lay above and beyond the tombs Gorias had slept inside. The series of switchbacks up the mountain were like a natural set of staircases he'd seen when traveling near Jericho. The children stayed back, knowing their place, allowing Gorias to ascend to a precarious spot near to where the dragon set her nest. Once the switchbacks petered out, Gorias hunched to the ground, surprised that a more level plain stretched out for about a hundred yards, and that the cone-like structure across from him was the dragon, wings about itself, curled up in a pyramid about its young.

He didn't comprehend just why the nest wasn't higher, or on a place of lesser access, but perhaps the dragon didn't think like birds or a crazy Thulite out to glean the approval of others.

There really wasn't any place to hide, so Gorias went back down the trail beside the elevated plain, and waited.

If he'd waved a flag at the kids, it wouldn't have fallen in line any better. The children of Thule started singing, pretty songs about war and the gods, their harmony very sweet to his ears, and suddenly annoying to the dragon. Gorias saw the almost rock-like structure of wings tremble, then unfold and shake. When the long neck reared up from the nestled spot, Gorias' heart stomped down hard and the folded cloak fell out of his armpit.

Fear can become so intense it defeats itself; he'd heard a

wise man say that once, but he grew very dry mouthed and waited for it to happen in the face of a blue dragon uncoiling. All of his anger and pain for what lay in Kemet melted at the specter of his possible death. True, he walked near death each day and often waved his cock at it, but feeling the ground move and his eardrums pop as the dragon unfurled made his soul freeze.

Almost a prayer to Wodan on his lips, Gorias cowered, hoping but not praying that the dragon would miss him. Unsure of the senses of the monster, he hoped and considered prayer. If he prayed to Wodan, the god would piss on his weakness. *Piss*, he thought, *I could really piss right now*. He truly hoped Wodan, or some god, was really there and not all was blackness beyond the veil of eyelids. After all, sending his enemies to the eternal fire was a better thought than just stopping them to breathe.

The dragon, a majestic creature even if a scary spawn of Hell, planted its clawed feet on either side of the oval-shaped nest and spread all wings out. A hundred yards didn't give Gorias a perfect image of the beast, but it was close enough to see the scales, the bat-like leather of the wings, and the curious smoothness of its long neck. He'd seen other dragons of varied colors, each a bit different in body than its brothers. This one's neck extended more like a serpent. He felt hungry to strike the dragon's throat, but comprehended he may as well slap it with his cock rather than his sword, because it'd be just as effective.

The great wings pushing down, the beast started to ascend. Soon, the wings beat so fast and the creature spun, pursuing the children as they ran like mad, still singing the songs, now switching to a cadence of marching tunes. Even with the shadow of death over them in the dawn's light, the barbarian kids played games.

Gorias didn't casually arise and stalk the nest. He got up, grabbed the cloak and ran across the expanse. Ideas that this might be another folly flew from his mind as the nest loomed. Truly like the creation of a fowl, the large nest sat as a conglomeration of branches, mud, grass and leaves, but it also sported cloths, bones and rocks in the mix. Gorias tried not to stare at the pelvis and skull on the exterior of the nest, almost looking like a warning sign to any.

He started to jog around the nest, looking for a proper spot to cut it open, and nearly ran over the edge of the mountain. Hand on the nest, Gorias cursed the dragon and threw down the cloak.

"Bitch, why would you build it close to the edge?"

While no one was there to answer him, something heard him. Three long, stalky necks arose from the nest, chirping like huge birds. Each creature, identical to its brother or sister, sat as a copy of its mother. Curious at the lack of variation, Gorias felt glad they weren't mobile. Uncertain of their development or ability to fly at any age, Gorias drew the broadsword from his back and swung it in an overhand arc, hard. It took several whacks before he could rip the nest open, as the exterior ran smooth and he had a vision of himself falling in and being unable to get out if he climbed it. Once the babies were exposed, he noted their legs not as long as their bodies would allow someday. True, each dragon was the size of a big man, but babies, all the same. Each, awake, extended their neck up, mouth agape like a bird, awaiting a feeding.

"Wyrmlings," Gorias named their stage of life, but didn't hesitate in his task. He took a step into the gap he created and climbed into the nest.

The wyrmling nearest him broke with the feeding ritual and moved toward him. Legs emergent, it lurched, but the long neck extended, and the beak looked strong enough to crush Gorias' face. Eluding it proved straightforward. He ducked low and back body dropped the wyrmling like he wrestled a fellow savage. When he heard the baby dragon squeal and then fall silent, punctuated by a wet snapping sound, Gorias grinned.

"Yer bones can break," he said with glee and swung the sword about to try to behead the wyrmling nearest him. The blade bounced off and the sharp edge blunted on the stalk neck. "That's the stuff, good," he commented, glad the overall plan would work well. Dropping his sword, Gorias got the one he struck in a headlock and twisted. "Ya wouldn't be much good it yer skin broke on that blade." Using all of his force, he tried to break the neck of the wyrmling, afraid the other would snap out of the feeding posture and attack fast.

The wyrmling's neck didn't snap like a limb, but something cracked in the stalk. Some fight went out of it, enough for the extended neck to wilt, so Gorias took his chance and grabbed up the broadsword again. With one hand on the edge, he leapt up to the lip of the nest, squared his boots on either side of the yawning maw of the hungry wyrmling and brought the broadsword around.

He didn't yell for God, Satan or any of their asshead minions as he stabbed the sword down the throat of the baby dragon. The beast gagged, convulsed and shook until Gorias hopped down, all of his weight on the blade, driving it into the innards. Hands on the pommel, Gorias twisted it, cranking the blade in a circle, clearing out a spot deep in the guts of the beast. It screamed but it died faster than he thought.

Sucking breath in fast, he didn't pull the blade free, as if that act might revive the wyrmling. Gorias moved around the wyrmling he'd just slain and grabbed up one of its arms. The limb, heavy due to the undeveloped wing webbing on it, was a tad bigger than his own arm. He gripped the wyrmling's limb by the elbow at first, smiling at the sight of the dew nails on the forearm near to where the wrist began.

He heard the distant bellow of the dragon and knew he'd best be fast.

So, with the dew nails of the dead baby dragon, he sliced the wounded wyrmling in the nest open. The nail cut through the armor plates and skin like a hot knife into spoiled cream. Once the beast was open, Gorias pulled the sword and performed a crude quartering, then did the same action of the other wyrmling.

Half out of the nest, he started to throw out parts of the babies onto the spread-out cloak. As he started to arrange the pieces and prepare to get them wrapped proper, a voice squeaked across the plain.

"Eyes up, Gorias."

He faced one of the Thulite children. It was a nephew of Rothwell, he thought, but couldn't recall his name.

The boy hollered, "Get your shit and run. We've done all we can do."

Gorias nodded and held up the head of one of the babies to the boy.

The kid grinned and disappeared.

Gorias brought the edges of the cloak in and tried to knot them. He armed up the parts, angry at their weight, and loped across the level plain.

The dragon trumpeted from afar, so he figured he had

time. He just hoped it'd be enough.

*****

Dozens of Thulites gathered about the space where the blacksmith's forge had been set up. Hundreds more tried to get in to see until Rothwell cussed them and ordered them to get back. The dawn's light showed those that could see what had been laid out on the ground.

"Sonofabitch, you did it," Rothwell chuckled as Gorias finished his cuts of the dragons' skins using the dew nails of the wyrmlings. "You really killed that thing's babies."

Someone in the crowd muttered, "Mama is gonna be pissed." This caused many to laugh but others to state the obvious that they were in real trouble.

Gorias turned and stood by the stout blacksmith. "Garretson, the village is in real trouble first."

Rothwell wore a confused look, then reached for the pommel of his blade as the dragon's scream echoed all around.

Unconcerned, Gorias turned to Garretson. "We have some time. I dropped some meat of the wyrmlings through the town as I walked, so that thing will be on a rampage there first."

Garretson grinned and looked at the skin pieces at their feet. "Yer a real asshole, Gorias. Let's see here."

As Rothwell told the tribesmen to pull up stakes and spread out, Gorias knelt by the pieces. "You see what I have in mind here?"

Garretson nodded. "Yeah, but I'll need a lot of time to cook these parts to make them proper, I think. I'll have some of the women design you a liner under it, but it's a helluva idea."

Rothwell guffawed. "Lots of balls or no fucking brains, that's Gorias La Gaul." He stopped smiling and looked down at Garretson with the skinned skull of the baby dragon in his hands. The smithy stood straight, then waited for Gorias to arise and raised the skull over his head. Slowly, he pushed the skull over Gorias' mane of hair.

"Nice helmet. No face plate, though."

Gorias kicked the other wyrmling head on the mat. "Can ya fashion a face cover out of the other skull?"

Garretson nodded. "Sure, and I can pull a rabbit out of my asscrack, given enough time and a rabbit. However, I think you have bigger concerns."

The squeals of the dragon grew closer and Gorias sighed. "You better get back, too. One of you fuckers leave me a horse, all right?" Gorias sat on the ground and took off his boots. He then slid the sections of the wyrmling's legs up to his thighs. The section from his knees to his hips came out perfect, same as the lower portion on his shins. These pieces even bore a pointy edge that acted as a natural covering for his exposed knee. It was then he discovered he couldn't pull his boots on.

Garretson remarked, "That'll be something to solve if ya live through this. I wouldn't fret a stubbed toe right now."

"Are you still here, Davin?" Gorias asked as he saw even Rothwell had departed, but indeed left a mount tied up not far off. Davin lingered near, but looked ready to flee.

Gorias stood and put on sections of the wyrmling's skin to plate his behind and then a crude codpiece over his groin.

Garretson said, "The way that midsection fits, you'd think ol' Wodan designed it for you."

His chest, stomach and back covered by the dragon skin, Gorias reached for the other pieces, ones that covered his biceps and then the armlets, each sporting dew nails. "I think the gloves might take some better design off of the claws."

Garretson coughed. "I'll get right on it once they burn yer ass and send your spirit to Valhalla."

Skull still on like a helmet, Gorias faced Garretson. "How's it look?"

"Pretty fucked up scary for a man about to be food."

Gorias faced the screaming noise over the village being destroyed. "I hope I gag that blue bitch."

Garretson handed him a spear and a sword. "That may work, climb out of her ass and all that."

The blue dragon spun about at the edge of the village, looking their way at last. It floated, pausing, staring their way.

"Get back, Garretson. She's mine."

The big man receded. "Fuckin' right she is…."

*****

Gorias ran for the lone mount, left tethered to a dying tree. He gripped the horse's brown mane and swung his leg over its back, feeling scant sorrow for the animal under him. After he kicked the horse with his naked heels, and yanked on the bridle, the animal lurched forward.

Off by the ruined village of Blackstone the blue dragon turned, head no longer scanning for victims, and saw him riding. The creature had expended a great deal of anger on the village, destroying almost every home and laying many a crude stone temple level. Blood spattered her mouth and she flittered her claws to get the flesh clear. When her great head aimed and focused on Gorias, she turned her body about, wings fast beating, flare position, spread out across the horizon, almost looking near enough to touch.

Gorias didn't cuss nor did he pray; he just rode hard forward, looking wild mad with his hair flapping under the bloody skull of the wyrmling. Oddly enough, the dragon skin, that felt so damned heavy to him at first, didn't feel really bad when charging into battle.

The dragon bellowed quick, screaming and then drawing its neck back, cocked like a cobra. She then started toward him, snakelike eyes blazing, arms ready to grapple so much the claws were flexing fast, fluttering like the wings on her back.

When they drew close to meeting, Gorias' feet clenched the sides of the horse and he leapt, rolling on his shoulders. The dragon noted the move and tried to adjust, but overshot his body. Still, her legs grabbed the galloping horse. Trying to pause in mid air, the dragon twisted, stabbed at the earth with her tail to anchor itself, and screeched loud. Gorias got to his feet. Standing behind her for a moment, he saw the exact nature of the wings in relation to her arms. They were attached like webs, but it didn't appear as such from the ground. She had more than two wings that she used to fly, he noted, truly a thing of beauty and terror. His assessment took but a moment for he leapt on the dragon's lower leg claw that ripped into the belly of the horse. Legs about the dragon's ankle, Gorias' arms embraced the leg like he hugged a lover, but this action was to better perform his next. Gorias sliced with both forearms, wyrmling dew nails rending open the dragon's skin on the shin. The skin peeled back like the cut belly of a freshly-caught fish and the scales popped off like tree leaves in the fall of a branch struck hard.

The dragon trumpeted like the mastodons the Thulites rode and kicked with her legs. Lucky, the claw Gorias rode had a horse in it or he'd have been brained. The shot knocked him off the creature and to his ass. As the dragon flew up a few yards, horse intestines covered him when she shook violently, but he lived.

Up and swiping off the guts, Gorias bolted toward the pit his brothers had dug to trap the dragon.

The dragon arose, wounded leg kicking more than the other, anger apparent in the deep growl of her throat.

Gorias reached the pit, but didn't dive inside the trap. It'd have been a jest of the gods had he leapt in and been impaled on the broken lances intended for the dragon. However, he stopped, went to his ass and hopped down at the edge. He pondered if the dragon skin on his flesh would save him from the brutal lances, and wagered it very well might. He started weaving through the unnatural thicket of the spear trap when the dragon arrived.

He crouched in the center of the pit, wanting the beast to stick its neck down. Unfortunately, she slammed the bridge of her head into him, sprawling Gorias to his back. Eyes of the dragon, red and striped, smoldered with anger as the jaws opened. Indeed, he'd fit nicely into that wicked mouth, rimmed with teeth a foot long each and hemmed in by a second set of canines ready to get at him. Before fear could take hold, his warrior's instinct kicked in and he pushed off with his legs, catching the dragon by the lips and stopping the bite for but a moment. In that pure instant, the long teeth grazed his legs, but didn't break his skin or armor.

Content she had with him with her lips, the dragon shot her tongue out, a forked serpentine thing, and enwrapped the Thulite fast. The only reason the dragon hadn't broken Gorias' legs was that she'd chosen not to, probably planning to suck him into her gullet with the tongue.

Gorias' arms, pinned to his sides under the wrap of the tongue, yanked up. The dew nails of the wyrmling sliced through the tongue. When the pain seized the dragon, she drew back and lifted her head. The dragon didn't withdraw from the pit, but she seemed in shock at the hurting caused by the human. Gorias got off his back and leapt at the thing's neck, holding on with his legs. Quickly, he performed the double swipe with the dew nails again, crossing his forearms on her flesh, this time laying open the scales and underskin of the dragon at the middle of her long neck.

The beast lifted up, wings beating, and Gorias became airborne with the monster. Fifty yards in the air, he pulled the sword from his belt and jammed it into the gap created by the dew nails. He sank his entire arm into the beast until the blade ran into something rocky, bone he prayed. Gorias twisted the sword as they went further aloft, and his hands lost the pommel as the blade sucked into the beast. The sword disappeared up into the long neck of the dragon and his hand closed, seizing a fistful of slick goop inside the creature.

Looking down, Gorias fixed his legs and other arm on the dragon more, even digging in with the other dew nail for more security, but understood he was screwed if he fell. Amazed at the sight from above, one reserved for ravens, and father Wodan, Gorias took a few breaths trying to not be overwhelmed by it all. Still, his guts turned and his ears popped, a sign of weakness he imagined.

The right arm of the dragon reached out and grabbed Gorias' body by the midsection. The dragon ripped him from her neck with great force. Gorias' arm, lodged in flesh, came out but the hard way, the dew nail on his forearm splitting the dragon's skin open a yard wide as his body came away.

The dragon screamed louder as the injury occurred, an agony brought on mostly by her own power.

The claw released, trying to send him to the ground, but with no force as its flight wavered. Gorias floundered for a moment, touching nothing, but instantly gripped the dragon. The dew nails accidentally clung in the edge of her right wing, the small webbing under the arm, not the chief wing on the right side that kept them aloft. When his weight went down, he flopped about and the dew nail tore the wing open, peeling the skin down. The dragon's erratic flying jerked and they lowered several yards. Gorias rolled onto the creature's back, sliding between the wings, heading for a sled ride down its spine to the tail and thin open air. He slammed the nails into her back for a hold. The dragon started to wavere more, and fell further. On either side of him the great wings beat rapidly, and he felt he'd be chopped up if thrown into that frenzy. She shrugged, trying to get him off, but instead the beast lurched and dived, crashing into the dirt. Gorias bounced off its back, ripping more scales loose and flew off, over into the area not long ago occupied by the blacksmith's forge.

The world rotated around his vision a few times before staying solid again. Terror burned in him and he couldn't immediately rise. At last, Gorias turned over and was stunned to see hundreds of his brothers nearby, all brandishing weapons and crouching low. Like one mass creature, the warriors of Thule rose up from the long grasses about the whorehouses of Leonore. He then noted the mastodons behind his people, four of them, also drawing closer, ridden by great hairy men almost looking like lumps on their hirsute backs. He got to his feet and ran over to the dragon. She choked, purple blood gushing from the wound in her throat. More blood came from places where Gorias had broken the scales. He jumped on the back of the dragon as it flailed, ripping again with the dew nails.

"What are you fuckers waiting for?" Gorias yelled at his brothers. "Go for an open wound!"

The mass of Thulites ran, men, women and children, fearless, to the dragon, stabbing axes and swords into the wounds created by Gorias' dew nails. Not many of the shots landed true. In fact, more weapons got ruined on the dragon than found a home, but a few spears were driven deep into the bloody areas provided. When the dragon moved and knocked a few warriors off her back, the creature looked to have sprouted many long spines minted in a land far away.

Gorias kept riding the dragon, ripping open new spots in the scales then moving on to break the wings, leaving a place for the Thulites to insert a hunk of metal and twist. He shredded the fabric of each wing, making certain she'd not soon rise.

The tail of the beast threw Gorias off, cracking him up side his head, but he got to his all fours fast, seeing a few of the kids loop ropes about the legs of the monster. All four limbs got a solid rope and when Gorias' eyes followed the heavy woven lines, he grinned. Each rope became tethered to a mastodon's harness and the teamsters quickly drove them on, in four different directions.

Air sucking in fast, Gorias got out of the way as the ropes became tight and started to haul the dragon away, then stop, and then jerk the body a different direction. Once the tension became high, the line to her left arm broke, but the ones to the legs stayed true and the great elephants moved on, ripping the dragon apart at the crotch. A ruined groin split further up the stomach, and a belly full of wound up guts spilled onto the sand. The screeching stopped once the dragon had been split like a crab.

Gorias staggered about and fell to his knees. He sucked in air as the children grabbed handfuls of the dragon's innards and ran. As the long lines of guts started to crisscross the former encampment by the whorehouses of Leonore, Rothwell slapped Gorias on his armored shoulder.

"So that's how one kills a dragon."

Gorias gagged and went to his hands and knees again. He didn't puke but it took effort to suppress. "Yeah, Simple. Huh?"

The kids sang and were not admonished to stop in their merriment.

The mastodons yawned and fed on long ferns by the edge of the savannah.

The men of Thule started to chant the name of Gorias La Gaul. Soon, the women and children joined in with them.

Gorias stared at the dead dragon and felt the bones of his daughter on his chest. They felt warm.

CHAPTER SEVEN
Father

The tribesmen of Gorias moved their encampment north for several days, not in a hurry to return to their homeland, and not giving an answer for Gorias' boon of vengeance. One village near the Bospurus land bridge they absorbed, used and burnt to the ground. The name wasn't known then nor will it ever be.

When they crossed that sector of land they came near to the edges of a series of mountains. At the base of these Ivor, the Oracle of Wodan, indicated one of his homes lay in the clefts.

Many a warrior oft stopped to look at the sheer cliffs on the edge of the mountain that dipped into the water of the small sea, by the edge of the bridge. Ivor listened to them speculate about the gods creating such a marvel and he scoffed.

Ivor shouted them down, saying, "Not everything is the work of the gods, foolish boys. Just because a land mass is deep doesn't always mean an angel crashed there. A pointed set of hills doesn't mean a goddess with a nice rack sleeps there under the earth. Sometimes, the earth is shifting beneath our feet and climbs atop each other and well, there you go. Someday, the earth will shrug and this land will all be a sea from the edge of the ocean to the border of Jericho."

One of the youths observed the snow high atop the mountains, and a few lodges up there, one belching smoke.

Gorias stared up there as well, and said, "The puffs are regular, like from the bellows of a smithy shop."

The boys all grabbed each other by the arms, again their superstitions running wild, but they spared their tongues.

Ivor filled in their thoughts, this time his manner grim. "Yes, children, I know what it is a sign of." He then leered at Gorias. "It looks as if the gods are smiling on you, or choosing to shit light on you, boy."

"What?" Gorias frowned, his mind and heart full of jagged edges.

"That gamy-assed parcel of dragon meat that killed the villagers when they tried to eat it? The one you keep packed on your mount? Why is that?"

Gorias bristled, hands in fists. "That's my own affair."

Ivor stepped closer and looked in the face of the taller youth keenly. "You plan to seek out the All Father when you return home, or a goodly blacksmith as the tradition goes, aye? You want to offer them the meat in exchange for an audience with the all father, to find a way to cure your aching heart." The last words were tinged in laughter. "It looks like the All Father has come unto you, so quit acting like a cunt and get up that mountain."

The youths muttered about the dragon meat being poison and a bad omen to ply a smith with it…a smith possibly the real all father hiding in his stead. Ivor cursed them again.

"You think the all father can be poisoned? Suck your own candles, dolts, and gather dinner." He glared at Gorias. "The boy here has a long climb ahead of him to reach the snows. It will take a few days."

Born of Swords

This scene played out in his head over and over in the next few days. After a two-day climb, Gorias thought the camp might be gone if he ever returned and all the words a fun ruse by Ivor to be rid of him. However, at night he could see the lights of the camps down the way.

With no horse, he lugged the packets of meat up by himself. Though heavy, he understood his burden part of the endurance. He thought this had to be foolish, but part of his broken heart clung to faith, clung to the possibility it could be true. On the third day he awoke before daybreak, just beyond the snow line. He stared down at the distant dying embers of the camp, or at least he convinced himself that is what he was seeing reflected off the sea. It was then he heard another voice.

"Are you going to school, my son?"

From the deep, raspy voice, he thought it his father, but no, whoever spoke to him wasn't his dad. However, the burly, tall, bearded gray man wasn't too far off.

"I haven't been to classes in years," Gorias admitted. "But when I was at Nineveh a few years ago, I took courses when I was on the fighter circuit."

The burly man coughed and stretched, his heavy buckskin overcloak expanded as he stretched.

Gorias stood, legs over the packet of dragon meat. "You are going to call me a foolish kid?"

A yawn later, the man replied, "When and if you get much older, you will understand that brevity of words is best." He coughed, spat, turned, motioned for Gorias to follow and added, "And that words are oft wasted on the young."

Gorias picked up his pack and followed into the shallow snows. "How would you instruct better than words? With a rod?"

Several paces latter, the man replied, "Suffering is good for the soul and mind. You'd be shocked at how much one can learn from suffering."

Gorias mumbled, "I'm a genius then?"

Again, a deep cough rattled the big man in front of him just as several huge wild dogs passed in front of them. Gorias stopped but the man trudged on, so he again followed him.

"A lost love, a lost brother, a lost fight, a small member--one of these on your mind? All of them disappoint how a father sees his son, but you can deal with each shortcoming the same way and move on in life."

"Yeah?" Gorias wondered, the boots he wore sinking deeper as they trudged to the long log house and brick shop, so out of place in the mountains.

"Sure." His big hands spread out to his sides as if he embraced the cabin. "Fighting and death, it solves everything."

"Even a little prick?"

The man nodded, arms down and turned to face Gorias. The old man wasn't shivering. "Chop off your opponent's arms, make him watch as you kill the maiden who laughed at a little cock, and yes, you'll feel more like a man. You might not really be one how women measure one, but the way you are measured in eternity is better."

Winded, shaking from the cold, Gorias put his head down a little. "So murder is the answer?"

"Murder," the man spat again. "That is a word cowards use, probably more with little pricks, but I digress. Death is just another part of the life-force. Flesh and bones are just a cage." The man held up his hands, and it was then that Gorias noted that in the gray hair wafting over his bearded face, he couldn't see the man's eyes. Still, Gorias figured he looked at his fingers. "A spirit, that is forever. That little bit of you goes on for all time, a gift from God."

"Not gods or goddesses?"

Hands down, the man frowned. He faced Gorias. "All right, you are sounding like a dumbass, son."

Shuddering from the cold, feeling silly, Gorias rasped, "You aren't my father." When he looked up, he saw the gray man only a yard from him, oddly closer than a moment before.

"On the contrary," the gray man said, his hands shooting out to grab Gorias by the shoulders in a vice-like grip...his right eye flaring at him...the only eye he had.

With no effort in a moment, Gorias flew through the air, struck a deep snow bank and found himself buried. However, the cover wasn't enough to stop him from hearing the words of the gray man.

"I'm everyone's father."

Gorias blinked and darkness enveloped him.

*****

Gorias floated in the darkness, but not for long. Soon, waves of violet swirled about him and it was like the stars fell from the sky to encircle him.

As suddenly as he slept, he felt his world crash back in. Instead of a snow bank, he saw a battlefield. He watched from above, and wasn't a player on the field. He thought the view amazing, like that of a bird, or truly one shared by the gods.

In his mind he wondered what he saw, and the voice of the gray man echoed in his skull, telling him, "The future."

Gorias heard a voice, a yarn spinner, telling him a tale....

*****

On a white horse that galloped across the grassy plains, the tall figure held the reins with blue fists. No, the gauntlets with an aqua hue held the reins fast. The color became clear in the vision all over the body of the rider…for the figure rode the draft horse clad in armor. Dragon skin armor.

It took a great steed to carry such a huge warrior, for the figure could be nothing else. No priest or scholar would wear such ghastly armor or could've attained it. The long cloak that billowed from off the back of the rider betrayed twin swords secured there. Though a helm obscured the face, there could be no doubt the ferocity of the rider.

About the helm, though, spilled long hair. Red hair. When other riders charged the figure, bearing spears but not similar armor as this figure wore, the swords came out. A spearhead blunted on the dragon-skin chest plate. The deathblow meant for the rider's heart went off to the left and the right sword of the rider stabbed home true, removing the right arm of the attacker as he passed.

The great white mount swung about as another spearman jabbed. This attacker swore, momentarily glancing at his screaming partner as he rode off, bleeding and maimed. That moment was all the rider needed to clamp down the spear under the left arm… and stab forward with the right sword. The sword tip just made it to the second rider's mouth. The blade inserted like a long bit of candy, smooth and sleek. The second attacker had a moment to contemplate he held that blade on his tongue before the weapon went in deeper and slashed out, ripping him loose from tonsils to his ear.

As wet, throaty howls emerged, the figure returned the swords to their housings, turned and rode on, hardly steering the white mount save for the big thighs, not desperate to take up the reins. Onward the figure rode, till a huge man emerged from over the crest of the hill. His hair ran dark and the sunlight refused to shine off it. A swaggering man, walking with arrogant power, looked to see the rider, and raised an eyebrow. In the sunlight, the mark on his forehead became clear. An "X" marked him.

A deep voice echoed across the valley from this man, saying, "So, you've come for me at last, La Gaul?"

The horse stopped and the figure reached up and remove the helmet. A mound of red locks flowed out and the rider cleared them to get a better look.

La Gaul answered, "Yes, Nosmada, first son of Adam, I have come for you at last." The voice wasn't that of Gorias, not even one aged centuries old. It was female, throaty and deep, but not Gorias.

Nosmada gave a deep chuckle. "Can't you hear the thunder? You know the deluge comes. I'll be drowned with everyone else if the tales from the Creator are true."

"No, I'm going to kill you first," the big, red-haired woman promised. "My father would've wanted it that way."

"You are not content to have me drown? You want to slay me with your daddy's swords?"

"Looks that way."

"Why?"

"Well, 'cause it'll hurt more."

Nosmada's mirth transformed to anger and his eyebrows lowered. "You are a silly girl, no matter the stories about you."

"Then you will have no problems getting rid of me."

"You think that armor of your daddy will protect you against the power of the son of Adam?"

The woman grinned. "No, not entirely. But I have a

confidence, don't ya know?" She put the helm back on but left the visor up. Her fist pounded her chest. "It's something in the blood. You should know that."

"You will scream my name before the day is done, ginger bitch!"

"I wouldn't dignify the name of Cain other than to laugh," La Gaul promised. "But I'll carve my name in your heart and on your soul."

She drew out the twin swords again and slashed them across herself. With her thighs, she directed the horse under her legs.

"Go Traveler," she whispered and the horse leapt forward.

Nosmada, Cain, the fallen son to Adam, reached for his sword and gritted his teeth, but not before he swore, "A curse be on you...Roan..."

"Deliverance has come!" Roan announced, heading right for him.

"Foolish girl," Nosmanda/Cain shouted. "Your daddy said Deliverance shall come."

Nearly on him, not caring if he heard her, Roan replied, "I know what I said."

*****

"What is that supposed to mean?" Gorias shouted, and sat up, but he wasn't in the snow bank, nor even on the strange mountain by the land bridge.

Gorias stared across different mountains, ones with sharper points and no tree line visible. His heavy fur overcloak moved with the strong wind. From behind him, he heard a voice, one he hadn't heard in some time.

"You return to the snows, seeking what?"

The voice rang old, cracking, and seemed to come from a

different time. He never turned to face the speaker. His mind blurred, almost frigid at times before returning to lucidity.

Gorias responded roughly, "I'm not yet thirty winters old, yet I find myself reflecting on life. It's a sign of weakness."

"No, it's a sign of being alive, Gorias. It's not a failing to think on matters, but it is real madness to reflect on them too long. If your mind becomes too clouded, it falls into your stomach and churns. Eventually, we know what comes from the stomach, so get that shit out of your mind and remember what you are."

"I know what I am," Gorias snapped, turning at last to face the older man. This action felt more like rolling in a snow bank than whipping about. "And you're dead. Am I mad to be talking to you, *father?*"

"And yet, you returned to the face of your real father when overcome by loss. How childish, how simple, and yet, how very human of you."

Gorias frowned at the burly man with white, flowing hair. He wished he couldn't see through the image of the old chieftain. Once again, he felt heavy, cold and tight. "You talk much for a dead man. I wish I were drunk; I'd write this off."

Ambiorix raised a gray eyebrow and pulled his heavy furs closer about himself. "I once had less time for whoring and more for the hearth. Careful it never happens to you."

"I'll try. Now you have time for haunting?"

"You trod in your dreams invoked by God himself and don't expect to see me? Don't be an asshead, son. What would you have done if you heard my voice longer ago? If I told you not to return to Kemet when Akhensobek asked for your services? Would you have listened? Of course not."

"I know." Gorias paused, eyeing for a moment a log

smokehouse jutting from the mountainside. Lost for a second in the smoke billowing from the stone chute, he shook his head fast. He searched for words and found them, saying, "At my birth, you left our home, and traveled far to save me. You slew the Nephilum at Larak so I could do no less for my own blood. I never thought it would be all of this." His hand touched his heart, the necklace of bones nearby, and it quickly dropped.

Ambiorix's glowing form said, "You decided to see the world beyond Thule long ago. Well, you saw it. This is what happens to you in the world. These folk of Kemet are not ours, not from our portion of the Earth and not of our land. I care little that you chose to breed with one of them, save for the fact that they valued you less than an animal if they sacrificed your daughter. See now what they thought of you and of us."

"Yes," Gorias nodded and turned to face the snowy slopes again. His ears popped and suddenly, his breathing turned shallow. He soldiered on in his head, not moving, though.

Ambiorix went on to say, "It's a hard lesson, one that cuts deeper than a rod or a whip. But as with any lesson, the wound in the heart heals, given the proper balm. Only blood can heal blood lost, son."

He turned back to the face of his father and responded, "I didn't come to you asking questions."

"Yet you desired answers. I know. However, you know the answer to the problem. It's in your blood, and in your mind or you'd not be hearing it now. You know the way of our kin and how it must be."

"But what I am feeling goes beyond customary payback," Gorias hissed, his voice dropping in tenor. The heat in his heart thawed his aching limbs.

Unfazed by these words, Ambiorix folded his arms under the furs and reflected for a few moments. "Perhaps that's a good thing. Every so often, the world needs to see what happens to bad people."

"Father, where do bad people go when they die?"

Ambiorix smirked, his leathery, weathered face cracking in folds as he did so. "The answer has not changed since you asked me that in your youth."

"Good," Gorias said, fingers and hands flexing, his ears sounding as if wind swirled down their canals. "I just wanted to make sure nothing was different. Will Donar, son of Wodan, accept me at his table in the land of eternal youth if I should fall?"

Ambiorix sighed, bored with the conversation. "You ask me so I can reassure you further. Drop the teat, son, and do what you must. I will go to Donar's table today. If I don't see you there soon, it'll be a goddamned wonder. But if you keep asking these questions, I'd think a serving girl's bodice would be ill-fitted to your frame in that hall. You were a male the moment I cut you from your mother's belly, Gorias. You became a man years later. Don't make me regret my actions against that bitch in Larak now."

No more words were spoken. Ambiorix disappeared and Gorias felt several sets of hand on his back. The illusion broke and his tribesmen lifted him from the snow bank. Frost caking the left side of his face, causing his beard to feel like stone, Gorias gaped at the others, and then down at his nude body.

The men chuckled as they dragged him back toward the smokehouse. One said, "Did you see the all father?"

Gorias didn't answer.

Another added, "It beats crucifixion or another of Ivor's

cures for spiritual oneness. Piss on all that. A good steam house bath and a toss into the snows will bring most things in life back tight." The men all laughed as they carried Gorias' trembling form back into the log house. "It will probably be a while before ya see yer nuts again, friend."

"I saw an adventure, one beyond our time. It was mad, the story I saw."

"You did see the all father!"

"I didn't understand his meaning at the time, but now, perhaps, I get it."

His eyes on the faces of his tribesmen, he looked across the glade and unto the valley full of the Ingaevones. So many stood there he could never hope to lay a number to them. The old shaman, Ivor, read the guts of a man from Shynar, by the looks of his tan skin.

No more words were needed.

CHAPTER EIGHT
Three to Fall

Gizane liked to fly. Of course, she couldn't sprout wings nor could the power of her demon grant her levitation, but in trances invoked with the power of meditation, it proved exciting.

Demon, she giggled to herself as she soared through the clouds above the Earth. Many thought the creature one of the gods, captured by her power. Gizane understood the truth that he was a monster barely kept in check by enchantments and made to serve her. For a being that oozed such power, few saw the beast it was, the very essence of evil that hated the eternal god-force so much it decided a putrid existence of freedom rivaled servitude beyond the sky. And it was evil. Gizane shuddered at its true abilities and appearance.

But this day, flying came to make her happy. When all the egos of the King's world proved tiresome, it made her full of glee to push off the world and take wing.

Even if she didn't leave her bath and flew under his eyelids, detached from her mind, all of her tingled at the flight. She soared above Kemet, into the clouds and away from the Earth itself. All her life she loved to fly above the ground, near to the abode of the gods. They weren't really evil demons, she couldn't accept that, and their adoration of infant sacrifice for these gifts of power was a small thing in the scope of the universe, she reasoned. Since a babe herself, when her mentor priestess marked her as special and decided to let her live, Gizane felt blessed and flew. She even created a glass representative of the gods and goddesses, all lined up in the stars, watching her fly. That model, over by her collection of captured souls, was the only thing kept from her youth.

Although out of her body, Gizane felt herself smile. Those people down there, especially the men, what gnats in the plan of the gods. Men, she laughed, how insular and petty, from the court of the King to the fields of the labor hands, they were no different. They fancied themselves so big, powerful and dominant…because of that flesh that dangled between their legs? What a joke. A few moments of pleasure and they were finished, done and sleepy.

So few men had the minds to dream. Oh, the King? He possessed an uncommon brain, one that let him see a longer view of his life, but he was still a bastard under it all, a little boy wanting more toys. He fancied himself on par with the gods. Gizane had seen gods. The King wasn't a god.

Flying over the vast jungles far to the south of Kemet, Gizane pondered the creature she kept hostage again. The demon she kept, while not a god, was more impressive to talk to than the King. The virgin serving girl and the three infants? Worth every drop of blood to trap him. True, he bided his time and would be free of her once she died, but she didn't worry about fencing with an immortal.

The demon hated her, and while it amused Gizane, that bothered her sometimes. No matter how much the demon was her slave, it held out the eternal hope of freedom, of revenge.

Born of Swords

The idea that she instilled hope in a demon amused her greatly.

Gizane arose from her bath, but didn't remove the plugs that allowed the water to drain. Her body glistening, she lay her hands on the edges of the stone tub and let her breath glide over the froth. She smiled, blew the waters a kiss, and felt the hairs rise on her body. In her mind, the chants rang out and the waters tainted by her bodily fluids started to structure images. Her confident expression churned to one of confusion as the profile of the dead savage Gorias took shape in the bubbles.

She shook her head and turned her face to the howls outside. Her look of puzzlement flowed to one of disgust over what Uylikla may be doing in his jackal form. When she gazed into the tub again, Gorias' face wasn't alone. So many faces akin to his filled the waters that soon, the image washed away in the water.

Composed and letting her indignation die down, Gizane dried her body with a long cloth. Her serving girl had gone and that made her anger rise again. She left the long wrap draped over her shoulders when she walked to the place of enchantments. Her eyes widened for the double folding doors stood ajar. A red glow with a golden corona flowed from her inner sanctum. With no fear, Gizane slammed into the shutters, hands to her hips.

The sight of her demon on the star didn't give her pause. After all, he was her prisoner, oft popping in and out of the star symbol. The shelves full of soul jars pulsing golden beams made her jaw tighten, but she never lost her composure.

Gizane pulled the towel from her chest. Her nails down between her small breasts, she rubbed both index fingers on a small spot between them. In a few moments' time, a tiny nipple protruded there, hardening and pulsing. She bent near the demon and offered the middle breast to the creature.

Balanced back on his goat-like haunches sporting hooves larger than a bull's, the scarlet-hued being extended its fin-covered spine out so that his jaw nearly touched the edge of the prison. Mouth open, fangs dripping yellow fluid, the demon let its long tongue roll out. Though the usual tickle at her teat commenced, a sharp pain knifed into her breast. Gizane glared down, seeing the blood bubble over the tip of the demon's tongue…but the end of the appendage wasn't forked like any other day. The two ends curled into an oval and a face emerged. Gizane found she couldn't move as the small face grew a little larger and opened its eyes.

"Feel the terror of those you've wronged," the voice from the face growled at her. "I tell you my name, Ivor, for I want you to carry that name into eternity as the one who set you to dust. Your demon is gone for his power is scant compared to that of my deity."

Terror gripping her, she tried to move, but found this impossible.

"I'm the throat of that god, a power who cares little of humanity, but allows me to be his gullet and Oracle in matters that I deem worthy of his time."

Gizane tried to think of enchantments, spells, and to formulate curses, but her mind swam with dull waters, unable to outline anything solid.

"He shall come unto you, woman. Be of good cheer, for all that will soon be over for you, in this world." The face of Ivor faded back into the persona of the demon. However, the demon itself started to melt away, but not into nothingness. The hooves dissolved and reformed into long feet. Wings and fins melded into a set of broad shoulders. In the place of the demon soon towering a giant of a man sporting flowing gray hair. He wore no clothing over his sturdy body, for really, why would a god get dressed?

"No…" she gasped, trying to run, but still frozen in place.

"Listen," the voice of Ivor rebounded in the chamber just as the tops of the soul jars all blew away. "Can you hear them? The footsteps of assassins…the beat of so many hearts…the coming of the gray man's children…."

The gray man raised his head, mane of hair draped over his bearded face and only one of his eyes open. The blazing single eye focused on Gizane and a voice liken unto thunder rolled in her chamber.

"You are the one who eats the souls of my children?" Like a belch under water, a deep echo thudded in the chest of the gray god as he laughed. The echoes of that voice rattled like metal scraping on stone. "You are no one, even a dog is better than you. But you have disturbed my matters and gleaned my attention at last. My children live their lives without my aide. They rise and fall on their own. But one who keeps them from my table in the afterlife…" his huge hand waved across Gizane and her frame took on a bluish halo, "that just pisses me off."

Her body lifted from the floor and Gizane floated closer to the one-eyed god.

His head cocked to the side a little, he said, "I see through the ravens flying above that my wolves have met your little jackal outside. Hmm. Torn to pieces by bitches." He grinned a mouth full of radiant white teeth. "As it should be."

Both arms extended, the huge hands of the god grabbed her shoulders. His smile faded to an expression of boredom as he ripped Gizane's left arm from the socket. She screamed, but no blood came out of the wounds. He held her aloft as he reached down and pulled her left leg off as easily as one would skin a rabbit. He then dropped a limb and removed her right leg before closing his hand about Gizane's throat. The right arm came free and the god sighed. A slanted chop let her torso bounce on the floor and land, tits up.

"Wodan…" she gasped, but fell silent when a thumb dominated her mouth, pressing her lips closed like a crude button.

"Now, little pet," the gray god said to Gizane's head, held in the palm of his hand, "what shall we talk about?"

*****

After a few days, the mystery of Gizane's disappearance continued to be written off as her off on an astral journey. However, Althea heard tell her father had sent many scouts out to search the complexes and surrounding territories for her. Althea smiled as she fed mice to her collection of asps in a long habitat covered by a heavy netting.

None of that really mattered. Althea didn't let matters such as a disappearing worker of magic concern her. In a filthy world, she loved to be clean. Her father had constructed a stone lagoon that engineers finished up, making a marvel of purification of the Nyle waters nearby. She oft swam in these warm waters, even though the danger of crocs ran minimal in such a domesticated area. True, she kept guards about her, many to tease, as they could look but not have her…yet Althea loved to live in their dreams. They'd touch themselves, unable to resist as she bathed, but not act on such matters. She oft wondered, albeit only for a moment, if they trashed their dirty wives or whores thinking of her perfect beauty.

She'd bathed in a tributary of the Nyle as a girl, but the

crocs the men thought hunted down soon came near. While only a slave girl perished, she'd not soon forget the blood in the water, and her screams. That reason alone, to stop her memories from returning, was enough for the high archer Skan to patrol the bathing area. Skan could cut a locust in half from twenty paces, and he'd slain many a croc, it was said, but Althea hadn't witnessed such a feat. She believed him very brave and virile, simply by his lean body, intense way, respectful attitude and the long member he oft stroked for her on command.

Skan wandered as she bathed, not staring her way, but focused beyond the short walls of the bathing complex. Though very late at night, he kept his vigil.

"What is it?" she asked, yawning, arising from the water, stretching.

Not looking at her still, Skan tilted his head. "Something is amiss in the night."

Arms dropping to her sides as she walked toward her drying towels, Althea asked, "What mischief do you see?"

"More of a sense," he said in a low voice. "I have a hunter's intuition, miss."

Drying her sleek legs, she pondered his words, and the idea that a hunter stalking prey might know the woods or a jungle better than a novice. His words usually ran on hunting or training, a man of such loves, she sighed. There was a good reason she trusted him and only watched him perform self pleasure, not taking him to her bed mat. Skan was a soldier, a great guard, a true hunter, but a slave, nonetheless. He did as he was told, but his passion was more for life, not her delight. That is why she reserved such matters for the Irado twins, Nubians from the south with members worthy of a Thulite.

At the thought of the twins, one who had a member near to as large as Gorias' one, she felt a twinge of sadness.

Skan asked, "Shall I go and see, miss, and leave you to your stargazing?"

Althea, still full of melancholy, followed the motion Skan made with his bow, pointing at the roof of the nearby abode, the place where she lay to observe the heavens. She nodded, sighed, not sad at the death of the barbarian Gorias, but lamenting the intense pleasure he gave her, and would no longer be able to give her. Yes, he reached a depth no man had, but wasn't a savage. Her legs quivered a little as she wiped off, recalling his gentle touch, how he used his mouth, and performed tender with her, far better than a rough servant told what to do.

Perhaps Gorias cared. She smiled. Well, he obviously fell in love with her. That greatly made her laugh. Most men who are that tender only want a woman to recall them better than others, what an ego! But Gorias was different. He dearly cared and wanted her to feel good. She giggled at his folly.

Skan departed and she walked to the steps, still naked, draping her towels on the ferns as she climbed the steps. Some memories of Gorias were fading, but his taste, scent, and member lingered in her mind. Once near the roof, Althea pulled a cord that would let the servants inside know she desired company later on. If she pulled the wrong cord, she'd be greeted with food, not the huge Irado twins.

While she awaited their arrival, Althea decided to relax and watch the heavens. It sounded a restless night in the city, not far from morning, really, but she ignored all that ruckus and revelry. None of it concerned her, only her life.

She lay atop the roof of the fine palace meant only for the

many children of the King and watched the stars. This practice ran so common, she oft waved at others across the land doing the same thing. In her fingers, she twirled the crystal that once rested in her necklace of bones. Many times, Althea held up the crystal and gazed at the stars through it.

The distant lights took on blurry likenesses but in the middle of her playful games with the cosmos, the crystal filled with a gray light. She blinked, thinking perhaps she spotted a shooting star. Althea squinted into the depths of the crystal. Her mouth fell open as she suddenly could see humanoid shapes, though there was nothing to fear. They were just many men sitting at a table that appeared impossibly long. All of them, bathed in gray light, seemed intent on their food and drinks. At the end of the amazing little scene, a single small form hopped off his chair. Puzzled, she tried to focus on the face, one that seemed oddly familiar.

When the child turned his head and faced her, she gasped and pulled the jewel from her eye. Althea rubbed her eye and looked back into the crystal.

The youth still faced her. This time, though, he extended both hands, pointed with each index finger and mouthed words.

She cried out and jumped up to her knees. The crystal fell onto the roof and Althea never touched it again as she slid toward the steps. Her legs shook so that she barely made it down the stone staircase.

"Impossible," she gasped.

Althea ran into the kitchen and scooped up water from a basin. Her face splashed wet, but her mind couldn't be cleared of a terrible image.

The foreign slave boy, Dog, Gorias' servant…pointing at

her...*with two arms*...and mouthing words over and over....

"He's coming for you."

She ran to her room, wondering where the slaves were, desperate to find a weapon. Tears streamed down her face, unable to comprehend the wrath of something unearthly. Many times, she tried to calm herself, saying that the savage was dead, and the vision came from weakness.

Althea opened the cabinet in her room and took out a curved blade. She held it up in the moonlight, but froze in place.

Dog's face grinned at her from the surface of the blade. This time, she could hear his voice.

"Dead or alive, he's coming for you, bitch. There's no escape."

Althea dropped the knife and thought of a way to prove the voice wrong.

*****

"She cheated me," boomed the voice throughout the bedchamber of Akhensobek. Though akin to a god, the voice was that of a man.

Immediately, the King of Kemet bolted forward in his bed, dagger in his hands. Never covering his nakedness, terror filled his mind. He knew the voice, but couldn't see the speaker in the shrouded room. Hoping for the veracity of a dreamtime delusion, his senses knew better.

"Savage?" Akhensobek muttered, as if he didn't believe his own words. He took several breaths, searching for a dream again before he spoke again. A greater dread struck his mind as he asked, "Gorias? Have you returned from the dead to haunt me?"

Not answering his question, but continuing to speak, Gorias stated, "Your daughter thwarted my plans for revenge. Again, she cheated me and eluded my grasp. Damned asps."

Suddenly, the samite curtains flew back, allowing the morning sun to spill into the perfumed sleeping chamber. At this sudden action, the King moved forward and stumbled. Falling to his chest and rolling over, Akhensobek raged, turning to face what impeded him.

At the foot of his bed lay the body of his daughter, Althea. Her slender frame not marred in any way, but her chest didn't rise or fall. Akhensobek crawled over to her, touched her throat and found it ice cold.

Still holding the knife, he faced the barbarian. "She's dead, you bastard! You killed her, one of my blood angels! How could you with the proper spells of Gizane in place?"

"Gizane is dead. I had to deploy a wizard of our realm, Ivor, the Oracle of Wodan. Yes, even us animals have our magic. He called upon the one true God and he bested Gizane and her jackal pet in the ether-realm, thus, no one saw our approach."

"You lie!"

"And yet, here lies your daughter, dead for fear of my arrival. Alas, she robbed me of proper revenge." Gorias' words seemed to seep in from all over the room, nearly to the level of a growl. "I see the bite of a snake on her throat. She knew that I was coming for her and all of her kin. Ivor couldn't blunt that sense of a woman or the vengeful spirit she helped separate from the world. She escaped me, but perhaps I'll have to see what I can do about that, in time. Althea will not run away from me forever."

Akhensobek took up a defensive stance. Veins popping

out of his neck and running in a tight network over his mostly shaven head, he raged, "You strike at me through my child? What sort of man are you?"

Gorias stepped into view, a silhouette on the morning light in the window. "You killed my daughter, Akhensobek. Killing you once will not be enough to extinguish the wrong you have done unto me and my folk."

Akhensobek snarled, "I fear you not, barbarian. You think I ever feared fighting a fool such as you? A powerful man can make others do his will, either by forces of the mind, magic, money or the lash. You speak so proudly of your blood and your kindred. I spit on your family and all of that blood you are so proud of. My children and their children will number in the thousands and be remembered forever."

Gorias stated calmly, "All of your children are dead. So are your grandchildren."

The King laughed. "I have over one hundred and fifty children, savage!"

With a steady voice, Gorias informed him, "You have no more children."

Suddenly, panic struck Akhensobek and he ran for the door. Though it was unlocked, he banished this development and scrambled down the hallway. He took a fast right, sliding on the marble floors with his bare feet; the King searched the nearby nursery of his year-old son.

It was empty.

After shouting out orders for servants that never appeared, Akhensobek sprinted down the halls, throwing open doorways, again, finding no one.

He ran out of space in the home and nearly out of breath. The King paused and bolted outside to the courtyard of obelisks. In this immaculate garden that led up to his palace relaxation deck, Akhensobek found his one hundred and fifty children.

On the pillars that lined his garden hung the bodies of his family. Save for the ropes around their necks or the garrote marks on the ones who lay on top of the hedgerows, they appeared to be sleeping. Boys and girls alike, young and older, there was no difference. They were all dead. One of his daughters, her belly once great with his child, had lost the King's grandchild. The babe hung from her mother, dangling dead like the rest of the bloodline of the King.

Akhensobek stumbled and fell to his knees, unable to take in what he saw. He screamed at the top of his lungs, and then fell silent, for his brain cluttered with the names and proper faces of every child he laid his eyes on. Over and over, he grabbed his head in horror, unable to accept that each one hung dead. A few he checked for a pulse, but gave up after the first dozen.

"Still," Gorias said loudly, revealing himself on the steps that led up to the observation patio, "a few hundred of your offspring doesn't amount to the life of one Ingaevoneos baby."

Hauling himself to his feet, Akhensobek's teeth clenched so tight he almost couldn't utter the words, "You son of a whore...."

"My mother would've gave me unto demons for sacrifice," Gorias related in a matter-of-fact voice. "It's a good thing I had a strong father who loved me. Ambiorix taught me something about love, Akhensobek. Love is worth killing for." Then, with a casual gait, Gorias turned and ascended the steps to the patio. "Many times."

The King ran a few steps, and then stopped, comprehending

that this is what the barbarian wanted. He called for guards, but there came no answer. Cursing, Akhensobek looked around the garden. He found a small sickle used for trimming bushes. He gripped this and the dagger before bounding up the steps after Gorias.

Akhensobek reached the top of the patio and looked at the rising sun. He heard little activity in the palace grounds around him, or the city for that matter. Nothing on the deck seemed out of order, for it was a sparsely-decorated place.

Across the deck at Akhensobek's extreme opposite stood Gorias, his back to the King. The Ingaevone faced the river Nyle and said, "Come see what blood sounds like as it races through the heart."

Akhensobek took a few careful steps and stopped. He tilted his head, swearing he heard thunder or the echoes of it. No, but was it the thunder of stampeding elephants? No…this sound came to him uniformly as if made by a giant.

Cautiously, the King crept up behind Gorias to where he could view the entire city and the upper lands of Kemet. Mouth agape, he gasped at the sight that greeted him.

Across the savannah outside the city walked countless men and women, clad in furs and rough mail armor. These hordes, fair of hair and skin, marched as one organism toward his kingdom.

"How many barbarians…?" Akhensobek murmured.

"All of them. Does it matter?" Gorias replied. "One hundred hearts, all beating together. One thousand hearts, one single beat, one right after another." He drew the sword off his back. He wore no armor, but stood, naked, unshielded. "The world may remember this damned land or that accursed cat god idol on the plains. They may even recall the name of this mighty river of crocodiles, but they will forget you, Akhensobek, and every one of your damned children."

Still stunned by the show of innumerable invaders in his land, Akhensobek said dryly, "They came this far for the life of one half-breed?"

"No," said Gorias and suddenly slashed with his sword, destroying the scythe implement in Akhensobek's grip. "That dead girl was for me to justify. They came for the life of one of their kindred. Mine."

"They will rob my land, rape my women!"

"More like rape the land as well, but yes. They'll kill them all. Death is final. All of your people will die." Hands tight on the pommel of his sword, Gorias said, "Mass killing works every time it's tried. Perhaps the Bantu will have their land back afterwards, it doesn't matter."

"You see this as good?" Akhensobek raged, spit flying. "You see this gathering massacre as justice?"

"No, I see the bloodletting as truth. As sure as if you roll over and get your prick in a scorpion's nest, if you murder an Ingaevone, you better make sure you kill all of them in his bloodline. That's truth, simple and clean."

The King looked at his dagger and then at Gorias' sword. "You will kill me in such a way?"

Gorias dropped the sword on the deck. The metallic echo barely sounded over the stomp of savage boots all around them.

Akhensobek wasted no time, rushing forward in his attack. Though nearly as tall as Gorias, and certainly well built for fighting, his dagger thrust fell short as the Ingaevone twisted. Gorias grabbed the King's wrist with great speed, but groaned as he recoiled from the power in Akhensobek's stab.

Grappling with him briefly, Gorias let all of his body weight fall back to the ground and drew his knees together. With little effort, he threw the King over his head and dropped him flat on his bare back.

Around fast on all fours, Gorias saw that Akhensobek swiftly recovered as well. Still holding the knife, the King made a desperate lunge. Gorias rolled over, avoiding the blow and was fast to a crouch. Springing, he swung both arms down. One fist connected with Akhensobek's head.

Knocked to the deck by this shot, the King shook his head and started to rise again. Gorias leapt on his back, straddling him. With a quick swipe, he grabbed the King's ponytail and looped it around Akhensobek's neck. Drawing back with all his strength, Gorias heard the King gag. He broke the hold for a moment, only to knock the blade out of Akhensobek's grip, and then Gorias pulled back again.

Akhensobek flailed, his long body nearly dislodging Gorias from his back. Still he rode him, sweat pouring from his digits. He lost some grip on the ponytail, so he struck the King's skull with a balled up first, once, twice, five times or more. Quickly, he grabbed Akhensobek in a headlock, determined to break his neck. Akhensobek proved strong and fought him hard every moment.

A roar rising deep in his throat, Gorias dropped his head to the side of the King's neck. Yanking the head to one side, Gorias bit into Akhensobek's throat, searching for a vein. Akhensobek screamed as Gorias drew blood and tissue away from his neck. Like a greased eel, the King slipped Gorias' grasp.

Up on two feet, Akhensobek teetered, but didn't fall. He held his neck, as if it would stop the life from flowing out of him. He faced out across his land and heard the barbarian horde yell for their god, Wodan. They attacked all over and carnage ensued.

Screams filled the air, Akhensobek turned and Gorias once again held his broadsword.

"To kill me, unarmed," Akhensobek gasped. "Is that the manly way of your blood?"

Gorias gave a mild shrug. "You killed my Dog. You killed my daughter. Is it the way of your folk to slay the defenseless?" Gorias drew back and Akhensobek turned his back on him. Gorias said, "It doesn't matter if you face me when you die, doesn't matter at all. It's all about the dying." He then made an overhand arc with the blade, connecting with Akhensobek's head. The skullcap bones fragmented in two, squirting brains on either shoulder of the King. "Die...." The heavy blade crafted by Garretson sank into the middle of the King's neck. Gorias turned the pommel and the King danced. The body fell, and then rustled as whatever was inside of him departed. Gorias looked down on him, spat, raised the blade again and said, "That's all that counts."

*****

As the cities of Kemet burned, Gorias placed a bloody canvas sack beside his horse. He reached into his saddlebag and took out the necklace of Althea, the one made of tiny bones.

Rothwell asked him, "What is that anyway, Gorias? I saw you wear it before, but not into battle here"

Gorias sighed and said, "Her name was Inge. It means *Hero's daughter.*" Swallowing hard, he then said, "Would that I have honored her this day."

"How did you keep them in the crazy journey you told

me about?"

"I held them in my mouth as I swam the Nyle. I then wore them."

Rothwell still nodded and asked Gorias, "Are you going to keep such a thing or cast it into a pyre?"

Gorias looked at the bones. "We shall wait until we are in the mountains of Thule. I wouldn't want to leave the skin of my ass, much less the bones of my baby girl here to be confused amongst their gods. There is so little of her left, I hope I honor the gods and they take her home."

EPILOGUE

Over seven hundred years later, in the chamber of Ivor, Oracle of Wodan, Gorias stared down at the curved stone basin. Jessica pulled the jewel from her head and leaned against the wall, exhausted. She blinked hard, trying to comprehend how the knowledge, the vision and all of it had been jammed into her head and hardly no time passed in the chamber. Perhaps, she wondered, the eyes of the Dragon weren't always fair in imparting their visions.

Althea, daughter of King Akhensobek, stared at Gorias with trembling eyes. Blinking repeatedly, Althea failed to produce tears from her resurrected form on the floor.

She croaked the words, "You cannot imagine the torment...in leaving the place of the damned...to know bliss but a moment...out here away from it all...once in the flames...."

Gorias nodded. "You're probably right." He then reached behind his back and drew out his twin swords. No anger marred Gorias' face as he said, "Same time next year, all right?"

With that, he swung the blades, angled, chopping her head off cleanly. The head rolled once, impeded by Althea's long hair. The newly reanimated body convulsed, spurted a small amount of blood and then collapsed.

Jessica gasped, mouth open, as the realization of it all sank into her mind.

Gorias eyed her but a moment, blew a little on his crossed blades up to his face as the wizard Ivor called for his servants. His ladies-in-waiting entered and started to clean up the contents of the basin. Among them was an older woman carrying a curved knife. With great skill, she gutted the corpse and started to extract bones. She placed these on a canvas blanket and diligently went about the work of scalping the head.

Jessica put her hand to her gaping mouth and ran out of the chamber.

Outside in the air, Gorias returned his swords to their scabbards and faced south.

In a few minutes Ivor joined him and said, "You need more food for your trip?"

"Some wine would be great."

Ivor nodded. "I'll send for some in a moment."

"Many thanks, Ivor, as always," Gorias replied and gave him a casual nod. "You will see her bones back to the monks?"

"Of course." Ivor stared at Jessica for a minute, the small girl over by her mount, face buried in the saddle, hands gripping the edges of it. He looked to Gorias, who wasn't watching anyone, just looking south.

At the door of the chamber, one of the women stared at Gorias. She talked in low tones to the other ladies, but Gorias heard one of them say, "How many more times will he visit us for this task?"

With great strength in his voice, Gorias retorted, "I'm

still alive, am I not?" He then said gently, "I have been visiting you for years, Ivor."

The wizard acknowledged this with a pat on the warrior's shoulder, saying, "I appreciate the practice and the spices you bring."

Gorias looked at the palm of his right hand and said, "I never saw my daughter, Ivor. I never held her nor did I feel her fingers grip my thumb." His massive hand turned into a fist and he said ruefully, "As long as I live, I cannot kill that bitch enough times to make up for that."

Lightly, Ivor asked, "Is it true what your name means? I was at a gaming house once and the topic came up."

Gorias turned his head, winked and then walked toward his horse.

Ivor sighed, knowing it wasn't that important if the moniker's meaning was true. He'd met and known the King of the Bastards, old wives' tales or no. He paused, eyes closed, looking through the eyes of the world…through the eyes of Traveler as Gorias spoke with Jessica.

"It's time to go."

Jessica's chest rose and fell fast. She was silent.

"I gotta get you home."

"How…could you do that?"

Gorias checked the cinches on Traveler as the ladies of Ivor brought him wineskins. He stated clearly, "How could I not?" He breathed in full, then coughed once. "We need to get going."

"Get away from me…." She looked at him, tears covering her cheeks. "All those people think you are so much, all so heroic, but…you…."

"Are a monster?" Gorias gazed over at her at last. "I kill

monsters, young lady. I am what I am. You'll not see home again without the aid of this monster, so ya better get over it fast."

She wiped her tears, both eyes with her right palm, swallowed hard and glared at him, then looked to the ground. "All of those people…all of those children…and what you do to that woman, that thing every year…."

He said, "Yer thinkin' too hard on it all. It is what it is."

"What they did to you wasn't right, but…why didn't you bring back your daughter if you could do that to her?"

"There wasn't much left of Inge for something like that, and this ain't real living, that resurrection…but it is the act of pulling them from Hell, that moment of hope that is the real kicker."

"Why didn't you do this to the King?"

"You ask too many questions. Have you ever had your heart broken?"

"No."

"Once you do, ponder that again."

"That's insane and monstrous, Gorias…"

"Are ya really that shocked, little sister?"

She shivered. "I need a bath." Jessica took a breath. "For a year."

"This entire fuckin' world needs a damned good one," Gorias said in a boisterous tone, waving his right arm out as if to paint the Earth. "And from the stories I hear, it's gonna get one."

"Oh, who can accept the ravings of a madman down in Shynar saying the world will flood? That's impossible. After all that you showed me, you are not afraid to face the real God if he indeed drowns this world?"

Gorias returned to Traveler. "After you've looked God in the face once, kinda lessens the sting to the whole eternity meeting thing, ya know?"

"And you are not afraid of what comes next after life?"

"Frankly, I'm not. Cowards are scared shitless. I'm Gorias La Gaul, and I have no fear of God or the Devil. But I would like a place to rest my head for a while. I do still have that bargain with the angels I didn't explain to you."

Jessica again wiped her eyes and face on her sleeve. "What?"

"How I got my swords, I never told ya that one?"

"No...."

"About me and the angels, the deal I struck with them?"

"No."

"Well, then, sister, saddle up. We have a long ride to Nineveh."

Jessica stood still for a few moments as Gorias mounted up. Soon, she did likewise, but couldn't look at him.

Ivor smelt her heavy conflict, her fears for herself, alone without the big warrior, but for her own weaknesses...what she was feeling for Gorias, and how it all became knotted up.

"Children," Ivor said as the pair started to ride off. "I'm so glad I didn't have any."

Overhead, ravens flew, shadowing Gorias and Jessica as they made their way toward the Bospurus land bridge and the direction of Nineveh. In the distance, wolves howled, but the barking of jackals was no more.

**THE END
Of
BORN OF SWORDS**

*But Gorias La Gaul will return
in*

USURPER

About the Author

STEVEN L. SHREWSBURY lives, works and writes in rural Central Illinois. Over 365 of his short stories have been published in print or digital media since the late 80s. His novels include WITHIN, PHILISTINE, OVERKILL, HELL BILLY, BLOOD & STEEL, THRALL, STRONGER THAN DEATH, HAWG, TORMENTOR and GODFORSAKEN.

He has collaborated with other writers, like Brian Keene with KING OF THE BASTARDS, Peter Welmerink in BEDLAM UNLEASHED, Nate Southard in BAD MAGICK, Maurice Broaddus in the forthcoming BLACK SON RISING and Eric S. Brown in an untitled project.

He continues to search for brightness in this world, no matter where it chooses to hide.

Check out the following pages
to see more from

 **SEVENTH STAR PRESS**

All Seventh Star Press titles available in
print and an array of specially priced eBook
formats.

Visit www.seventhstarpress.com for further
information

Connect with Seventh Star Press at
www.seventhstarpress.com
seventhstarpress.blogspot.com
www.facebook.com/seventhstarpress
www.twitter.com/7thstarpress

Transcend Reality!

Want Sword and Sorcery?
Pick up the anthologies *Thunder on the Battlefield:
Sword*, and *Thunder on the Battlefield: Sorcery,*
from editor James R. Tuck!
(author of the Deacon Chalk novels)
Available in print and eBook!

Thunder on the Battlefield: Sword
Softcover: 978-1-937929-24-4
eBook: 978-1-937929-25-1

Thunder on the Battlefield: Sorcery
Softcover: 978-1-937929-26-8
eBook: 978-1-937929-27-5

Gorias La Gaul adventures from Steven Shrewsbury!
Enter an ancient world of heroes, blood, and steel in the
tales of Gorias La Gaul! Hard-hitting Sword & Sorcery in
the vein of Robert E. Howard!.

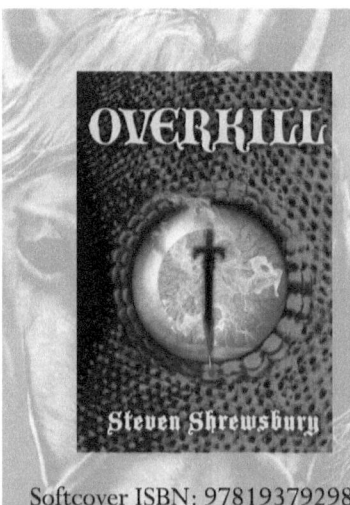

Softcover ISBN: 9781937929800   Softcover ISBN: 9780983108634

eBook ISBN: 9781937929831   eBook ISBN: 9780983108641

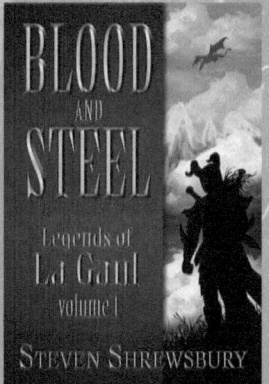

Softcover: 978-1-937929-28-2

eBook: 978-1-937929-29-9

Now Available from Seventh Star Press,
the horror stylings of
Michael West!

Trade Paperback ISBN: 9780983740209
eBook ISBN: 9780983740216

Trade Paperback ISBN: 9781937929718
eBook ISBN: 9781937929725

Trade Paperback ISBN: 9781937929954
eBook ISBN:9781937929831

Trade Paperback ISBN: 978-1-937929-18-3
eBook ISBN: 978-1-937929-19-0

Shadows Over Somerset from Bob Freeman!

Softcover: 978-1-941706-11-4
eBook: 978-1-941706-12-1

Michael Somers is brought to Cairnwood, an isolated manor in rural Indiana, to sit at the deathbed of a grandfather he never knew existed. He soon finds himself drawn into a strange and esoteric world filled with werewolves, vampires, witches... and a family curse that dates back to fourteenth century Scotland. In the sleepy little town of Somerset, an ancient evil awakens, hungering for blood and vengeance... and if Michael is to survive he must face his inner demons and embrace his family's dark past. Shadows Over Somerset is the first Cairnwood Manor Novel.

Urban Fantasy from John F. Allen!
Meet Ivory Blaque!

Softcover: 978-1-937929-16-9
eBook: 978-1-937929-17-6

In The God Killers, the first book of The God Killers Legacy, former professional art thief Ivory Blaque is hired to procure a pair of antique pistols and gets much more than she bargained for when several attempts are made on her life.

Her client turns out to be a shadowy government agent who reveals that she is descended from a race of immortals, and that the pistols are linked to her unique heritage and the special psychic gifts she possesses. He uses the memory of her father to guilt her into working for him.

Ivory eventually gives in to his request, and in return, he presents her with her father's journal, which was written in an unbreakable code. Bishop believes that she is the only one capable of breaking the code and unlocking the plans of the vampire hierarchy. But when the city's top vampire is a sexy incubus with an attraction for her and she's assigned a hot new lycan enforcer to protect her, she finds herself caught between two sets of rock hard abs.

To regain her autonomy, clear her name, unlock the secrets of her past, and protect the lives of those closest to her, Ivory must play along with the forces trying to manipulate her. Ivory's life is rapidly spiraling out of control and headed for an explosive conclusion which she just might not survive.

16 Tales of the Paranormal and Ghostly from editors
Alexander S. Brown and J.L. Mulvihill!

eBook ISBN: 978-1-937929-14-5
Softcover ISBN: 978-1-937929-12-1

From the shadowed realms of the paranormal comes 16 chilling
tales that dwell in the South and South West. From 16 authors,
learn of haunted homes, buildings, landmarks and roads where
restless entities from beyond the grave desire acknowledgement
amongst the living. Become acquainted with the aftermath of
an eclipse that awakens the dead in a Memphis cemetery, see
what horrors dwell in the woods at Hell's Gate, learn the dark
secrets of Sidney's Cotton, and dare to travel down Ghost Road.
These and many other tales are sure to keep you awake as you
are introduced to what makes the South and South West so
unique.... History and GHOSTS!!!!! So, sit back, dim the lights
and prepare yourself to face the spirits that walk among us.

Sword and Sorcery from Stephen Zimmer!

Softcover ISBN: 978-1-941706-21-3
eBook ISBN: 978-1-941706-23-7

Rayden Valkyrie. She walks alone, serving no king, emperor, or master. Forged in the fires of tragedy, she has no place she truly calls home.

A deadly warrior wielding both blade and axe, Rayden is the bane of the wicked and corrupt. To many others, she is the most loyal and dedicated of friends, an ally who is unyielding in the most dangerous of circumstances.

The people of the far southern lands she has just aided claim that she has the heart of a lion. For Rayden, a long journey to the lands of the far northern tribes who adopted her as a child beckons, with an ocean lying in between.

Her path will lead her once more into the center of a maelstrom, one involving a rising empire that is said to be making use of the darkest kinds of sorcery to grow its power. Making new friends and discoveries amid tremendous peril, Rayden makes her way to the north.

Monstrous beasts, supernatural powers, and the bloody specter of war have been a part of her world for a long time and this journey will be no different. Rayden chooses the battles that she will fight, whether she takes up the cause of one individual or an entire people.

Both friends and enemies alike will swiftly learn that the people of the far southern lands spoke truly. Rayden Valkyrie has the heart of a lion.

Heart of a Lion is Book One of the Dark Sun Dawn Trilogy.s

Appalachian Gothic! Jason Sizemore's Irredeemable!
18 Tales of dark fantasy, science fiction, and horror

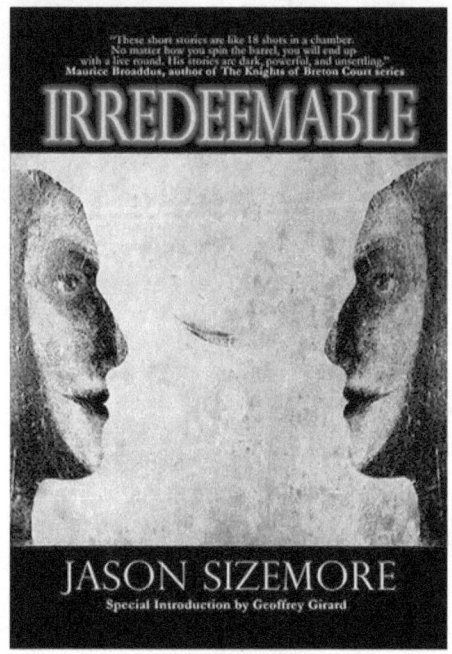

Softcover: 978-1-937929-59-6
eBook: 978-1-937929-68-8

Flowing like mists and shadows through the Appalachian Mountains come 18 tales from the mind of Jason Sizemore. Weaving together elements of southern gothic, science fiction, fantasy, horror, the supernatural, and much more, this diverse collection of short stories brings you an array of characters who must face accountability, responsibility, and, more ominously, retribution.

Whether it is Jack Taylor readying for a macabre, terrifying night in "The Sleeping Quartet," the Wayne brothers and mischief gone badly awry in "Pranks," the title character in "The Dead and Metty Crawford," or the church congregation and their welcoming of a special visitor in "Yellow Warblers," Irredeemable introduces you to a range of ordinary people who come face to face with extraordinary situations.

Whether the undead, aliens, ghosts, or killers of the yakuza, dangers of all kinds lurk within the darkness for those who dare tread upon its ground. Hop aboard and settle in, Irredeemable will take you on an unforgettable ride along a dark speculative fiction road.

Post-apocalyptic, zombie-infested military thriller from Peter Welmerink!

Softcover ISBN: 978-1-941706-03-9
eBook ISBN: 978-1-941706-02-2

The HURON, a 72-ton heavy transport vehicle and an army of four; tracked, racked and ready to roll, to serve and protect the walled metropolis of Grand Rapids-both her living and her undead. Captain Jacob Billet and his crew patrol the byways, ready for trouble. William Lettner, the North Shore Coalition High Commissioner, has enemies from the mainland to the lakeshore and needs to be covertly transported home after his helicopter is shot down en route to Grand Rapids. He has no love for a city that give unliving civilians the right to survive. Lettner's venomous outbursts assaults Billet and his crew along every mile travelled as they are assigned to safely bring him through the treacherous landscape outside the city back to his hometown. To complete their mission, the HURON and her crew will have to face domesticated zombies and the feral undead; marauders holding strategic chokepoints hostage; barricaded villages fighting for survival, and a group of geneticists who've lost control of one of their monstrous experiments. The crew will need to stay strong and trust one another in order to finish the mission and bring their "precious" cargo home, even knowing, all the while, the terrible deeds Lettner has done. Travelling through West Michigan was never so dangerous. Transport is the first book in the Transport series!

Powerful fantasy from A. Christopher Drown
A clash of the realms of magic and knowledge!

Softcover: 978-1-937929-53-4
eBook: 978-1-937929-58-9

Myth tells how magic came to be when the fabled gem known as the Heart of the Sisters was shattered by evil gods. The same tale speaks of the Heart being healed one day, unleashing a power that will bring the end of humankind.

While traveling to begin his magical studies, young apprentice Niel finds himself suddenly at the center of the Heart's terrifying legend. Caught in a whirlwind of events that fractures the foundation of everything he's believed, Niel learns his role in the world may be far more important than he ever could have imagined, and ever would have wished.

A Mage of None Magic begins an extraordinary adventure into a perilous land where autocratic magicians manipulate an idle aristocracy, where common academia struggles for acceptance, and where after ages of disregard myth and legend refuse to be ignored any longer.

A Mage of None Magic is Book One in The Heart of the Sisters series..